The Can

A B Morgan

To Sarah.
With thanks for all your
support !

Ali Morgan.

x

First published in 2018 by Bloodhound Books

www.bloodhoundbooks.com

Print ISBN 978-1-912175-94-9

Praise for Divine Poison

"The pace is great for the plot, which is well thought out and planned thoroughly to give it an added edge..." **Donna Maguire - Donnas Book Blog**

"I would highly recommend this book to so many readers. And I'm definitely going to be reading so much more by this author." **Ami-May Smith – Shyla's Uncensored Opinions**

"This story was full of intrigue and mystery that kept me turning page after page." **Lorna Cassidy - On The Shelf Reviews**

"Divine Poison has a tangled web of lies and secrets lurking within the pages along with a few surprises thrown in to make things interesting." **Rachel Broughton - Rae Reads**

"DIVINE POISON is thrilling to read and a book to keep you on your toes!" **Sooz Barthorpe - The P.Turners Book Blog**

"Again AB Morgan has used her own career experiences to add her own unique style to this story." **Yvonne Bastian - Me And My Books**

Praise for A Justifiable Madness

"I was in my element here it was like One Flew Over the Cuckoo's Nest." **Susan Hampson - Books From Dusk Till Dawn**

"This is a fascinating and insightful thriller about psychiatric treatment and diagnosis." **Caroline Vincent - Bits About Books**

"This is a really well written and unique storyline. As an avid blogger I crave unique storylines and I applaud the author on such a brilliant debut novel." **Philomena Callan - Cheekypee Reads And Reviews**

"A fantastically gripping read that I struggled to put down!" **Kate Noble - The Quiet Knitter**

"This story will make you wander who is the madman and what goes on within the system...A dark little twister of a read..." **Livia Sbarbaro - Goodreads Revewier**

"This is a great book that will keep you gripped throughout" **Julie Lacey - Goodreads Reviewer**

For Andy: You bring me sunshine.

Chapter 1

Turning slowly, Konrad Neale faced the film crew and directed his words at the watching audience behind the large lens of the TV camera.

'If Matthew Hawley were a woman would his sentence have been so harsh? The answer, in this case, is probably yes, for the simple fact that the level of premeditation could not in any way support the suggestion that he was of an unstable mind. Unbelievably, this was the case strongly argued by his barrister in court, but how on earth can we accept his story? Based on what we are about to show you, how is that possible?

'If you are of a delicate disposition, I strongly advise that you look away. What you will see next is graphic, brutal and sickening.'

There was a momentary pause before a series of still colour photographs appeared on the television monitor, and were commented on in finite detail.

'Here we see the mutilated body of Helena Chawston-Hawley, on the expensively tiled floor of her substantial kitchen. It is the morning of the first of March 2014 and her own blood surrounds her. The skid marks that we can see in the lake of red, we are told, were made by her husband, Matthew, as he carried out the deliberate surgical removal of certain appendages and organs. Not, as you would suppose, to make life easier for himself in the disposal of his wife's body, and not even to aid his attempt to hide her, because Matthew Hawley made no such attempt. He killed her, neatly laid out her remains, and dialled 999.

'He mutilated her, as is plain to see from these police photographs, by removing her eyes with the implement pictured to the left of her head. The eyeballs are on the right, on the floor amongst the blood, and quite difficult to distinguish. The order in which these disfigurements were carried out is not known but we have to ask ourselves why would he do that at all? Why did he cut off her breasts? And bizarrely, why did he make careful incisions to remove her lips?'

The camera cut back to a shot of Konrad leaning forward earnestly as he sat to one side of a functional desk in a prison interview room, where the stark grey walls contributed to the slightly hollow sound when he spoke, 'Welcome to another case of "The Truth Behind the Lies" with me, Konrad Neale.

'Over the four days that I interviewed Matthew Hawley, here at HMP Longlees, I have probed into the unbelievable chain of events that led to the brutal murder of his beautiful wife. If what he has told me is the truth, it does not change that one simple fact. Matthew Hawley did murder his wife, Helena Chawston-Hawley. He remains guilty of a heinous crime and he accepts that, so why are we here if there has been no miscarriage of justice? I'll leave you to decide for yourselves once you've heard what he has to say.' Konrad leant back in his chair with his hands together, as if in prayer, placing the tips of his fingers to his lips.

The scene changed, although the room remained the same.

Sitting on a plain plastic chair was a slim, almost gaunt, Matthew Hawley.

*

'Yep, I'm happy with how the intro is looking, Konrad. What do you think?' asked Annette the editor, as they sat together with two other members of the production team, beginning an initial run of the material recorded by Konrad and the film crew at the prison.

The first thing that had struck Konrad about Matthew Hawley was that the greying hair and prison pallor could not belie the man's underlying distinctly handsome features. A strong jaw, chiselled nose, intense but alluring green eyes and not a tattoo in sight. His modest intelligent air coupled with his good looks shattered the stereotypes that could potentially define him as a monstrous killer. When Matthew spoke, he did so with consideration, careful with his choice of words but he didn't shy away from answering questions. He was believable.

'Yeah, good. I guess we can get hold of a recording of Matthew's call to the emergency services if we need to make use of it, but overall, I'm comfortable that our outline plan is a sensible order of events. Goodness me, he comes across frighteningly well on film…'

'Doesn't he just. You know, watching this and transcribing every word freaked me out quite a bit, I can tell you.' Annette brushed cake crumbs from her enormous trouser-clad thighs. She hadn't stopped eating so far that morning and this was irritating Konrad, who had to suffer the endless moaning about her weight, for which she blamed her thyroid. His own eating habits were overshadowed by the constant fear of putting on the pounds. The slightest weight gain would be magnified in front of the television cameras where he earned his living, when he wasn't writing newspaper columns, or fronting chat shows. He had thought his best days were behind him as far as fame and fortune in the fickle world of television was concerned, but his move into documentary and real crime had reignited the nation's interest in what he had to say.

'I can't believe how lucky we were to get the green light on this one. It's a hell of a story,' Annette said as she stood up, gently patting the presenter's designer-dressed shoulder. 'Great interview. Do you realise he could be your younger brother, in appearance I mean? Similar features. You make quite an attractive pair, which will please our female audience members, I'm sure. What would you say, there are five years or so between you and Matthew Hawley? Good looking man, but shit, I can't quite comprehend what sick and twisted stuff he told you, you know.

'So, what do you want to do now?' Annette turned to ask her team. 'Shall we let it roll as usual, and get this firmly into our heads before we finally identify the selects?'

A young intern, by the name of Joe, bravely interrupted to ask what that turn of phrase meant.

'Slow Joe, you didn't do your homework, otherwise, you would know what the selects are.' Annette had been ironic in nicknaming him Slow Joe. Konrad knew that she was impressed by how swiftly an enthusiastic Joe absorbed information and by the intelligence with which he used the latest sound technology.

'Actually, that's a fair question, Joe,' Konrad interjected before Annette had a chance to enlighten her protégé. 'The art and craft of producing, and especially editing, a documentary is entirely different from a fiction film. Although there's a chronology to the interview itself, it has to be edited with the viewer in mind. We don't change what has been said, but we do develop a working structure and identify scenes, ideas, thoughts that can be separated out. The selects. We can trim the long pauses or the repetition of the same argument, do you see?' Joe mouthed his thanks and received a thumbs-up in return.

Annette had obviously decided to ignore the interruption, and she continued without needing to contribute to the response. 'This transcript's a long one. Mind you, having looked at it again, I'm beginning to think we have enough juicy solid material to make a two-parter and I'm loathed to bin anything. What's your feeling, guys?'

'I don't think we can argue for two episodes of the same case,' Konrad replied. 'The executives won't agree to a change in the fundamentals of the contract, so let's watch and aim to eventually edit to the required sixty minutes. I can précis certain parts to camera if necessary or as voice-over material during those odd shots around the prison that we bagged. It'll provide atmosphere and break up the face-to-face sections.' The assistant editor, Mike, signalled his approval. Konrad was explaining in more detail than was strictly necessary just for Slow Joe's educational benefit.

'To be frank with you, this one's had me awake at nights ever since we started filming. I wasn't expecting to like Matthew Hawley, but he's so bloody convincing on camera, and the viewers are in for a rough ride when they see and hear what he has to say. I wanted to hate him, but I couldn't. Anyway, let's crack on before the coffee goes cold.'

Chapter 2

Konrad waited patiently for Matthew Hawley's reply to his first question. When it came he sensed the pain and anger in the words, although the man sitting in front of him appeared, on the surface, to be focussed and in control of his body language.

'My legal representatives didn't fabricate an unbelievable story, as you suggest, Mr Neale. What I told them was the truth, most of which was deemed inadmissible. How the evidence was perceived and twisted by the prosecution made the truth appear to be a lie.'

'But you must be aware, Matthew, that what the public heard during your trial was that you had a fantastic life with a beautiful, kind-hearted woman, who worshipped and doted on you. She even accepted your son to live with you both. You were a phenomenally well-off family, and willing to share that wealth you raised thousands of pounds for charity. When you have a life of stable privilege it simply doesn't make sense that you would murder your wife.' Konrad left a three-second pause before asking his question. 'What can you say to help us understand why you snapped and killed her? Did you snap?'

He couldn't read Matthew. He could usually pitch his questions in a particular way by watching for signs of discomfort in his interviewee, but Matthew Hawley was giving nothing away. The man was distant: cut off but not aloof.

'I didn't snap, Mr Neale, that much is obvious.'

'I see your point. Of course, it can't have been impulsive or an act of self-defence. You took your time to mutilate Helena and, from what we have seen from the evidence, there appears to have been a reason behind how you laid out her body. Tell us then, if you would, how you came to the decision to kill your wife. Try to build a picture that will serve to detail the events leading to your actions, two years ago, when you deliberately killed and mutilated Helena.'

'Mr Neale, I believe that is what we agreed. I'm happy to recount my story because this is for my son. I want, above anything else, for him to hear and know the truth that the court failed to examine. But please don't expect me to tell you, in gory detail, every incision I made.'

'Your son, Josh, was how old when you left your first marriage?'

'Let's straighten out the facts, Mr Neale. I did not leave. Amy had an affair and I went through the painful process of a divorce, being obliged to leave the home I had worked so hard to build for my family. Instead of a contented life, I had my heart broken. I vowed to do whatever I had to in order to keep alive the relationship with my son who was only twelve. Unlike my ex-wife and her exaggerated claims of irreconcilable differences, I remained adult and compliant with Amy's wishes in order to keep the peace. Somehow, I even learnt to tolerate "Pete the wanker". No apology for referring to him in that way, the bloke is a twat, and I still hate him for decimating my family. If you have to cut that bit then so be it, but he's still a wanker.'

Konrad was supposed to be listening hard to pick up a cue for his next question. He didn't worry about the fruity language as it made for a gritty edge to the documentary and revealed a small glimmer of emotion breaking through from Matthew Hawley's well-guarded inner feelings. Instead of concentrating on the words being spoken, he had found himself wondering which idiot researcher had got the facts wrong about Matthew Hawley's first marriage, and in doing so he almost missed the opportunity for a swift winning question. Almost.

'Can I ask you to think back to that time and explain to me why you didn't kill your first wife, Amy? Or her new lover Peter? You say they "decimated" your family and it sounds like a desperate time for you. So why not kill them?'

Matthew sighed. 'I'm not a serial killer, Mr Neale. I was an ordinary man whose wife did the dirty, and I had to live with the consequences of not paying her enough attention. She wasn't the only one at fault. Just because I speak my mind about hating what they did, doesn't mean I would kill them.'

'What made you kill your second wife then, if a painful divorce and betrayal wasn't enough to drive you to any sort of violent reaction, what did?' Konrad had floundered. He hadn't expected Matthew Hawley to be so grounded, rational and implacable.

The best psychopath I've ever met, he decided.

*

Annette piped up. 'Stop there a second. Where were you going with these opening questions, Kon? You let him sidetrack you. I think we may have to cut that bit of waffle. Scoot through to the question about first meeting Helena.' The editing suite was silent again as they identified the moment Matthew began the details of his relationship with the woman he would eventually kill.

*

'We met through a dating site. Yes, I know, not romantic or original these days, but I'd avoided any form of relationship for at least two years after my divorce from Amy. I focussed on Josh and we had loads of good times together every Saturday afternoon. We played football, went roller-skating, fishing, that type of boy's stuff. It was great, and I enjoyed time with Josh, but I'm human after all and hankered for female company that was a bit more meaningful than a quick bang with the barmaid at the Bird in Hand.'

The interview, with the cameras rolling, became more of a natural conversation as the two men settled into the rhythm of the story. Matthew's facial features had relaxed as he spoke, remembering with fondness the times together with his only son.

'Whose idea was it to try Internet dating?'

'Gary at work. He's a bit of a wag on the surface, but he's a nice bloke who eventually convinced himself that I was heading for eternal solitude and blindness due to nights playing with myself.'

Konrad chuckled.

'It was Gary who helped with the wording on the application for one of those dating sites for professional singles, and we tinkered about with photos on my phone, trying to make me look macho and confident. Anyway, it worked. I had at least three disastrous dates before I met Helena.' Matthew rubbed his hands up and down the length of his thighs before being able to continue. Knowing Matthew didn't react like that when he spoke about Amy and his divorce, Konrad made a mental note to check with the editing team whether that movement was clear to see on film. Matthew gave a short cough before he recommenced.

'She was an absolute stunner. I remember we'd agreed to meet at Gino's, an Italian restaurant. We'd chatted online about everyday mundane nonsense, you know; books we'd read, sports we enjoyed and food, which is why we settled on Italian for dinner. I'd promised faithfully to arrive early because she said she was worried about turning up on her own and being left in the lurch. So, I made sure I was there sitting at a small table facing the door and I happened to be chatting to the waiter about... I can't think now, the weather probably, when Helena walked in. My heart sank.'

'Did it? Why?' Konrad asked without hesitation.

'Because there was no way a woman like her was going to find a man like me the least bit attractive. I was fit and healthy all right, but not your toned tanned beefcake, and I wasn't wealthy or powerful either. I didn't stand a chance; all the aphrodisiacs were missing.'

*

Annette paused the run-through in the editing room. 'Do we have that photo of Matthew from when he was first dating Helena?

Having sight of that will give the audience a better idea of how much change he went through from the exercise regimes and the surgery, don't you agree? Let's make a note of that then. Good.'

Slow Joe put the digital photo of Matthew Hawley on the computer screen in front of them and Konrad shook his head in disbelief. 'Christ, he looked like a different man back then. When was this taken?'

'The date says twelfth of April 2013.'

'Bloody hell, what a difference between that and the photo of him with Helena at the charity gala a year later. Have we got that one to hand, Joe?' Konrad asked, intrigued by the contrast between the pictures. After some mouse clicking, Joe managed to get the images side by side on one of the three screens.

'Save that please, Joe,' demanded Annette, who, like Konrad, was staring at the monitor in awe. 'The nose job is amazing, and look at the difference in his physical shape, he must have spent hours in the gym to get like that.'

'Nice teeth. They're definitely expensive. Now look at her, look at Helena, in those pictures. Are you seeing what I'm seeing?' asked Konrad.

The other two men in the room nodded emphatically, but Annette shook her head. 'No, what about her?'

'Her tits have got to be two sizes bigger at least.'

'Are you sure? They can't be plastic; they look too real. It could be the camera angle, or a better bra. But look at her mouth… see? Fewer lines. Botox probably. Nice lips. She's a beauty, there's no doubt about that.'

'Was a beauty.'

'Yes, you're right on several counts. We'll use these contrasting pictures for sure. Nice work. Thanks, Joe. Take a note of the time code at that section, would you. What a lovely sound bite from Matthew. "I didn't stand a chance; all the aphrodisiacs were missing."' Joe looked around as if searching for someone else called Joe, but once it dawned that Annette had paid him a compliment he beamed across at Konrad for confirmation.

Following the pause in proceedings, the team returned to the task in hand. Watching and making notes about the interviews with Matthew Hawley in HMP Longlees, Konrad could recall every minute and as he watched the playbacks he relived and analysed each moment.

*

On the screen he was seen smiling amiably at Matthew. 'That was your view but it seems, from the evidence, that Helena must have found something attractive about you, because you had a whirlwind of a courtship leading swiftly to marriage six months later. Most people would say you landed on your feet there, Matthew. Helena Chawston was a wealthy lady, so she wasn't looking for your money. She ran her own successful business and was a bright, intelligent woman by all accounts. What was it she found in you, do you think?'

'A sex toy.'

'Pardon?' Konrad sat back in his chair pulling away from Matthew in surprise. *What the hell? Where did that reply come from? He didn't say that in court.*

'There wasn't much mention of that specific side of your relationship during your trial, so I find myself wondering why you've just made that comment.'

'You're right, Helena didn't need money, but she was attracted to my vulnerability and potential to be the man she wanted in her life. What she needed was my obedience, my loyalty, and undivided attention to make her life complete. I'm not an idiot, but because she took her time to win my affections she made certain, once I had fallen for her, that I couldn't bear to leave.'

'Why do you think that was?'

Matthew took his time to find the right words. 'Absolute and overriding dread of rejection was her driving force. Only with hindsight can I see that she continually tested my devotion to alleviate her fears. Although I'm sure any good psychologist could tell you that, if they cared to examine the right evidence. I didn't understand her motives at the time but I wouldn't have wanted to leave; she gave me everything. You need to understand, Mr Neale, that Helena was amazing. When I first met her, I thought I'd died and gone to heaven.'

*

Konrad couldn't help himself. As he watched the interview in the editing suite, he thought of his own wife, Delia, and began to drift into a reverie. *God, she was the sexiest bitch I'd ever had the pleasure of bedding. Those were the days when we first dated… shagging anywhere and everywhere. Legs up to her armpits and the best tits in town. Nowadays, sex has to be booked into Delia's diary and it's a rare treat. "There's a good boy, thanks for the new earrings, if you really insist on a quick one, do it now before I have to get ready to go to book club. I can spare five minutes. Help yourself and don't make a mess".*

It took determined mental focus to shake himself back into paying attention to the monitor screens before him, and to Matthew's words.

Chapter 3

'Sex was the carrot she dangled in front of me. She was good at it. Really good. You have to remember, Mr Neale, that I'd chosen to be without a regular relationship for nigh on two years, and to have a woman who resembled a 1950s pin-up girl in my arms was a miracle. Helena had an hourglass figure, not flat thin and scrawny, she was soft and womanly, and smelt amazing. I'm not a lover of strong perfumes, and in my view stacks of cosmetics slapped on a woman makes her look cheap, whoever she may be. Helena had it right. A subtle smell of perfume always greeted me as I nuzzled her neck, with enough make-up on to accentuate her eyes and make her lips seem moist and inviting. Sounds too good to be true, doesn't it?

Konrad had to agree. 'Yes, it does.'

'It was, and for the first few months I walked around in a permanent state of sexual excitement. It was blissfully excruciating and exactly what she wanted to achieve. Helena would look at me across a room full of people when we attended those endless charity functions and she would only have to run her tongue across her lips to have me dribbling.

'Don't get me wrong. I wasn't bought that easily; you see I didn't trust her to begin with. Let's face it, I was having a good time, but there was no way I was contemplating a long-term relationship with a woman who most men would give their eye-teeth for. In my mind, she would be off with the first Adonis that caught her attention.'

Konrad sympathised with Matthew's assessment of the situation. 'Divorce can have that effect, can't it? That... lack of trust. Still, she didn't seem to be interested in other men, did she?

From what was described in the evidence to the court at your trial, almost the opposite occurs. She builds a life with you and around your needs.'

*

Sitting watching in the editing suite, Konrad had vivid recall of this part of the interview. He had become determined to catch Matthew out, to trip him up by finding any inconsistencies in his story of the events, but as hard as he tried to keep his focus on teasing the next fact from Matthew, he couldn't stop picturing the luscious Helena. Watching the interview again, he was caught in the same trap.

I'm turning into a filthy lascivious middle-aged tosser. What's wrong with me? I shouldn't have been imagining my head between her boobs. She's a dead woman, for Christ's sake.

*

'It appears that she built her life around me. That's the impression she wanted everyone to see. You're right, she focussed on me and she built trust by creating dependence.

'Let me try to explain. With Amy, I hadn't taken enough time to be with her and do things together. We'd allowed our lives to drift apart and I spent too many hours at work. Even so, I never thought she would cheat, and that was crushing. Helena spent time with me, we had a lot in common: music, film, a love of the outdoors, and she had a sharp mind. The more conversations we had the more she gained an understanding of my insecurities; my underlying fears, likes, dislikes and she also lavished presents on me. Not just sex, but treats and gifts, as I did for her. We did things together for fun and she made me laugh.'

'I'm sorry, Matthew, but that sounds to me as if what you had was a normal, healthy relationship.'

'Yes, I know it does, and it was normal and healthy until small things started to happen to change the balance of power.

She worked hard to help me build trust, and once she had that, I was hers to do with as she pleased.'

Matthew pointed to the desk at which Konrad was sitting. 'You have an iPhone. Then you'll understand what I'm talking about. We used Find Friends to keep track of each other and it helped to identify where she was. I could press a button and have confirmation that she was at home in her office, at the hairdressers, having her nails done, or having coffee with a client. Helena took the time to meet my work colleagues by coming along to a couple of evening socials with my team and their other halves, and I had regular contact with her staff.'

'Tell me about them.'

'Helena's? There were only the two of them: Naomi and Richard. Richard was quite young, but he had been with Helena since he'd left school and he lodged in the upstairs flat above the offices. Lovely chap, hard-working, efficient but quiet. Naomi joined the business a year or so before I came on the scene. She and Helena were like two peas in a pod. More like best friends than a work relationship I would say. Their offices were in a separate annex to our main house, so as far as work was concerned they didn't interfere with our private lives. Not in the beginning anyway.'

'What about your family? How did that work?'

'Helena came with me to meet Josh within a month of our first date, and eventually she met Amy, which wasn't as awkward as I expected. Without me interfering, they seemed to be able to negotiate when Josh would spend time with us, and as the weeks went by, Helena organised really brilliant days out. She seemed to instinctively understand that being fourteen, Josh was at the most treacherous age, and so she didn't try too hard with him. Initially she tagged along with our boys' adventures or left us to it. You can't imagine the relief when it became obvious how well Josh had taken to Helena. You're right, it was normal and healthy. Even when she asked me to move in with her, it felt right. We talked about the pros and cons, and agreed how we would manage our relationship and seeing Josh. The things I worried about.'

'Where were you living at the time?'

'I'd been staying with Gary as a lodger and it was great. Two blokes in their thirties drinking, watching sport on the TV, and even shagging occasionally… not each other, you understand. Do you remember the series on TV, Men Behaving Badly? It was the same set-up. But, you can't go on like that forever if you want to be taken seriously, and I had a decent career. Once the maintenance money was paid, I actually had enough left to think about buying somewhere, a small house of my own.'

Konrad interrupted. 'Just to check the facts here, Matthew, if I can. You were a marketing consultant for a well-known company who provide medical and surgical equipment for hospitals. Is that correct?' He looked down to a clipboard lying on the desk to his left. 'You had a company car, and earned around eighty grand a year with bonuses. That's an exceptionally good income.'

'Yes, it was, out of which I had to pay an extortionately high amount of maintenance to my ex-wife, despite the fact that "Pete the wanker" had moved in with Amy as soon as the divorce was settled. I'd paid off the mortgage, everything. Try it yourself some time, it's like being robbed.'

The challenge didn't go unrecognised. 'I don't intend to find out.'

*

Annette gave a snort as she turned. 'What did you have to make a personal comment for? We'll have to cut that. You know the rules.'

No sooner were the words out of his mouth he knew he'd made a mistake in rising to the bait. Matthew had been testing him out and he'd failed to recognise the fact until it was too late. Subconsciously, Konrad looked down at his crotch as he thought about how he'd practically had to pay his own wife for the privilege of sex in recent years.

As his popularity with the viewing public had waned, so had his wife's interest in him. Unfortunately, without a bunch of expensive flowers, a dinner date, or jewellery as a bribe, she didn't seem to find him enough of a turn-on to bother with.

Mrs Delia Neale had expensive tastes, and therefore with the thought of the astronomical cost of legal proceedings, the public humiliation and negative impact on his future career, the idea of divorce had barely ever crossed Konrad's mind. He'd had extramarital flings to fill the void, and he'd fallen in love with his last – until Delia had put a stop to that. But until he had started his series of interviews with Matthew Hawley, he hadn't thought about whether he truthfully wanted to spend the rest of his life married to Delia, and pandering to her requirements.

Every evening in the last three months, he had made a point of purchasing a gift for his wife to buy back her affections, even if his only reward was a soft touch, a kiss on the cheek or the occasional brief lacklustre coital encounter. He was so sexually frustrated he'd had to lower himself to these degrading bribery tactics.

This was inescapable.

It was Delia who had marketed them as a golden couple to keep their public profile alive, landing him advertising jobs, and voiceovers. Her PR efforts eventually served to resurrect his place in the affections of the public and the television producers. He owed it to his wife, and she knew it. Delia was also well aware that he'd had a wandering eye for years and that his most recent affair had threatened their business-like partnership. She put a stop to that, and thus, inevitably, the price paid for fame and celebrity was a private life so dreadfully dull that only desperation to hold onto his career remained as the sole impetus enabling him to return home at the end of the day.

He was now wallowing in the realisation that his decision to patch up his marriage three months previously, to salvage his career, had been disastrous. He had behaved like a shallow, selfish bastard and he could barely look in the mirror each morning without being disgusted at the man he had become.

Chapter 4

'If you were planning on buying your own house why did you agree to move in with Helena?' Konrad asked Matthew, genuinely puzzled as to why that decision had been made.

'I told you, it was impossible for me not to be with her. The thought of sex on tap was too much for my feeble mind to argue with. Besides which, Helena ran her office from home and it made sense for me to move in there, but for her own reasons she didn't give me a set of keys until I had proved myself.'

'Are you saying that you had to ring the doorbell to gain entry to the house? Had you forgotten to pay your bed and board money?' He was sceptical, as was reflected in the tone of his question.

Matthew held his gaze. 'It was only for a matter of days. Actually, I'd set up a joint account with Helena and we used it to pay bills, so please don't mistake me for a freeloader; I paid my way, Mr Neale, more than you'll ever imagine. She dangled the house keys in the same way that she dangled her sexual enticements. There were to be long lines of "special challenges," and rewards that Helena had in mind. The first was designed as a surprise. I was so excited, like a puppy, Mr Neale, and I couldn't do enough for that woman. Believe me, she did everything for my benefit, short of wiping my arse. On the day, she outlined how I was to earn my own set of house keys; she sat me down and handed me a card, properly printed, about A5 size, and on it was a description of the surprise she had arranged for me: skydiving.'

'Okay, that sounds exciting.'

'Not if you're petrified of heights it doesn't. It gets better. She filmed me with her phone to capture my reaction to the surprise and continued videoing as she handed me another card. This one confirmed that Helena had pledged to make a five thousand pounds donation to Cancer Research.'

'I see.' Konrad smiled appreciatively towards Matthew.

'No, you don't see. My parents died of cancer within a month of each other in the same year that I was divorced from Amy, and I'd been raising small amounts by doing fun runs at the weekends. Helena's pledge was astounding and her thoughtfulness made me break down in tears. Embarrassing as it was, she filmed me crying like a child. I didn't suspect a thing.'

'But you agreed and did the skydive.'

'Of course. I had two sleepless nights to get used to the idea before the actual jump, and somehow, I managed to convince Helena that it had been exhilarating and the best thrill ride of my life. The sad truth was that I had been petrified the whole time. But as promised, I was handsomely rewarded with a set of my own house keys, a donation to a charity close to my heart, and shortly after landing, at the back of the aircraft hangar building, I was treated to hot risky outdoor sex against a wall and confirmation of the date for our wedding.

'I was over the moon, Mr Neale. Not just because of that, but because she wanted to meet with Josh to tell him about the wedding plans personally, and she even insisted that if Josh was not happy, then we would postpone until he was.'

*

Annette stopped the play back. 'Kon, do we really need this soppy sentimental stuff?'

'Have you read the whole transcript? You have, I know you have because you wrote the bloody thing. In which case you must have missed the relevance of exploring the special thrilling treats that Matthew was being given. Anyway, we said we'd watch the whole thing again, make notes and get this into our heads. Can we please stick to the plan?' Konrad had heard what was about to be revealed over the next hours and days of the editing, and he was unable to emphasise enough the importance of retaining the integrity of the whole interview. 'No cuts. Not in the first run. Tell you what, shall we stop for lunch? I think we could all do with sustenance and a comfort break.'

Nobody argued with him, and the three men left Annette to secure the door.

'Back in an hour – a walk in the park is called for,' Konrad snapped, distracted by a personal quandary, fuelled by the interview re-run. He didn't crave food; he needed to hide away in selfish misery to deal with his inner turmoil.

Sitting on the park bench, he played with his mobile phone, moving his fingers across it. Pressing the contacts button and then reverting back to the main screen. He was wearing a shabby baseball cap to hide his face. Despite having a particular dislike for that particular type of headwear, he had to take some precaution against being recognised if he wanted time for quiet contemplation in a public place. 'What have I done?' he said aloud to a passing squirrel.

Prodding a finger onto the tiny phone keyboard, he formulated a message.

"Lorna. I can't do it. I can't live without you. Bollocks to my public profile. Bollocks to everything. Please. Please, let me see you and I beg you to forgive me. K xx"

Not giving himself time to cancel the words, he pressed the send button, hoping that his self-inflicted broken heart could be mended. He waited. A reply arrived moments before he was due back in the editing room.

"You either haven't read my letter or you haven't received it."

This was from a phone number that Konrad didn't recognise.

"Lorna? Is that you?"

"No. Who is Lorna? Has she made you sad? You look so dejected."

He scanned around him, trying to spot a familiar face. *Who's messing me about?*

Nearby, there was an elderly couple walking their equally ancient West Highland Terrier, a young mother with a baby in a pram, a middle-aged man cycling past, three people on the next bench along eating sandwiches and snacks for lunch, and dozens of people meandering around for as far as he could see. He decided to ignore the message. Time was slipping by, necessitating a coffee stop on the way past the street kiosk on the corner of the main road. Nothing was heard from Lorna. A dispirited soul, he plodded back into the uninspiring high-rise building where he would be incarcerated for the foreseeable future.

Every editing workday he was welcomed by two receptionists who never seemed to tire of greeting staff and answering the phone. On re-entering his workplace, through the automatic revolving door, he took off his cap and smiled at the immaculately coiffured, uniformed pair behind the desk.

Lillian picked up the ringing phone. 'Good afternoon, Marriot and Weston's, how may I help you?' she chirped. Her colleague, George, had a poorly disguised crush on Konrad.

'Good afternoon, Mr Neale. I hope you've had the most amazing lunch break.' George was incredibly camp. He flirted unashamedly with men and women alike, and got away with it.

Konrad found him amusing, and was always cheered by Gorgeous George, as he was affectionately known amongst the office staff. 'Not quite up to the usual standard, George, I have to say.' Konrad raised his coffee cup. 'I didn't quite manage to eat anything. A business call, you know how it is, but thanks for your concern. I don't suppose I could trouble you to order a Caesar salad from Poncho's Deli around the corner. Could I?'

'Oooh, I'd be delighted. I'll deliver it to you personally, Mr Neale. Give me five minutes.'

I know you'd love five minutes with me, young man, but I don't swing your way.

He watched, entertained, as George minced from behind the reception desk, took the twenty-pound note offered by Konrad, brushing his fingers on purpose as he did so, before prancing towards the door. 'Lillian, I shall return forthwith once I have completed a most urgent mission for the lovely Mr Neale.' Lillian acknowledged this with a wave. She was still chatting on the phone, repeating the phrase, 'Yes, I see,' peppered with the occasional, 'Oh dear.' She gestured to Konrad by raising one finger and handed him a registered letter as he headed for the lifts while resurrecting his flattened hat-hair, smiling to himself.

*

'You say the skydive was the first of many special events, but the impression we have of you and Helena is that you willingly organised charitable fundraising activities and you raised tens of thousands of pounds. Are you saying that these formed a systematic plan of Helena's making?'

Matthew replied with impatience. 'Yes, that's exactly what I'm saying. Don't you see? Helena had me cornered. Cancer Research is a noble cause, and one which was part of my grieving process for my parents, so I was hardly going to refuse. But as you will no doubt have noticed, the events were all organised by Helena and Naomi, but carried out by me. The abseiling was next on the list. Then came the bloody wing walking…'

As Matthew recalled the order of his challenges he counted them on his fingers. 'I've no idea how I didn't throw up. This is where you've missed the central motive of Helena's actions, Mr Neale. She would offer me a number of rewards, which would be in the form of money to Cancer Research, adoration from my son for being heroic in his eyes and a direct physical treat for me.

'Once I had completed a challenge, whatever it was, we would pose for the obligatory publicity shots, and having promised me a kinky thrill as a reward she would delay our return home, or drive me insane with frustration by flirting with me. Sometimes, even when we did get home, she would sit me on a chair and walk naked in front of me not letting me touch her until I was about to explode. You understand?'

Konrad desperately wanted to hear the details, but knew that would be for his own guilty pleasure and wouldn't help to reduce the fantasies in his mind that were tormenting him. He changed the subject before embarrassing himself on camera.

'You mention the publicity shots, were they the reason you both had your looks enhanced?'

Matthew glanced towards the floor before he answered. 'That's a yes and a no. It began as a treat for us. Helena told me to take the day off work one Friday. It was July or August, I think. Helena woke me on the morning of that day and, as predicted, gave me one of her "surprise cards," which had by then begun to fill me with dread. However, by way of an unexpected change, she'd arranged a whole day at a health spa.'

Chapter 5

Konrad inclined his head, encouraging Matthew to continue. He had decided to let the story flow. There was something in Matthew's tone of voice indicating the importance of this particular reference.

'It was just what we needed. Helena had booked us into a swanky spa hotel for the night because we had a charity zip wire event to attend the next afternoon. The hotel was about halfway there. Josh was taking part in the sponsored junior event and he met us there with a couple of his mates. If I remember rightly, he had a lift from one of the other dads.

'The zip wire was an enormous long death-slide across a rock-strewn valley; one of those new adventure attractions for the ultimate thrill seekers and adrenalin junkies. Helena and Naomi, with their magical powers of persuasion, had negotiated with the owners to publicise the opening of "Europe's second biggest zip wire" by having a charity event. We dressed up as superhero characters and launched ourselves down the almighty wire. The boys loved the experience; I hated every minute. My fear of heights had worsened with each event, but I had at least learnt to put the terror aside until the moment of no return. Even so, it was petrifying.

'On the drive to the spa, Helena and I talked about wedding plans. That discussion continued throughout most of the day, as we made final decisions on music, confirmed the number of guests, talked about the honeymoon, the usual endless organisational nightmare that had dominated our waking hours.

'She had a clear idea in her head of how she wanted our special day to unfold and initially I went along for the ride. It was to be her day. Our parents were dead, and I only had distant cousins and Josh as family. The rest of my guests would be friends from work, Josh's gang of spotty mates and my old university pals, so it didn't matter to me, as long as Helena was happy.

'It was a wonderful time at the spa; although, there was one unsettling incident that has played on my mind ever since.'

'Go on...'

'We'd been chatting in the steam room as Helena went into the finest details of the arrangements, and to be honest I had tuned out. The last lady had just left the spa area, probably sick to death of hearing about flowers and table settings. Anyway, I found myself disagreeing with Helena about the scale of the plans. I didn't want a fuss and yet she was describing this great lavish affair with a horse-drawn carriage, chandeliers, a full orchestra and a dress of biblical proportions. I didn't remember agreeing to what sounded like a ludicrously expensive and ostentatious affair. That's not my style. When I broached the subject, she reacted as if I had made a vicious attack on her dreams, which I probably had, and, as a result, she stormed out of the sauna, heading back towards the Jacuzzi in a magnificent sulk.

'I sat silently for a matter of seconds before shouting my apology to her and after sufficient begging she stepped reluctantly from the hot tub and back towards the sauna in the corner of the room. She made mocking faces at me through the small pane of glass in the sauna door, making me promise that she could have whatever she wanted for our wedding. I caved in without an ounce of resistance. What was the point? Then she said she couldn't open the door. Or she pretended that she couldn't.'

'You don't expect us to believe that, do you?' Konrad said impassively.

'You can decide for yourself, it's my observations and my perspective. For all I know the door was stuck, but the expression on Helena's face was of pleasure, not concern, as she held the handle. She could easily have had her foot against the bottom of the door, so I thought she was messing about at first. Which is what she said had happened. It was only after I collapsed that she went for help. She said the alarm hadn't worked. The manager came back with her and they freed me without too much trouble, apparently. I'd passed out.'

'You weren't angry?'

'Not at the time. I thought it was an accident.'

A doubtful look crossed the interviewer's face. 'I see. So, what was next on Helena's itinerary?'

'Over carrots and quiche, she informed me what was in store for the rest of the day. In brief, I had to endure the spa treatments of medieval torture to earn my reward. While Helena had her nails done, I had my eyebrows shaped and my nose hair removed. That really makes your eyes water, I can assure you, Mr Neale. After which she revealed my next hair removal experience.'

'All involving wax?'

'You've got it. "Back, sack and crack" the next one was called.'

Konrad winced in sympathy as Matthew continued his description of events.

'Good God, no man should have to endure that indignity. But it pleased Helena so much she squealed with delight at my protests and manly screams. The result was fascinating to her, which led to her suggestion about plastic surgery and veneers for my teeth. Just rhinoplasty and new teeth, that's all I had done. The rest was my own hard work. She'd had me pounding away in the gym at home, and I have to say I was pleased with the results. The more toned I became, the more attractive Helena seemed to find me, so it was a win-win situation.'

'I'm still puzzled; why did you agree to something as drastic as plastic surgery, Matthew? You seem like a reasonable man, a bloke's bloke who likes a beer and a night out with the lads, so why would you agree?'

'I didn't at first, but that's where I began to lose myself.'

*

'Hold it there please.' Annette confronted Konrad again. 'This drags on too long, it's way too lovey dovey and poor-man-needs-sex, don't you think? Now, having said that, I like the phrase he uses here – "that's where I began to lose myself" – so can we make a record of that please?' Annette, clearly not content with having had lunch, was now devouring a packet of chocolate digestives that she was dunking in her coffee and selfishly hadn't offered one to anyone else. Konrad had finished his salad and risked being given a slap on his wrist as he could resist no longer and helped himself to a biscuit. Annette scowled at him as he offered the packet to Slow Joe, and then to Mike who hardly ever expressed a controversial opinion in case he offended his colleagues in the production team; instead he worked silently and diligently to earn the reward of approval from Annette, the undisputed queen of the editing suite.

The afternoon had been uninspiring apart from the dramatic entrance from Gorgeous George who had them in fits of giggles for a few precious minutes. George had caused a stir in Poncho's Deli when he had decided to buy a treat for his colleague Lillian.

'She's partial to sickly cakes and puddings, and there was a special offer on. I spoke to the lady who was serving and she was happy to sort out a takeaway salad for you, Mr Neale, and then I got my words in a muddle and I asked her for a "stiffy cocky pudding with cream" for Lillian. I didn't know where to put myself! Anyway, Lillian knew where to put it. Know what I mean?' George had then swanned out leaving a cloud of aftershave in his wake.

'That boy should be on the stage.'

*

'How did you lose yourself?' Konrad asked, following the hook.

'At first, the suggestion of plastic surgery was ludicrous to me. I'm not that vain, but when I declined, Helena became really upset. She turned my argument around reacting as if I had offended her by rejecting her idea. "You don't want to be more attractive to me?" It wasn't a moment of slight offence, Mr Neale; she shunned me for days, so eventually I did what she wanted. It was easier. After that, I conceded to every challenge and every request, because I had to have her affection and that's what I mean when I say I lost myself.'

Konrad didn't speak, allowing Matthew to complete the full answer to the question.

'You're correct, I wasn't the sort of man to have plastic surgery, but I agreed to it because the rewards were worth it. The more I became the man she wanted, the more she provided.' Matthew sat back in his chair, breathing out as if he had unburdened himself.

'You mean sex.'

'Is that all you think about, Mr Neale?' Matthew had caught him out again and he could have kicked himself for lack of judgment.

'I'm talking about the rewards from the charity work, which were far-reaching in terms of the publicity for Helena's business. Not surprisingly, my company bosses were also pleased with the attention. There was such a strong link between our products and cancer care, and they quite rightly took advantage of the positive press by sponsoring quite a few of my daredevil challenges. Work mates would make up the crowds cheering me on. To be frank, I think the lads in the manufacturing side were running a betting ring on whether I would die, or at least end up seriously mangled in hospital. I let them down in that regard, but I did earn their admiration. Can you imagine how proud Josh was of his superman father? It was almost worth it for that alone. I felt like the greatest dad that ever lived.

'My fundraising isn't why you're here though, is it? And it's not the most fascinating of subjects. I do appreciate that you are far more interested in my wife's ability to lead me around by my manhood, and why I killed her, are you not, Mr Neale?'

Konrad deliberately kept a straight face and maintained full eye contact with Matthew. *You're not getting me this time, you bastard. I'm not going to bite.*

'I'm still no clearer on why you killed her, Matthew.'

'I killed her, but I never wanted to. I know I killed her because I've seen the photographs; my fingerprints and my DNA were over everything at the crime scene, even on the bunch of flowers that I don't remember buying for her. What I do know is that over time I became more confident and with confidence came more self-assurance that I could keep a woman like Helena. I had the stamina, I willingly accepted her challenges and her rewards, but, and there is a big "but" coming here, Mr Neale, don't ever underestimate the pressure to perform. Helena had to be satisfied first and foremost. I was not permitted to orgasm before her.'

'Not permitted?' On screen, Konrad's pupils had enlarged. He shuffled uncomfortably in his seat and frowned as he could not help himself from enquiring further.

'Correct. The punishment if I did?' Matthew asked as if guessing what the man opposite was thinking.

Got me with that one, he thought, and with a circular gesture he encouraged Matthew to answer his own question.

'That varied depending on what mood Helena was in, but it was always disguised as a playful flirt with another man or woman, a game, a tease, or the next well-publicised charity challenge. I had eight hours a day at work to imagine what was coming my way when I arrived home. It could be pleasure, it could be pain, or it could be both. Are you beginning to understand how my life was changing?'

'And yet you still married her?'

'Are you mad? Of course I married her. My life with Helena was the best thing imaginable – paradise. I was obsessed with her, every waking moment at work and every night, even in my sleep. I couldn't wait to marry her before she tired of me or I failed to please her. In the same way that she wanted me, I had to own her and possess her.'

'Wasn't there one niggling doubt?'

'I had no reservations left. She adored Josh and he adored her, and the wedding was to be perfect, fucking perfect. We had to look flawless for the day, for the photos and for our public face of marital harmony and generosity to charity and do you know what? We looked sensational.' There was a raw edge to Matthew's voice and a creeping anger rising to the surface. Konrad took a chance and pushed for more of a reaction.

'Did you pass the test on your wedding day? Did you behave like a good boy or did you incur a penalty?'

Matthew sneered. 'I'm not a child, Mr Neale. I wasn't her pet or a plaything, this was a serious relationship built on mutual trust. If Helena thought that she couldn't trust me then she would react. Once that was made clear to me it was not hard to remain within the parameters. However, Helena was not the sort of person to be satisfied with the status quo. She would become bored without a threat or a challenge and that's how I kept her interested in me. Do you see?'

Konrad shook his head. 'No, I'm sorry, I don't see. What you describe is a game being played by two people who receive equal amounts of pleasure from the relationship.'

'It was to begin with. But as I have just said, Helena would have been bored if our marriage had maintained the same routines. The special challenges for charity and her personal surprises provided her with a way of testing me even after we were married. It kept the excitement alive.'

Chapter 6

Konrad hailed a cab at the station and sat back resting his head for a few precious minutes before putting on a brave face and greeting Delia with a bunch of expensive flowers and a loveless kiss when he strolled through their front door.

God, I hate this bloody house with its white walls and shining surfaces. It's unforgiving, empty of character, like Delia.

'Hello, darling. How long 'til you can be ready?' Delia asked, bustling in her crispy dress as she hung her husband's jacket up inside the sliding doors of the cloakroom. No shoes or coats, tennis rackets or umbrellas were permitted to be seen on display in Delia's house, and neither was dust nor a cushion out of place.

'Ready? Ready for what?'

'Please say you haven't forgotten. We've promised to go to Pippa's book launch for nibbles and wine. We must be seen to be supporting her cause.'

Must we? I can't stand Pippa and her simpering entourage. Bunch of morons, the lot of them. Give me strength.

'What did you say, darling?' Delia asked, and for a brief second, he thought he had accidentally spoken out loud. 'Nothing…'

'What do you mean nothing? When are you going to be ready?' Delia swished past him again on a mission to put the flowers in water and to find her clutch bag.

'I'm not.'

'Not what?'

'I'm not going to be ready because I'm not going. For a change, real life is beckoning me in the shape of a pint of beer in the pub. Not a cocktail or a glass of Prosecco with false people in a pretend world. Delia, I've had it with launch parties and luvvies getting married. Enough, do you hear me?'

Delia teetered back across the hall in her high heels and smiled. 'I'm sorry, darling, I missed all that, what did you say?'

'I can't go, I'm shattered and I fancy a drink in the pub, Delia. Forgive me just this once, please.'

The smile on Delia's face slipped away to be replaced by a scowl. 'Do as you bloody well like, Kon. I'm trying to do my best to support your career and you throw it back in my face. If that's your decision then I'll represent us both, in style, and I do it willingly. Money?' She held out the palm of her hand expectantly, onto which her husband placed a layer of mixed notes. She nodded when she thought he had handed over enough for her needs that evening. With her hair sprayed solidly in place and make-up checked, she left, taking his shining-clean white Range Rover, ignoring her Mini alongside it in the garage, and roared out of the drive to make her feelings known.

He couldn't believe his luck. The sense of freedom he felt as he walked to The Valiant Soldier only served to remind him of the life he had wanted to lead with Lorna. He should have been walking along, going for a pint, holding her hand, but he wasn't and it was his own stupid fault. He had been checking his phone all afternoon in the agonising hope that she would reply by asking to see him immediately. Nothing. Not a word.

'Oi, dopey, wake up!'

A familiar voice roused Konrad from his self-pity. 'Barney Ribble, as I live and breathe. Where have you been?'

'I ain't been nowhere, mate. It's you that's been missing. We don't see you no more. She let you out for once, The Camp Commandant?'

'Now then, Barney, that's no way to speak about my lovely wife.'

'She ain't lovely and you know it. She's a prize bitch and after one thing mate: your money. Come on, I'll buy you a pint, you must be boracic if The Commandant has let you out, she'll have fleeced you for that.' Barney chuckled and clasped his friend by the elbow, dragging him through the doors of The Valiant Soldier. A cheer went up from the locals in recognition of Konrad's appearance and Barney's announcement that his mate had made a successful bid for a night of freedom.

The beers flowed as easily as the conversation, and Konrad wanted to stay in his local pub with his friendly neighbours forever, telling jokes and swearing, being lewd and revolting without having to worry one tiny jot.

Marvellous, fucking marvellous. I'm never going home again.

He caught the new barmaid sizing him up. She had a certain glint in her eye, he convinced himself.

'Barney, what do you think? Sarah has the hots for me wouldn't you say?' Konrad waggled a finger rather rudely at the well-proportioned lady serving behind the bar.

'No, Kon, me old mucka. I would say that is a trick of the beer. She's not that desperate.'

'Well, I am.'

'You're out of luck, mate; she's taken, but I do know where you might have some chance of clearing your pipes.'

'Really?'

'Genevieve's massage parlour.'

'Oh, piss off, Barney! I'll catch a dose at that filthy whorehouse. If it were a classy joint I'd consider it, but I don't want to have to pay if I don't have to.'

'No? I thought you already did?'

The pair of them chuckled into their beers and chatted amiably into the early hours about women, and their own love of things mechanical.

*

'Good morning, Mr Neale. How are we today?' George asked brightly as Konrad made his way towards the lifts.

'Keep it down, George, there's a good chap. I'm a bit delicate.' He was late and had not been brave enough to take off his sunglasses or baseball cap, which were, in his opinion, preventing his throbbing head from physically splitting wide open.

'Don't you worry; I shall rustle you up a cure with my own hands. Always a pleasure, never a chore for you, Mr Neale.' Pirouetting, George stepped through the office door at the back of the reception desk, shouting over his shoulder, 'You pop along to the editing suite and settle yourself down, I shall be with you pronto tonto.'

Roughly an hour later, George received a personal phone call from Konrad Neale who failed to choose his words with care. 'George, I could kiss you. Whatever was in that hangover cure, I want the recipe. It's a miracle. I feel alive, thank God.'

The phone was instantly removed from his ear when a high-pitched squeal erupted from the receiver. 'Oh my God! Oh my God! He wants to kiss me. My dreams have come true, Lillian. Thank you, Mr Neale. Can I expect delivery of my kiss at lunchtime?'

'A small peck, George, if you're lucky.' Konrad hung up while he still had his hearing intact. As he looked up, he caught Annette having another fit of the giggles. 'And you, stop laughing, this is a serious situation.'

'You're not kidding. You sure know how to make a catastrophe out of a cock-up, don't you? From what you've said so far, not only did you stagger home in the early hours blind drunk, but your wife, she of the searing eyeballs, caught you piddling into her best vase, and then you had the gall to fall into her arms calling her Lorna and declaring your undying devotion. Your solicitor will be rubbing his hands together in anticipation. What a plonker.'

'I know, I'm in the running for "prat of the year". It's actually worse than that. I deposited my shoes on the hallway floor and dropped my jacket in the lounge as I headed for her expensive ceramic-ware for a piss, all of which is "verboten" in our house.'

'I think peeing in a vase is forbidden in most peoples' homes, to be fair.'

'Good point, well made. I might have got away with all of that if I hadn't woken her up. You see, trying to find my way to bed, I knocked seven bells out of a full-length mirror thinking it was someone walking through a doorway.'

Annette let out a series of donkey braying laughs, splattering the digital equipment with jam doughnut before the story could be finished. 'But in my defence, it was dark. That was the crashing noise that woke Delia. Still, at least it was quiet over breakfast this morning. The Camp Commandant is currently doing her impression of a faulty television set. Picture and no sound. It usually lasts for a good week. I'm not sweating it.'

'You bloody-well should be,' Annette warned.

'No, the twins are home from uni this weekend, and she'll put on a good show for them. She always does. She'll soon forget about this small misdemeanour when I hand her more cash to buy a present for the returning children. They'll protect me.'

'That reminds me,' Annette said. 'While Slow Joe and Mike aren't in the room, have you heard from Lorna recently? You know she's moved, I take it. The pictures are on Facebook… Did you hear what I just said?'

Konrad's heart had plummeted into his expensive boots, and he struggled to find a response. 'No, you know I don't do Faceache. Delia deals with the social media crap. When did Lorna move, and where's she gone?' His voice cracked.

'You really didn't know did you. I'm sorry, Kon, I thought she'd have told you.' Annette's face had softened even before she reached out to touch her colleague's hand. 'She took a promotional marketing job with BBC Wales, so basically she's gone home. Haven't you two at least stayed in touch?'

'I sent her a text yesterday, but she hasn't replied yet,' Konrad answered Annette like an automaton, his head spinning with despairing thoughts.

Fucking hell. I've lost her. What do I do now? She's gone back to Wales after all these years. Christ, I can't not see her again.

Chapter 7

He watched himself on the screen, trying to concentrate on the details of his interview technique, and in particular paying attention to Matthew Hawley's body language. Reliving the interview, working, took Konrad's mind away from the bitterness of losing Lorna, and allowed him to re-enter the fantasy world in his head where Helena Chawston-Hawley had taken up residence.

*

'You say your workmates, and particularly Gary, wanted to please Helena, so they clearly liked her as a person. You also mentioned that Amy managed a friendly acquaintance with Helena allowing a smooth transition for Josh between the homes of both his parents at the weekends, I would imagine.

'I mention this because we've accessed the Facebook accounts for you and for Helena, and the posts seem to support the prosecution's assertions that you and Helena were fun-loving, happy and adventurous as a couple. There was not even a hint of animosity or distance between the two of you. But after your marriage, your friends do occasionally comment on how much you changed as a person. Indeed, the social circles in which you used to move in seemed to fade away, and become less important. How and why did that happen?'

When Matthew stared back, a slight twitch of the mouth occurred only fleetingly, but enough to alert Konrad to the fact that he had initiated a line of questions that could prove fruitful. Matthew bowed his head, and rubbed the palms of his hands together before replying, again choosing his words with care.

'Yes, the social media aspect of our relationship was carefully managed, not by me, by Helena and sometimes by Naomi. Your research appears to have been more thorough on this aspect, Mr Neale.' Konrad knew that it hadn't. This was pure luck.

'Are you confirming that Helena wrote her own and also wrote your Facebook posts and comments?' There was a significant inflection at the end of that question.

Matthew nodded once, slowly and emphatically.

'So, Matthew, you wish for us to believe that the Facebook interactions between you and your friends, your work colleagues and even between you and Josh, were mostly written by Helena. There is no way of proving that of course, one way or the other, but it does help your cause to convince us that it's true.'

Konrad believed him. His wife Delia did the same thing. Facebook, Twitter, the social media nightmare needed a PR approach if not to prove fatal to his career.

'You are also, therefore, leading us to believe that she somehow steered your social life. Allow me to return to the Facebook evidence; your honeymoon photos were plastered over it. An adventure to the icy wilds in Scandinavia followed by beautiful beaches with palm trees in Sri Lanka, for ten days, wasn't it? A great choice for a late autumn wedding, and filled with thrilling adventures. How dreadful for you to endure.

'Forgive my sarcasm, and explain to me, if you will, just why your legal counsel insisted in court that this was torturous, Matthew, because the pictures tell the story of a blissful honeymoon, and so do the Facebook posts.'

Matthew sat up straighter in his chair. 'Of course they do. Mr Neale, I have nothing more to lose in life, and I certainly have nothing to gain by lying to you when my intention is to record the truth for the sake of my son's future. I don't want him to go on believing for the rest of his life that his father killed his stepmother out of a sick and twisted need for revenge or of jealous anger. I have to accept that I killed Helena but, as I have always insisted, I did not carry out a wilful murder.'

There was a lengthy pause. 'How can you expect people to believe that your wife's death wasn't wilful? You not only killed her but also disfigured her, and decapitated her as if it were fuelled by the most incredible rage. When did things shift from an exciting adventurous relationship to one that ended in death?'

Matthew Hawley gazed down at his feet for several seconds before he raised his head to look his inquisitor in the eye.

'When Helena and I went on our honeymoon, I was the happiest man on the planet because we had arranged our two destinations to please each other. Mountains and fjords, lakes and snow excite me. The silence and the clean air are magical, as was the thought of sleigh rides and skidoo experiences – it was great. Of course, I hadn't taken into account Helena's habit of planning surprises for me, as well as the games she loved to play with my mind and, as it turns out, with my body.'

'Go on.'

*

As Konrad watched himself on the screen in the editing suite, he noticed how his breathing had quickened when he encouraged Matthew to tell the story. As he viewed the events in front of him again, he closed his eyes. Knowing full well what was about to be revealed. He wanted to listen to the description again, and immerse himself in Matthew's experiences of Helena's game.

'She organised a sauna again, but this time it was by a frozen lake, a short walk from a stunning farmhouse where we spent the night sleeping on fur rugs by an open fire in a log cabin annex. We had supper by candlelight and a hearty breakfast in the morning, provided by the owners. They were lovely genuine people who couldn't do enough for us and yet respected our absolute privacy. I can smell the place now; fresh pine, candle wax and smoke from the log fire. The sauna was the treat, to help rebuild my faith in sauna doors I think.' Matthew smiled and seemed to be living his recollections as he spoke.

'The torture was the dip in the frozen lake afterwards.'

'Body shock…?'

'No, I'm kidding, that was part of the treat. It sounds terrible but once you're brave enough to try it, you reap the benefits. Very invigorating, it is too. Helena insisted that I had behaved like a coward by hesitating for too long before working up the courage to take the plunge into the icy black water beneath the thin frozen surface of the lake. On top of that, I had apparently ruined the video she was making of me as I ran gingerly from the sauna to the lake. I waited for her in the icy waters before she made a dash to join me and screamed with the shock, just as I had done. Because I'm a man, I was deemed inadequate for having done the same as her, and therefore the video was unusable. She laughed as she explained this, of course, but I was to be punished for behaving like a sissy, as she put it, by being given one of her "special" massages.'

'Please feel free to explain…' Konrad encouraged with an open wave of his hands.

'I'll try not to be too explicit, Mr Neale, but this isn't for the faint-hearted.'

Konrad had laughed briefly, under the impression that Matthew was being playful with his humour. He stopped abruptly when Matthew's face indicated otherwise.

'As you will no doubt have guessed, Helena used sex as the enticement and her next treat. After supper, and to allow enough time for our meal to be digested, we sat in front of the warm log fire, nursing a glass or two of red wine. Later, when we were mellow and glowing, she instructed me to close both eyes, and lay face up on the heap of fur rugs in our cabin, naked of course. When I was permitted to open my eyes, she stood over me, feet either side of my pelvis, with a long-rounded icicle held in a leather-gloved hand. She forbade me to move my arms from my sides while she entertained herself with her other hand and the icicle, allowing it to melt inside her, just enough for drips of freezing water to land on my genitals making me flinch. "No moving," she said.'

'Torture.'

'Not yet, Mr Neale. You are impatient.' Matthew chided, raising one eyebrow. Konrad pulled back into his chair realising his error and finding Matthew infuriating.

He knows this kinky shit is getting to me.

'The candle wax was the torture. A step too far. Helena crossed an invisible line that night. She took a large candle from beside the fireplace. Not one of those common-all-garden household candles, no. This was one of sturdier proportions that developed a crater full of molten wax. She dripped that wax onto my genitals, Mr Neale, begging me to be a man and not to make a noise. She deliberately and slowly spilt the molten wax and then took the burning pain away by dripping the melting ice from her frozen dildo onto my balls. The finale, Mr Neale, was my second experience of having my pubic hairs waxed. Helena was thrilled. Not a sound did I make, not a wince or a yelp, and I was rewarded for good behaviour with a sound seeing to, Mr Neale.'

'Very poetic, Matthew. Thank you for taking the trouble to avoid offensive sexual language. Your point is well made, but again what I'm hearing is the story of a man who has chosen to explore the kinkier side of sexual practices. I'll have to leave it to the viewing public to decide whether that is considered to be torture.' *She could torture me like that any day.*

'Mr Neale, not one of those special massage treats made it onto Facebook. The pictures of me completing the skeleton luge run at over eighty miles per hour were there, the gruelling ice climb, and the vertigo-inducing base jump were posted, as were the shots of us during a snow sprinkled dogsled experience, but never my vomiting with fear beforehand, and never my burnt skin or rope marks.

'Did your researchers tell you that each one of those extreme winter sports challenges were sponsored? I was even raising money for charity on my honeymoon. How about that?'

Konrad spotted again how Matthew counted each of the sponsored challenges on his fingers with a bitter edge to his voice.

'Did Helena count on her fingers like that?' He asked, struck by how often Matthew would repeat this gesture.

'That's an interesting question. Yes, she did as a matter of fact. She would recap for the press doing the same thing. It irritated me. Strange that I should do the same thing…' Matthew stared down at his hands as if seeking an answer there.

'Is that why you cut off her fingers and toes?'

'I suppose it could be. I don't remember,' Matthew said, as his thoughts took him away to a half-forgotten memory. 'She used to count on her fingers and say, "More events than you could count on all your fingers, toes, and then some". The press loved it.'

'Did you have a rest in Sri Lanka?'

'I was hoping to. Helena had organised a retreat. "A yoga health retreat for relaxation and rejuvenation". Doesn't that sound lovely?'

Konrad did not reply.

'When we arrived in the warm sunshine, the yoga and meditation featured heavily in the photos that Helena posted on social media, as did the swimming pool and the beach. Everyone was amazed that we didn't put on weight during our luxury honeymoon. "You must have exercised it all off, you naughty people!" was the type of innuendo in comments we received. Well ha, bloody ha! I had an enormous appetite and needed every ounce of strength to cope with Helena's honeymoon programme, but the word "healthy" seemed to have been interpreted as "starvation rations" at our holiday retreat. To top that, and to ensure I was exhausted and detoxified, I had the shit washed out of me several times by a small Asian woman who hooked up a tube from a bucket containing warm, strong, fully caffeinated coffee, while I lay flat on a white, ceramic, sloping sluice. The noises and the stench were indescribably dreadful. Colonic irrigation was degrading. Utterly degrading. Ever had a tube wedged up your arse while your wife watches, Mr Neale? No?'

*

'Look at your face. What a picture,' cried Annette with glee.

'You can cut that shot, most definitely.' Konrad found enough humour left in reserve to accept Annette's ribbing and find himself funny. 'Oh my God, I remember this so well. I didn't know where to put myself. I had this ridiculous cartoon in my head of Delia shrieking at me not to shit on her clean bathroom floor.'

*

'I can't say I have, Matthew. No,' Konrad replied, grateful for a reprieve from descriptions of sexual acts involving the voluptuous Helena. 'I believe I understand the argument you're putting forward, in which case, can I take you back to the time of your wedding preparations?'

Chapter 8

'In court, a letter was produced, which you say you received before you married Helena, and although not signed, this letter was sent to your place of work and was from Helena's sister. Why was it that Helena never mentioned to you that she had a sister?' Konrad sat back, watching for Matthew's response.

There was a long pause, and the muscles in Matthew's cheeks twitched as his jaw clenched. 'I don't know if I have a definitive answer to give you.'

Konrad stepped in. 'Perhaps I should expand for the benefit of the people who will watch this film. I have a copy of the letter you received, and I also have a short excerpt from a story written by Helena's sister when she was a young child, also sent to you. Both are very telling. I should let you know that we are making on-going efforts to trace Helena's sister, just as your defence team did. There are requests for information on social media, and via missing persons' charitable organisations. We have even scoured CCTV footage from around the Crown Court at the times of your trial in case she was tempted to make an appearance. She remains elusive.'

Matthew was impassive, but his interviewer could sense tension as he sat opposite. He continued. 'This first letter was read out in court, and in brief it warns you about the potential difficulties you may face if you decide to proceed with the wedding to Helena. This paragraph is particularly interesting:

"I knew Helena throughout my childhood, but I didn't live with her for many of those years. Her jealousy was so consuming and her hatred of me so intense that she couldn't bear to look at me without resorting to vicious assault, either verbally or physically. I did nothing to deserve this other than being born. She hated me from the moment I arrived. Mum and Dad tried to explain to her that there was to be a new baby girl or boy arriving in the family, but she couldn't comprehend what that meant. They said she was too young to understand, but she was old enough to have had their undivided attention for four whole years before I arrived on the scene. Helena was furious, outraged and inconsolable. Mum could not leave me in the same room as Helena, unattended. I have the scars to prove that."

'You are aware, Matthew, that Helena had a sister by the name of Tessa.'

'Call her what you like, I have no clue if that's her real name or not,' Matthew said with an irritated tone Konrad couldn't quite fathom.

'You know that Chawston isn't even Helena's real surname, because the court proceedings referred to this fact.'

By the look on Matthew's face, Konrad confirmed what he had suspected. There was an awful lot about his own wife that Matthew hadn't known until he was told during his trial.

'Her surname was actually Carlton. Tessa says, in her letter, that child psychologists and numerous therapists saw Helena in an effort to get to the bottom of her jealousy, but in the end it was Tessa Carlton who had to live with her paternal grandparents. The two sisters couldn't go to the same school or be at family events together. It was attempted, but failed and drove the family apart in the end.

'Not the parents, no. According to this letter they stayed together meeting Helena's every demand, but Tessa hardly saw them. Helena went to university, moved on and abandoned her parents, denying their existence. She changed her surname and told everyone she was an only child and that her parents were dead.

'They were very much alive until after your wedding, as it happens. Shortly after that they died due to carbon monoxide poisoning. Their rented flat was in a shocking state of repair and the ancient gas boiler was deemed the cause of the tragic accident. Odd isn't it that Helena had so much, and yet her parents lived in poverty.' He took his time, leading Matthew from the charade that Helena had created and towards the truth.

'Now then, Matthew, you had this letter in your possession, which gives fair warning about Helena's potential to harm those close to her. What did you do with that information? Nothing?' Forthright in his presentation, he had pushed for an overt emotional response.

'Far from it, Mr Neale,' Matthew replied. 'The court dismissed the evidence, as there was nothing to prove Helena's sister wrote it. It was a typed letter that anyone could have produced. In court, the prosecution asked the jury to believe I had written the letter myself, after Helena's death, which was an insult to their collective intelligence.' Matthew sighed. 'Of course, when I read the letter, I had no idea of Tessa's existence and I was besotted with Helena. What would you have done? I showed it to Helena. Her initial reaction was not extraordinary in the least. She read it several times and declared that I had managed to attract a nutter, a psychopath who was jealous of our relationship, and she even asked me questions about past lovers and girlfriends. We traced one or two on Facebook but found nothing untoward. So, you see Helena found a way of convincing me that the letter had been sent because of actions I had taken. Not because of her.'

Konrad was hitting his stride, knowing he held some information that Matthew wanted.

'But those letters continued after you were married, didn't they? Helena was so insistent you had attracted a stalker that you reported this to the police. Why did it have to be a stalker? Couldn't Tessa feasibly have been an envious sister who didn't have the wealth and lifestyle of her older sibling?'

'Yes, quite easily, Mr Neale, but what Helena and I believed was also plausible. A stalker, a jealous individual who wanted to scare me away from Helena, who herself reacted in the only way she knew how. She protected me from predators and ensured that I would never consider taking the advice in those letters. As far as I was concerned, Helena didn't even have a sister.'

'Those letters told you that she did, and you could have tried to find out, one way or the other. You chose not to. But they weren't just giving you advice or trying to warn you, were they? Tessa appeared to give you evidence. Let me show you a copy of something Tessa sent to you, as a reminder. She sent an extract from some English homework written when she was about ten. It doesn't sound like much at first but it's so powerful in this context. It reads as follows:

"The girl with beads in her black hair, and with straight teeth, was there peering through the window. An older girl with curly golden locks and big blue eyes was hugging her. She was called Helena and we heard the other girl shouting, 'Get me the antiseptic cream!' and Helena said 'stop crying,' sniggering away because Helena was a sour girl. She looks cute and innocent on the outside but inside she's as sour as a lemon. She had cut her sister with the scissors in her hand, and she smiled when she saw the blood. 'You didn't do what I asked you to. No reward for you,' Helena said to her little sister. 'You did, one two three four five and six, but you didn't do seven.' Helena counted on her fingers all the scary things her sister had done, because Helena told her to."

'What does that tell us now do you think, Matthew?' Konrad sat back, proudly.

'I'm sorry, Mr Neale, I must have misunderstood the significance of that reference. When I was sent that by the lady you call Tessa, who is apparently Helena's sister, it was another piece of evidence to strengthen our hypothesis that a stalker was hounding me. Anyone could have picked up on the habit Helena had of counting on her fingers. It sounds the same as it did then; coincidental.'

*

'He's right, you know,' Annette said, stretching her arms up in the air and thrusting out her enormous overhanging chest. 'That was a pathetic story, which anyone could have written pretending to be a child. It could be about our Helena or any other Helena. But we may keep it in, given that we don't have any footage from an interview with Tessa, because she may not exist.

'I was thinking; you know we talked about putting in a clip or two of the videos showing Matthew and his extreme challenges? I think we should. That poor man has flown, bounced, and teetered on tightropes for two years without getting seriously injured or dead. It's hard to believe really, after all that effort, success, money raised for other people, notoriety and adulation, and he turns out to be a psycho-slasher.'

'I thought we'd identified the videos on his Facebook as being too staged, too perfect to bother with.'

'Yes, we did, which is why I set Joe here a task to find other sources. Can you do some homework on the ones he found, Konrad? I can't give the job to Mike, he doesn't know what to look for, but you do, and if they're of good enough quality we may be able to get a close-up headshot when Matthew's in action. Let's see if we can find evidence of the fear of heights he talks about, or the rope burns. Slow Joe has put the clips on a hard drive for you and he's trawled YouTube, other posts on Facebook, and the rest of the Internet to find a selection of the best.' Annette leant across to whisper in her colleague's ear, 'He's not a bad lad really.'

Evidently Slow Joe was making progress and Konrad was pleased for him, but it was the junior editor, Mike, he felt sorry for. Annette never allowed him to take responsibility for anything unless it was under her strict guidance. He was a wizard with the equipment, and it was strongly suspected that Annette was trying to delay Mike's career advancement. She clearly wanted him by her side to make up for her lack of technical ability when it came to innovations in the digital world, and Mike was too nice to see it. However, on this occasion, Konrad latched onto the fact that Annette was not undermining faithful lapdog Mike. Keeping Konrad's mind away from Lorna by setting work he could do at home would help to avoid the inevitable conflict with Delia; Annette was trying to do him a favour.

Hiding away in my little office playing with video clips of a cold-blooded killer enjoying himself, just to avoid having to be around my wife. Is that what my married life has come to? Is this a taste of my future?

'Coffee break, children. Your turn to make a mad dash for the bargains at Poncho's please.' Annette was talking to Mike and Joe, who willingly took up their challenge and a chance for time away from the confines and intensity of watching the endless screening.

Konrad stood up to alleviate the numbness in his behind, and to stretch, synchronising with Annette who was doing the same from a seated position.

'Shit. That's reminded me. I need to phone the kids to see if they're catching the train from Bangor tomorrow and how long they're staying for. If they're back for a week or more I might have to collect them.' He paused. His arms dropped limply by his side. 'Bloody hell, I hope not, Delia might want to come along. Can you imagine how that journey would pan out? Hours of silent bitterness followed by a return journey the next day filled with plastic pretence and false laughter. Pukesville.'

Annette gave a sympathetic glance. 'Why don't you go to collect them tomorrow? We'll carry on here. You can always put Delia off the idea of spending two days with you by placing sex firmly on the agenda. Tell her your drunken exploits were caused by testosterone overload and that a night in a cheap hotel being filthy will cure you.'

'Annette, sometimes I think you're wasted in this business. Agony aunts earn a lot of money working in the glossy magazine sector. You're a relationship genius.'

'I know... While you're in Bangor you could stay at The Management Centre at the university, they have beautiful bed and breakfast accommodation on site and it's within walking distance of a great pub and BBC Wales. You could look Lorna up while you're there. She's working on site, I checked.'

Konrad was still for a while. 'She's in Bangor? But I thought she was based in Cardiff…'

Annette pleaded with him. 'Kon, you're a good mate, and I can't take the heartache I see in you much longer. Your mind is all over the place and you've been acting like a lost puppy since we finished filming the first series. You're an idiot. The Truth Behind the Lies became a sensation and suddenly your wife goes into overdrive to sell you for more money, and blackmails you into saving your washed-up marriage. Money, not love, is what she wanted. You don't need to spend the rest of your life with a dried-up cold fish like her. Grow some balls for fuck's sake. Life's too short.'

Konrad was momentarily stunned into silence, and there was an uncomfortable pause before he simply held Annette's rounded face in his hands and kissed her full on the mouth. 'Why didn't you say this three months ago?'

He turned as if to leave the room but Annette had to call him back. She took a minute to recover from the unusual show of personal affection, despite knowing there was no romantic connotation to Konrad's kiss. It was one of friendship and gratitude, but even so it had taken her by surprise.

Desperate for a trip to the ladies' toilet she had tried to stand, but her thighs had taken up the available space beneath the arms of her swivel chair and over spilled the seat to such an extent that she found herself moulded into it. It took a gargantuan effort on her friend's part to help prise her free. 'Thanks, Kon. I know… I should see if the doctors can review my thyroid function…'

Konrad was left alone in the editing suite allowing him privacy while he checked his phone for messages again. Nothing.

Disappointed, he diverted his attention away from his mobile and picked up the registered letter that Lillian had given him after lunch the previous day. He'd thrown it on top of a pile of correspondence that he was hoping would miraculously deal with itself. Reading the words in front of him, it dawned that the team's search for Tessa had taken a dramatic step forward.

"Dear Mr Neale and colleagues,

Please do not persist in trying to identify me. I understand your wish to interview me for your documentary and I'm informed that you are busy editing the final product as I write, but I don't want to be found. (Forget the postmark... I don't live there.) Helena is dead and for that I am profoundly grateful to Matthew, because I can now be free, but only if you leave me alone. My expectation is that you will announce on social media that you are no longer seeking me out. You don't need me. You have what you need from Matthew.

Kind regards."

The letter was dated but not signed. Konrad did not need a signature to identify the author, as far as he was concerned, it had to be Tessa, and far from having any intention of withdrawing the search for Helena's sister, he was determined to redouble the efforts.

'Who has access to The Truth Behind the Lies' Twitter page and Facebook?' He asked Mike when he returned, cheese twists in one hand, coffees in the other.

'There's a whole department for that upstairs. I'll give them a ring for you.'

A new useful contact was made – Raj – who was extremely helpful in allowing Konrad to explain his intentions and in getting a strong message across to Tessa on social media. 'Raj, you're a star! That should hook her in, enticing words and a video clip. Lovely. A short, personal filmed appeal for information. That has to be one of the best ideas anyone has come up with so far. Nice doing business with you. Be in touch again soon.'

Chapter 9

The house was warm, but the reception received when he walked in was decidedly frosty. Delia was not expecting an expensive gift from Konrad and he knew better than to consider such a cheap trick after his drunken antics in the early hours. Besides which, he had resolved to confront his shallow cowardice when it came to his future with Delia, and had put his plans in motion to make an escape from a life of hen-pecking.

'I'm going to Bangor tomorrow to collect Freliza.' Konrad made use of the appalling collective name given to his twin children by their friends. This infuriated Delia and set the tone for the evening. She would accept that he was in no mood to placate her. He had judged this correctly.

'Please don't call our children by that dreadful nickname. They are two individuals. When are we going tomorrow? It'll have to be later in the afternoon, I have a hair appointment at eleven.' It was clear that Delia couldn't bear to look at her husband and she busied herself realigning ornaments on the sideboard in the lounge.

'You're not coming with me. I've arranged with Freddie to meet him and Eliza before lunch because they have to change their digs, so I'll be moving boxes and furniture for the day, stay overnight in a B&B, then bring them back either Saturday or Sunday depending on how the move goes. I'll let you know.'

'What on earth do you mean? How fucking inconsiderate and thoughtless of you to make these arrangements without me. You owe me, big time, for your disgraceful drunken behaviour last night. You're a bloody disgusting creature urinating in my investment piece. You shattered a mirror, you left clothing all over the floor and you insulted me by calling me her name. Yes, The Whore. Her. Miss Yoyo Knickers.' Delia was spitting the words out like a machine gun, and her eyes had become slits from which emerged tiny arrows of hatred. 'If you think I'm ever letting you into my bed again you've got another thing coming!'

Konrad held fast. 'While I'm away you'd better move my stuff into the spare room then, hadn't you? Oh, don't worry. I'll tell the children my snoring had become intolerable and that you need your beauty sleep. They won't believe me, but it'll make you feel so much better. Another charade to convince people what a wonderful marriage we have.'

At this, he ducked as a cushion was launched in his direction, followed by another accompanied by a screeching siren. 'Don't push me any further, Kon. I'll take you to the cleaners. I'll have every penny and the car and the house. You know it.'

I do. Guess what, Delia…? You can have it. I hate this house, I want a Land Rover not a Range Rover, and I'd like to spend the rest of my days with a soft supple woman who wants to live in the real world, who laughs at silly things, farts in bed, dances in her bare feet, drinks for the hell of it, and sits on my fat cock because she enjoys it, thought Konrad. But he didn't have the guts to say those words. Instead, his sensible head persuaded him to hold his tongue for the present.

'I'll play it your way, Delia, but if you want to keep our public face and our pretence of a cohesive showbiz couple intact, I suggest you reconsider your threats to withdraw conjugal rights. It's the only weapon you have left and if you remove it from the battlefield then you lose.'

Delia stared at her husband in disbelief. He'd never spoken to her in such cold and calculated terms before. He sensed her uncertainty. 'Right, I'm going upstairs to pack a bag for my trip tomorrow. I take it you won't be following me stripping off your clothes and kneeling before me, so I suggest you trot along to Sainsbury's or Waitrose to buy delicious and expensive food for our offspring to devour when they return with me. As I said, we'll let you know when to expect us home.'

With that masterstroke, Konrad strode confidently towards the stairs. 'And don't organise a stupid party. I hate them. Freddie and Eliza are going to have a barbecue and invite their friends. We shall be upsetting the neighbours with loud music and drunken behaviour on Thursday night. I might invite Barney and a few other real people. Yes. That's a great idea.' Delia looked about her as if she were figuring out which world she had just landed in. She knew she wasn't in Kansas any more.

He found a suitable holdall, and threw it onto the bed, into which he chucked a couple of pairs of underpants. 'That'll do for starters.' Stripping off, he headed for the clinically clean en-suite bathroom, and as he did so he was whistling, something he hadn't done for months. His phone buzzed with a message and he performed an immediate about-face to pick it up, pleading with it to put him out of his agony. 'Please be Lorna, please be Lorna.' It wasn't. It was Barney.

"Part two of the plan is in place. You can pick up your new toy this evening. Tax is sorted. Bring the old one as part exchange. See you at the yard 8pm."

'Cheeky bastard.' Konrad smiled and headed back towards the shower, flicking his underpants in the general direction of the laundry basket.

Not in the mood to talk to Delia during the rest of the evening, Konrad phoned Barney and they agreed to meet earlier to sort out the new purchase before an alcohol-free supper at the pub – where he would find out how much apologising he had to do, and to whom. His recall of the previous night was sketchy.

'There she is. Much more sensible than a sodding Range Rover Evoque.'

'Cor, you're not kidding. I'm glad to see the back of the bloody thing. It's like a giant posing car for a hairdresser. Useless.

This is much more the business.' Konrad took a long admiring look at his new wheels. 'Lovely green colour too. She'll really hate this.'

'I don't want to be anywhere nearby when The Camp Commandant clocks what you've done.' Barney was giving his friend a worried look.

'Have faith, old pal, it's worth it to see her squirm with embarrassment in front of all her posh friends. Anyway, I can't see what's wrong with this one; it's a bloody good vehicle. Just the job for moving the kids' belongings around in Wales at the weekend. Right, here are the keys and the documents for The Commandant-Carrier, get what you can for it. I'll drive this gorgeous green beast home, park up, take the flack, and see you at the pub. No beer this time. I've got to drive tomorrow.'

'Just a couple?'

'No, Barney. I'll buy you one, though, for getting this sorted without The Commandant finding out. Listen for the explosion. I'll see you in ten minutes.'

Delia's radar was working perfectly, and she appeared at the front door as Konrad drove in at the wheel of the used Series 4 Land Rover Discovery, in dark metallic green livery. He stepped out and walked towards Delia, putting the keys into his pocket as he did so.

'Whose is that?'

'Mine.'

'Where's my car?'

'Yours is in the garage, dear, where you left it I expect.'

'Not the Mini, the Range Rover. Where is it? In for a service, I suppose, with that idiot Barney who's had the gall to lend you this ugly monstrosity.'

Konrad revelled in announcing that he was the proud owner of this lovely low-mileage Discovery.

Delia's furious snobbery came spilling out. 'You can take it back. It's second hand on a twelve plate for God's sake, and it's green!'

'It's mine, and I like it,' Konrad replied as he threw some waterproof clothing and walking boots into the rear of the Land Rover, in case he forgot to pack them later. After which, he left Delia stewing on the doorstep as she sent daggers into the back of his head with her withering stare.

'You out and out arse, Konrad Neale. What will people think?'

I couldn't give a flying fuck.

Having avoided a direct hit from Delia, he strolled sedately towards The Valiant Soldier, but because his phone beeped at him, he stopped to perch for a while on a low stone wall. Taking his mobile out of his pocket to read what he hoped was Lorna's response, he prayed silently.

"Hello, Kon. So, she's finally had enough of you has she? You want to come creeping back into my life now, just when I thought I had begun to get over the pain. If you can find me, I'll listen to what you have to say. If you can't, then it's goodbye. I give you forty-eight hours. Lorna."

Konrad tilted his head towards the clouded sky and thanked a God he didn't believe in. Then he remembered to thank Annette, and was about to call her as another text came through, which he assumed was an afterthought from Lorna announcing her undying love. It wasn't.

"You got my letter and you chose to ignore it. You will not find me, but I will find you and show you how it feels to have your life ruined."

Good grief, we've rattled Tessa's cage. He checked the phone number on the text, another different one. *Clever. She really doesn't want to be found.* His thoughts were brave, but he could only hope that Tessa was making idle threats to keep him away.

*

54

A belly full of food and a couple of pints of shandy later, Konrad took a deep breath, walked into his house and straight upstairs to finish his packing. 'Laptop, don't forget the bloody laptop.' Locating his wash bag, he made certain that he packed Lorna's favourite aftershave, clean shirts, decent jeans, walking trousers and more clean underpants. 'Two pairs might not be enough.' He pictured himself and Lorna ripping off each other's clothes in a wild sexual frenzy of reunion, and then he crash-landed back to reality, knowing how unlikely that would be.

The house was empty and eerily noiseless which was unnerving. It was a while before he realised that Delia seemed to be missing. No one was nagging at him.

What day is it? Thursday. Her night for swanning around at the golf club though neither of us plays. Good, she'll be late.

With the car packed and laptop placed on the hall table to remind him to take it along on his trip to Wales, he phoned Freddie to confirm his plans for the following day.

'I should be there late morning, depending on the traffic, so I'll see you and Eliza at your place. Got everything packed?'

'Yes, Dad. Liza became bossy and fucking irritating, so I let her get on with it. She's so anal. Our stuff is packed, boxed and labelled. There are hardly any big items, so we'll probably manage the move in a couple of runs. The new place isn't far from The Management Centre and the best pub in town, which is handy. I'll stand you a pint or two in the evening if you're lucky.'

'Very magnanimous of you to spend my money on me, son. You'll go far.'

'See you tomorrow. Love to Mum. Did you mention the barbecue by the way?'

'Yes, I did. Brave of me, don't you think?'

'What did she say?'

'There were no objections.'

'Really?'

'Yes, really. See you tomorrow.'

*

Konrad had trouble sleeping. The bed in the spare room was comfortable enough, but his anxious anticipation about seeing Lorna the next day kept him tossing and turning. He heard Delia come home, slamming doors and clip-clopping across the tiled floors to let him know her foul mood was still very much present.

I really can't find any love left for her. She's turned into a self-centred, bitter and cold cardboard cut-out.

Eventually, he drifted off into a restless sleep dreaming about an escape from Colditz, until he rose well before six in the morning to head north and west to Bangor. His alarm didn't wake him, a text message did.

"Your wife doesn't think much of you. She and the other Stepford Wives had a mammoth bitching session at the golf club last night. Fancy getting drunk and pissing in her best vase, you naughty man. What would your public think? Your wife may have closed her fanny, but she's good at opening her mouth."

He stared at the phone in disbelief. *Tessa? Could she really be that serious?* He read the message again, before deciding to deal with Helena's sister when he returned from Wales. She would have to fester until then.

Chapter 10

She set the camera up on a tripod to give the desired angle and checked the viewfinder to ensure the placement was correct. The record button was pressed. She then stepped towards the tall stool only three feet away, turned, sat down and spoke briefly before rising slowly, and stopping the recording.

When the short video was replayed to her satisfaction, she grinned to herself. Initially, she had tried to film using a bookshelf as a place to stand the camera, but it was at the wrong height entirely and resulted in her having to hunch her shoulders to remain in the shot.

Although at first, she had resisted having to unpack the small tripod stand, this set-up was much more stable. There was nothing in the out-of-focus background identifying her surroundings. No pictures on the walls, no personal items in the shot. Just her head and shoulders with a plain wall behind her. Although the lighting was poor, it would have to do. She didn't have much time.

She pressed the record button again. As she took her seat on the stool, the floorboards creaked and the small red light on the front of the camera flickered slightly as the tripod shifted on one of its legs. She waited for the camera to become still before she spoke, looking into the lens as if talking to someone she knew well.

'Your wife, Konrad Neale, is one of the most unpleasant people I have had the displeasure of eavesdropping on. There she sat in the corner of the golf club bar, on a comfy leather sofa, with her so-called friends sipping wine and discussing the most intimate details of your private life. She didn't even take enough interest in me to give anything other than a cursory glance in my direction. I could have been anybody.

'You should have seen her taking great delight in demeaning you, her own husband. She sounded so false. Everything about her is pretence, apart from her tits. They are real, I think. Pretence and pretentiousness, that's Delia. I listened to her as she made it clear, to anyone who cared to listen, how much she despises you for not wanting to be in the right social set. How unhappy she was that you didn't go with her to Pippa's book launch. She had to drive herself there and back again which upset her plans for parading around with her famous husband clutching a glass of Prosecco. How thoughtless of you, Konrad.

'Your wife has told the freaky-faced, plastic women of the golf club how you disgraced yourself by getting drunk and pissing in her vase. You have more spirit than I gave you credit for. In fact, you've surprised me once or twice.

'I watched you sitting in the park. I sat close by with two strangers. We ate sandwiches together and chatted like old friends about the virtues of avocado.

'You made for a pathetic sight in your baseball cap trying to make sense of your personal world, which from an outsider's view may appear ideal but, from the look on your face, has become a dreadful burden. It took me a while to get hold of your mobile phone number, but Lillian on reception at your offices is so innocent that she believed my simple story. "Good morning, I've had a message from my studio asking me to call Konrad on his mobile, unfortunately the number they gave me seems to have one digit wrong. I have a zero too many. Can you confirm the number for me please...?" and she did. What a helpful girl, and so polite with it. I thought you would have received my letter by then, but obviously that was not the case, judging by your text reply. You were hoping to be contacted by someone called Lorna.

'Your wife told me all about her. She also told each and every one of the Stepford Wives at the golf club. I listened enthralled, Konrad, as she spilled the beans on your dirty affair. Over twelve months of clandestine meetings, rendezvous, fictitious film location visits, rehearsals and trips took place, during which

Lorna would be at your side and not your wife. Delia found out. Tonight, she has confessed to her friends that you called her "Lorna" when you were pissed up last night. She's angry, Konrad, but she's willing to maintain the status quo for now. She likes the fame and money you bring to your sexless marriage. Yes… she told them that as well, in a public place, in a loud whisper. I like her style. She knows when you're gagging for a shag. She's amused by your pathetic endeavours to buy affection and by how you try to bribe your way into her frosty knickers. Did you know she has a vibrator hidden in the bathroom? You don't know do you, Konrad. The Stepford Wives are all aware of the fact because Delia has told them how thrilled she is that you're going to North Wales tomorrow to collect your twins from university. She dotes on them, doesn't she? It was Freddie this and Eliza that. Nauseating.

'While you're away she won't miss you.

'She's going to lie on your bed fantasising about the new golf professional, Rolf, and she'll thrash around with her costly exclusive vibrator, which she does several times a week. One of her friends has recommended mint lube for additional tingling sensations, so she doesn't need you for affection or sex; she wants your money and the kudos you bring. How shallow.

'I'm feeling a certain sexual stirring myself, a little thrill at what you have set in motion with your challenge. You were warned not to try to find Tessa Carlton, but you can't resist. You seem to think you have a God-given right to seek out whosoever you choose to interview, but not everyone wants their lives exposed and put on display for the sensation seeking public to mock. So as an inevitable result, I'm drawn to your gauntlet. I warned you, and still you have chosen to ignore me. It looks like I'll have to catch a train if I'm to get to Bangor before you. I'll leave now. I do love to travel by train. I can spend the time usefully on the journey, researching into your children. Certain that you'll be meeting up with Lorna, I'll be watching both of you.'

Chapter 11

The Management Centre at the university in Bangor was not what he had expected. The beautiful Edwardian stone building overlooked the Menai Straits, and from his spacious, dual aspect room, Konrad had a clear view of the sea rushing towards the Swellies, and of Anglesey beyond. From the other window he could see across the grassy courtyard bordered on three sides by the impressive building. The bed in his room was vast, its size serving to remind him that, regrettably, he would be sleeping in it alone that night.

As he placed his bag on a chair, he berated himself yet again for turning his back on Lorna by putting his career before a life in the real world. He also began to recognise the rising panic setting in each time he considered the possibility of being single and alone, should she decide to send him packing when they met. There was no one else he wanted to be with.

Konrad had spotted the BBC offices from the car park but had not yet formulated a plan in his head about how best to approach Lorna. Strolling into the bright, breezy morning air, he found a useful vantage point to spy on the BBC building, vainly hoping to catch a glimpse of her, like a naughty schoolboy. Then he saw her. Lorna was with a tall man, chatting amicably as they approached the entrance.

Shit. I feel sick.

The fear of rejection was gnawing away as he sent the text.

"Found you! Meet me later for a drink at the pub nearest the pier? K xx"

Lorna must have picked up the text almost straight away as she appeared back outside the entrance doors turning her head left and right, looking for him with a shocked expression on her face. She set about replying, by which time Konrad had made a hasty retreat, wanting time to gauge her state of mind rather than rushing headlong into being permanently shunned by her, face to face.

"No. Bad idea. Meet me on the pier and we will walk and talk without alcohol being involved. 5.30pm."

Short, sweet and to the bloody point. It's going to be a long day.

Much to his relief, Freddie and Eliza were pleased to see him, even without Delia in toe, or possibly because of it. After warm greetings and disparaging comments about the new car, they set about loading up dozens of bags and boxes, keeping him occupied.

'Tell me again why you're moving,' Konrad demanded as he puffed and panted to the car carrying a heavy box, followed by Freddie and then Eliza laden like pack animals.

When they were younger, Freddie and Eliza had a confusing habit of saying the same thing simultaneously, or alternating information in order to complete a sentence between them. However, since reaching adulthood, and becoming more individual in their attitudes and tastes, they deferred to each other. Freddie took up the role of explaining the reason behind the move.

'The landlord here wants to squeeze more tenants into the house to earn himself additional income. We were cramped enough as it was so Liza and I have found ourselves a two-bedroom flat instead, that way we don't have to worry about anyone else getting on our nerves. The rent's not too much more and we've got part-time work. In fact, Liza has an offer of full-time employment over the summer, working for an events management company.'

'I think I can get Freddie at least a six-week stint covering bars at the summer gigs and the festivals. It's not bad money.'

Konrad spotted Freddie frowning at the mention of bar work.

'So we won't be seeing much of either of you after this week then?' Konrad asked, secretly relieved that neither of his children would have to witness their parents at each other's throats, bickering over who gets what in the bitter divorce looming large on the horizon. 'Bugger. I'd better phone your mother and let her know I've arrived. That'll keep her quiet for a while.'

As soon as he had announced he was with their children, Delia held her vicious tongue and sweetly asked to speak to Freddie and Eliza in turn. Both rolled their eyes.

'She sounded a bit pee'd off.' Freddie announced. 'Still, it looks like we're on for a barbecue...'

*

The day flew by in a series of loading and emptying the green machine, and much sweating and cursing. 'We'll get the rest of the stuff tomorrow. I'll leave you to make beds and get yourselves sorted. See you in The Tap and Spile at about seven-thirty. We'll have dinner together.' Konrad had made the excuse of meeting an old pal, meaning that he would have to catch up with his children for a beer later in the evening than anticipated. He wasn't even thinking about that. He was as nervous as a testosterone-driven youth on a first date.

Showered and clean, sunglasses on to hide his features, he walked down the hill to the pier arriving a good ten minutes ahead of schedule for his meeting with Lorna.

Wandering through the ornate wrought iron entrance gates and past the pagoda-like shelters with their distinctive domed roofs, he made his way to the end of the delicate Victorian pier. He gazed through the wooden slats to the sea below. Filling more time, he chatted with a gentleman who ran a tiny kiosk café called Whistlestop, where they sold tasty looking chowder. 'You look a lot like Konrad Neale, you know.'

'So they say.'

The man introduced himself formally and Konrad refused to believe that the café proprietor was called Terry Thomas. He was laughing heartily when Lorna suddenly appeared at his side.

'I see you've met Terry then.'

They walked and talked. Despite being somewhat stilted at first, Konrad felt they soon rediscovered their underlying friendship, allowing them to settle into reasoned conversation.

'Lorna, if I'm honest, I want to grovel and beg you to take me back and forgive my pathetic, selfish, idiotic plan to put my career first. I'm not proud of myself. I'm ashamed at what I've done to you. It's the biggest mistake I've ever made. But this is your decision and I'll accept my fate. Whatever the outcome, I'm leaving Delia. Just so we're clear on that.' Konrad and Lorna were leaning on the handrail looking out towards the boats moored at Beaumaris, letting the strong breeze wash over their faces.

'I'm not rushing into anything, Kon. You'll have to prove I can trust you again. You leave her and I'll believe your intentions. Until then… let's say, you're on probation.' He wanted to kiss her but held back, not wishing to make the wrong move.

His phone beeped, breaking the moment.

'That's Delia, I take it.' Lorna said, her face falling.

Konrad took a quick peek, but then declared, 'No, I think this is from my stalker.' His tone was serious enough for Lorna to appreciate that he wasn't joking. 'Jesus, I think she's here,' he said glancing back up the length of the pier towards the pub and the public green.

'She?'

'I've never met her. But I'm pretty sure who it is.'

'What's her name? Can't you simply report her to the police if she's bothering you? Or block her number.'

'I would if I knew her name and if she didn't change her number each time she sends a bloody text. I think she may have a screw loose. One of those obsession things you read about. It's to do with the documentary case we filmed recently for series two. We were searching for this person and she didn't want to be found. Now it seems she's got the hump and has turned the tables on me. It's a bit of a nuisance. She'll give up soon.' By saying this aloud, Konrad was reassuring himself; his inner voice was less confident. *Why would she go to the trouble of following Delia last night and then travelling all the way here to follow me?*

The subject was dropped. Lorna reiterated her terms and conditions to which Konrad readily agreed. 'We'll take it slow. No secrets, no selfish career moves, we start as we mean to go on. I'm taking the twins home for a week and I'll be back next weekend. After that, I'll move in with Barney or take a room at The Valiant Soldier until I find a place to call home. Maybe rent somewhere.'

Lorna squared her shoulders and dug her hands deep into her coat pockets. 'I mean it, Kon, no more heartbreak. You found me, thanks presumably to Annette, and I've listened to what you have to say, but this is it. Your only chance. Our only chance.'

'How about a drink and dinner tomorrow? You know the decent places to eat. Book somewhere and call me.' Konrad held her hands, kissed her cheek, then watched as Lorna strode back up the hill towards The Management Centre, and breathed a sigh of immense relief. He sat down on a bench and put his face into his shaking sweaty palms. *Don't cock this up, Kon, you utter muppet. Just don't cock it up.*

He looked again at the text from his not-so-mysterious stalker, Tessa Carlton, or whatever she was calling herself these days.

"So that's Lorna. Does Delia know you're meeting her this weekend?"

Konrad snorted at his phone. *You're out of luck, love, Delia already knows about Lorna, and that our marriage is over and when I get back home she will finally grasp that I am leaving her to spend my life with Lorna. You can't hurt me with this one, Tessa, old fruit. So fuck right off.*

Needing a moment to ground himself, he phoned Annette to give her the update on his reunion with Lorna.

'Thank God for that,' Annette said, heaving a sigh. 'I wouldn't have slept all weekend if you hadn't phoned. This is so exciting, just like a proper love story. Can I be bridesmaid?'

'Hold up a minute, I've got a hideous divorce to get through before we get to that stage. I've also got a lot of wooing to do before she'll say yes.'

'Wooing, is it?'

'Yes, Annette, there's work to be done. And talking of work, it appears that Tessa Carlton has deliberately turned the tables on us and has tracked *me* down. Since I opened that letter from her on Thursday and we challenged her on Facebook, she's decided to threaten me and turned stalker.'

'Bloody hell. No kidding? That's great news.'

'It's not so hot from where I'm standing. I'm pretty certain she's right here and watching my every move, but I can't see anyone who fits the raving psychopath bill. She's made some veiled threats but nothing reportable. Spooky though.'

'Can you ask the two whiz kids if they can do more detective work? Can we find out who the Carlton family GP was and try to get an NHS number or an NI number for Tessa? If Mike and Slow Joe can work from there onwards we might be able to trace an employment record or a health record that will get us what we need to identify her. A proper photo would be really helpful right now.'

'I'll give them a call. Joe's going to love getting his teeth into this. Right, you enjoy the rest of the weekend; take it slow and no flowers. They're a sign of guilt.'

'Yeah? Very funny. Of all people, don't you think I already know that…? See you Monday, and thanks, Netty, you're a good pal.'

*

Friday night, and the pub heaved with students and families drinking, eating meals and chatting animatedly. It was a second or two before Konrad registered that Freddie was already at the bar in deep conversation with a brown-eyed, auburn-haired beauty. Not wanting to cramp his son's style, he took his beer and sat at a table, which was neatly positioned up a short flight of stairs and tucked behind a wooden bannister from where he watched the mating rituals of the bright young things. His only son was doing a magnificent job of holding the auburn girl's interest and she was flirting in return. Freddie's efforts were not undermined by the arrival of his sister, who bounced up to the bar, kissed hello and embraced several of her fellow students, including the barmaid, and was eventually introduced by Freddie to his new female friend. Eliza seemed to respond positively and the three of them continued an easy conversation with smiles and laughter punctuating the discussions.

Eventually, Eliza spied her father and excused herself from the three-way social banter. 'How long have you been sitting there, Dad?'

'Long enough to work out that Freddie has pulled. Shall we leave them to it for a bit before we think about dinner?'

Eliza laughed at her father and ruffled his hair. 'You're so thoughtful.'

Konrad and Eliza had a father-daughter catch up for nearly an hour before they were joined by Freddie and his friend. 'Sorry to keep you waiting. Dad, this is Chloe Jordan.'

He approved of his son's choice, and of her firm handshake.

'Chloe's staying at The Management Centre too, so you'll see each other at breakfast,' Freddie joked.

'Just passing through?'

'No and yes, I'm overseeing a conference event for an outside company. Not very exciting but it pays the bills.'

Freddie my boy, you've got yourself an older woman, and you have no idea how lucky you're about to be.

'I'll be here until a week on Monday,' Chloe confirmed.

'Great,' Freddie gasped, 'we could perhaps meet up again. Eliza and I are only going home for a few days but we'll be back before the end of the week.'

'I'd really like that.'

He's in.

'Look,' Konrad said. 'It seems a waste for you to spend your time with Eliza and me this evening. You two go and enjoy yourselves. We have plenty to entertain us.'

Eliza gave her father a look of admiration and pride, before chirping, 'Yeah, we don't want you two hanging around, bringing down the tone. Now bugger off.'

Freddie and Chloe didn't need another unsubtle hint; they held hands as they went back to the bar.

'How old do you think she is? I find it hard to tell these days,' Konrad confessed.

'Twenty-five, maybe older, she has to be about that age. Who knows, but she seemed nice enough. Freddie's practically drooling.'

'Lucky blighter.'

'Things with you and Mum still no better then?'

'Eliza, there are things we need to discuss. Shall we find the best curry house in town? I feel like blowing the diet out of the water.'

Chapter 12

He nearly choked on his morning coffee when he saw Freddie and Chloe walk into the dining room at The Management Centre. They were subtly touching each other as they proceeded to fill their plates at the breakfast buffet, barely registering the other diners. Konrad was appalled when they made their way towards him.

This is a bit awkward.

'Morning, Dad. Hope you and Eliza had a good evening.'

'And I hope you are going to pay for a night's accommodation and that hearty breakfast, son.'

'You worry too much. It's all legitimate and paid for, so there's no scandal here for you to fret about.' Freddie shot a conspiratorial glance at Chloe who appeared as freshly made-up and fragrant as she had the night before. Konrad thought his son had a slightly smug air about him, as if he had excelled at his favourite sport, and he caught Freddie licking his lips deliberately at Chloe.

'I'm sorry, Mr Neale, we didn't mean to cause any embarrassment. I don't usually entertain men in my room, but Freddie and I couldn't resist each other. It's not a one-night stand.' Chloe was touching Freddie's forearm tenderly with her fingertips, while with her cow-brown eyes holding Konrad's gaze a little too long for comfort.

'You only live once…' Konrad stood up slowly. 'Sorry, I'll have to love and leave you. I've work to do on my laptop for an hour or so, please excuse me.'

He cut his breakfast short, not wanting to have any further blatant foreplay thrust in front of him while he was eating.

Besides which, he was envious of Freddie's success and Chloe had a distracting cleavage, which didn't help the situation.

'I'll see you at the flat a bit later, Dad. I've one or two matters to deal with here first, if that's okay.' Freddie had the audacity to wink at his father when he said this.

'See you later. Take your time.' *You lucky little bastard.*

Konrad's fertile imagination was doing him no favours, neither was his lack of meaningful sexual contact for the past three months or more, unless he counted himself. He called it "playing solitaire".

"Your son and his girlfriend seem to have trouble keeping their hands off each other. Why did you leave the dining room so soon? Was it difficult to watch or were you enjoying it too much?"

In his room, he leapt towards the window, which overlooked the courtyard and footpaths of the main building. The dining room could be seen from there, but no one was standing peering through binoculars or texting, which meant that Tessa had either moved away or must be in the building spying on him, and watching Freddie and Chloe.

Don't reply. That's what she wants you to do.

He fired up his laptop to check his emails. There was a brief message from Slow Joe confirming his willingness to accept the mission impossible; finding the current identity of Tessa Carlton. It was time to do some work and examine the video clips that Joe had collated for him of Matthew Hawley and his derring-dos.

The aim had been to find a clip which demonstrated Matthew's fears and might provide visual clues of physical torture. 'Rope burns, let's see if we can't find evidence of them somewhere,' Konrad said speaking to the screen.

'There she is, the luscious Helena, waiting by the side of the pool while poor old Matthew is on the high board ready to leap.' The camera shot zoomed in on Matthew who was apparently mentally preparing himself at the far end of the board. He turned around for a moment facing away from onlookers and cameras.

'There. Did he throw-up behind that pillar? It looks like it.' He zoomed in on the laptop and smiled. 'Well done, young Joe, first one and we have the jackpot.'

The scene showed Matthew Hawley placing his arm against an angular white concrete pillar and leaning forward, retching. As the toned figure in swimming trunks turned to face his fate, Konrad spied a line of small bruises on each inner thigh. He examined the film several times; following Matthew's every move.

'What else do we have here?' There were a few key scenes to choose from to support Matthew's assertions about his fear of heights. 'Poor bugger. The things we do for love, and a shag.' Another text beeped making Konrad jump. His mind had been elsewhere.

"They're at it again. Banging away and making filthy noises. He must be good, your son, he's making her beg for more. She's loving it. Room 107."

He couldn't resist. He knew it was risky but he wanted to catch sight of Tessa, so he crept silently as he approached the room along the corridor from where he was staying. The "do not disturb sign" was hanging outside the door, which he found ironic given the noises emanating from within. Looking around him, he could see no cameras in the corridor, although there was one close to his room in the stairway overlooking the exit door to the courtyard. With the stairs so close by, he checked to see if Tessa was hiding there.

After walking to the next floor level and down again, he hesitated outside the door of room 107. He could hear Freddie's throaty voice, grunting, and Chloe declaring a faith in God, before a pause in the familiar rhythmical thudding of a headboard on the wall. Konrad shifted his weight which made the floor creak, and with that he scuttled back to his room, embarrassed at what he had done. He felt like a Peeping Tom as he checked behind him to confirm that no one had seen him listening to the bawdy noises.

Reaching the safety of his room, he glanced out the window into the large courtyard area where he saw a woman on a bench playing with her phone. He stood still to get a better look. Early thirties, sunglasses, petite, neat and with thin lips. *Could that be her?*

His phone beeped, making him flinch involuntarily.

"You didn't stay long."

Konrad marched outside, into the courtyard, and made a complete fool of himself.

'Excuse me, did you just send me a text message?'

The woman on the bench took off her sunglasses and simply replied, 'What? Why would I do that? I don't know who on earth you are.'

He knew instantly that he'd made a mistake and all he could do was to humbly apologise.

Tessa was pulling the strings and making him dance.

*

Later, over dinner, he managed to laugh sheepishly about the whole fiasco when he told Lorna what he'd done.

'You idiot.' Lorna shook her head in disbelief although she still retained a bemused smile, letting Konrad know she was finding his story amusing. He had already regaled her with his drunken exploits and the story of the vase urinal.

'I'm dreading the journey home now. I'm sure I'll get flashbacks to Freddie's bedroom romp and I won't be able to look my own son in the eye. It's not something I'd prepared myself for as a parent.'

'You'd better stand by then because I'm sure Freddie will be seeing a lot more of Chloe. They sound well suited.'

'That's not funny... Look, Lorna, I'll be here again next weekend to bring back the twins and finish off odd jobs in their flat, so can we meet up again for longer? We could go for a decent walk, Newborough Warren, or out to the unpronounceable island with the ponies and the lighthouse, like we did last year, do you remember? What do you say?' The more time he spent with Lorna again, the more desperate he became to regain her trust. Taking things slowly was already becoming difficult.

'Ynys Llanddwyn. It sounds like a great idea, I love it and yes I do remember the last time we were there.' Lorna looked down at her plate, appearing suddenly embarrassed at the recall of events from their walk through the pines to the beach nearly ten months earlier. She blushed. 'Will you call me while you're at home for the week, to confirm?'

'I'll phone you every day. I'll FaceTime you if that would be better, in the evenings. We can see each other then.'

Chapter 13

Another hotel room, with better lighting this time. She quickly checked her phone, making certain that it was switched off during the recording. The camera's red light was on as she settled into the functional chair placed against the plain magnolia wall of the neatly appointed double room.

'I'm starting to have some fun now that you're so dangerously exposed, Konrad. If it weren't for Lorna, you'd be more difficult to play with, because without her you'd not have so much to lose. I've watched you and her together and your transformation has been quite magical. You are a handsome couple: well matched, natural together and clearly in love. Let's face it, Konrad, you're a catch, and good looking for your age, in my humble opinion. As for Lorna, she's younger of course, and she has that amazing fresh face and softness that Delia doesn't possess. You must be having a hell of a struggle in your underpants right now. You took Lorna to dinner, but she didn't put out. Poor you. You never even managed to kiss her. What are you scared of, Konrad? Is it rejection?

'Delia's rebuffs don't hurt so much, do they? No, they don't, because there are no meaningful emotions involved. When you try to coerce your wife into a quick one, it's a selfish act on your part. You don't care about her. You do care about Lorna, which is why you didn't push your luck.

'Freddie can't have meant to rub it in when he arrived for breakfast with his new girlfriend. I watched your expression as he touched her at the table and I'm sure you were envious of him. Did you have to go back to your room for an emergency wank? Is that why you took so long to respond to my text? The closest you got to a fuck was listening to your own son having sex. You dirty bastard.

'I'm going to stay on your trail a while longer before I decide how to proceed. I have plans forming but the next move is yours.'

She rose from the chair, and waved at the camera before switching it off and placing it in its compact black holdall with the tripod.

Chapter 14

Annette was eating again. Chocolate éclairs. She licked her fingers and spoke with her mouth full. 'So, Delia is taking the news well, in the circumstances.'

'It's hard to tell.' Konrad passed his colleague a paper serviette. 'I suspect that without the twins being at home I'd need a stab vest, but at least I did the decent thing and explained to her why I was leaving. We had to sit in the summerhouse at the end of the garden, so the children didn't overhear. She swore a lot but managed to keep the volume down to a dull roar, and only hit me three times.'

'Sounds like a success to me.'

'Without a doubt I've done the right thing. The main issues on her mind were: what other people would think, and how much money she would be getting. Shallow, wouldn't you say? She wants to stay in the house, so I've spoken to Rob at The Valiant and I'm renting a room there, although the separation won't be official until next week when the children have returned to Bangor. Rob's discreet enough to preserve my privacy for a while. Formal announcement to follow. The PR machine will handle that.'

'You mean Delia?'

'Yes. It wouldn't be in her best interests for there to be negative perceptions of our split. The money might dry up. She'll make herself look good by presenting an amicable parting of ways and an amazing friendship. That sort of bollocks.

'Then the real battle will commence behind solicitors' doors, and they'll take what's left of my money. Anyway, enough, woman. Back to work. Did you get those photos of Helena and Tessa when they were younger?'

Slow Joe and Mike grinned like two playful children. 'This is definitely going to help you work out what Tessa looks like now. Take a look at these beauties,' Mike said with sarcastic overtones.

On the screen in front of him, Konrad noted the blond curls and blue eyes of a young Helena, slightly chubby and awkward, beaming at the camera with a fixed false cheesy grin. She held a doll in one hand, dangling it, uncared for. The next photo was presumably of Tessa, a scrawny sallow-faced child with tangled mousy hair wearing a grubby dress and dirty shoes and socks, as if she had stepped from a puddle.

'Poor kid. She looks like little orphan Annie. She has the same blue eyes as Helena, but almost everything else is different,' commented Annette from over Konrad's shoulder. He scrolled again and again through the dozen or so photos that Mike and Joe had sourced. Helena grew into a pretty, confident teenager, posing with pleasure for the camera. Her huge eyes were a mesmeric blue-grey colour.

As the school years progressed, her figure changed from a slim boy-like shape to the hourglass curves of more recent photographs, and the camera somehow captured her allure. Tessa, on the other hand, remained plain, sullen and developed into an anorexic Goth. Clothes were black, her blue eyes were caked in black make-up and her hair was dyed an ebony colour, left long and severe. Her face was pasty white.

'Is that the last one we have of Tessa? Really? She looks like every other teenage Goth on the planet. Hopeless. No wonder they couldn't identify anyone likely to be her from the court cameras.

'Do we have any photos of the staff who worked for Helena?' Konrad enquired. 'It might help with the next section of the film to add some depth about Naomi, and we also need photos of Josh at around that time, if we have them.'

The screen in front of them bore the familiar image of interviewer sitting facing interviewee, in the confines of Longlees Prison.

*

'Why did your son Josh end up living with you and Helena?'

'Amy had a car accident. It was serious enough for her to be in hospital for three weeks and then need physio when she eventually went home. Helena offered to have Josh as he'd finished his first year of A-levels, and we thought he could cope better with the pressures of his last year at school if he stayed with us. Pete the wanker only had a few hours help from Amy's parents, and it took the pressure away from Amy, to be fair. She was happy enough with the arrangement. Once he'd passed his driving test, Josh went to see her whenever he could and we bought him a run-around to give him his freedom and keep up with his sports and seeing his mates. He was practically a young adult by then.'

Konrad was keen to steer the story in a particular direction.

'How long was it before you and Helena picked up on his infatuation with Naomi, her office manager?'

Matthew smiled weakly.

'That didn't take too long to figure out. Josh asked Helena if he could get some experience over the summer by working for her and obviously we interpreted that as an exceptionally mature attitude, not realising that he had an ulterior motive. Naomi's an attractive young lady, a few years older than Josh, bright and witty. She didn't do anything to lead him on. She didn't tease him or flirt with him, or not that we noticed anyway. He was a young man with the sap rising and fate played him a helpful hand, that's all.

'He was a good worker too. He became the office junior, handling calls, taking messages, even setting up interview dates. Quite often we left them to it while Helena and I escaped for charity events. The office only closed on a Sunday, so most Saturday mornings Josh worked with either Naomi or Richard to cover the calls. Sundays was sport for Josh. Tennis mostly. He kept himself fit in the gym and we worked out together when we could.'

Konrad kept his cool approach as he raised the next query with Matthew. This incident had been mentioned in court but questions had remained unanswered.

'When did you and Helena twig that there was a physical relationship happening between Josh and Naomi?'

'I'm not sure it's right to revisit this issue, Mr Neale. You seem to have a need to explore every sexual aspect of my story and this part involves Josh. It was his private life and we should respect that.'

'I agree, Matthew, but your wife didn't respect Josh's privacy, did she? She had a most unusual reaction to discovering what your son and her employee were up to. She filmed them, didn't she? Don't you find that bizarre?'

Matthew sighed as if exasperated. 'As I have explained, she loved sex, Mr Neale, and she found watching others having sex a turn on. No harm was done.'

Konrad was stunned at Matthew's dispassionate response. This made him delve deeper to gauge whether there was more to this story than Matthew was letting on. 'We're talking about your son here. Not just someone else. Who else did she watch having sex? Did you join a special club?'

'You're being coarse now, Mr Neale. Josh and Naomi had made the mistake of having sex where there were CCTV cameras. We had a comprehensive security system in place for the house, the outbuildings, the gym and the offices. Only Helena and I had access to the recordings and only we knew where the cameras were hidden.'

'But you didn't see fit to tell Josh, or at least warn him?'

'I'll be honest with you, the first time I saw Josh in action I was proud of him becoming a man, but I didn't register that Helena's interest had increased. When I did, I began to feel envious of my own son. For some reason, Helena became obsessed with watching Naomi and Josh, although I didn't realise what was going on at first, not until I stumbled across Helena watching recordings of them. Not just when they were having sex, but in the office as well. I once stood undetected, keeping a close eye on her facial expressions as she watched Josh with Naomi. I'd seen that look before. Many times. Usually aimed at me.'

*

'This is really unhinged stuff. I'm not sure we'll get away with showing these descriptions,' Annette commented. 'We might have to narrate the general gist. Forget my idea of making two episodes, we'll never be given the go-ahead. It's far too depraved.' Annette looked at Konrad for reassurance, but his phone distracted him.

'It's her again. I don't think she's here, but she's heading back my way soon by the sounds of things,' he said showing Annette his latest text message. She screwed up her face in response.

"Missing me yet?"

'That's a bit freaky,' she said. 'I'm glad it's you she's pissed off with, and not me. You're sure it's Tessa Carlton sending these texts, aren't you?'

'I can't think who else it could be. Where have Joe and Mike gone off to now?' Konrad asked, as the two assistants left together saying "cheerio" and "see you later". 'Have you sent them out for rations again?' He had swiftly changed the subject. He felt more vulnerable each time another text arrived from Tessa Carlton, which was made worse by the fact that the only picture he had in his head was of a bitter and twisted self-harming Goth; and yet, he hadn't seen anyone fitting that description since walking home from the station late on Halloween the year before.

'Apparently they're going to use some high-tech equipment at Mike's place to hack into the NHS data spine to locate twisted Tessa's health ID. We're not to know that, of course, because it's highly illegal and involves something called "the dark web." I innocently assumed that was to do with spiders, but I was laughed at by the pair of them. The word dinosaur was used, can you believe?' Annette coughed, choking on a peanut for a few seconds before continuing. 'While they're indulging in their underground activities, they also hope to come up with a few photos of Helena's staff as you requested and they're thoroughly enjoying themselves. I'm sure Joe didn't envisage his internship being quite so fascinating, or raunchy for that matter.'

Annette and Konrad turned back to face the screens and recommence the lengthy task of watching the first run-through of the documentary material. 'You can feel where this is going, can't you? Jealous father catches son with sexy stepmother and kills wife in fit of rage…'

Chapter 15

'Matthew, can I ask how you reacted when Josh took on a more responsible role in Helena's business? As I understand it, he was asked to help with finding suitable applicants and dealing with customers, often being out of the office. That sounds more than a part-time Saturday job or work experience.' Konrad had assumed an easy manner and had decided to focus on the father-son relationship to help the audience understand the bond.

'As I said, Mr Neale, Josh seemed to have an aptitude for dealing with people. He has a certain charisma; he's affable, intelligent and articulate. Throw good looks into the mix and you have an employee guaranteed to get business from female bosses. He's also a sports man. A man's man and therefore an all-rounder when it came to sales and contract negotiations. Helena behaved like a proud parent almost as much as I did. She could send him out with Naomi or with Richard and they would always return with the deal done. The biggest problem we had was getting him to focus on his A-levels and aim for university. He was far too hungry for success to want to stop his progress.'

'Did you spend much time with him?'

'Oh, God yes. The life of the daredevil appealed to him. He did sponsored triathlons, cliff dives, endurance tennis, and all sorts of stuff. He and I trained for the tightrope walk together. I expect you remember that one. It hit the headlines. There was Josh, me, and the girl from Blue Peter. She got the glory, of course, but we were up there too. Josh was as shit scared as I was, but the exhilaration of completing it and not falling was unforgettable. We raised about ten grand that day, which was phenomenal. I still remember Josh and myself standing on the platform at the end of the tightrope, hugging and patting each other on the back, practically crying with relief. After that, he did most of the extreme challenges with me, and some of his own. It was excellent publicity for the company.'

'So, in effect, Helena had both of you working for the business?'

Matthew nodded. 'Yes, but I still had my own career. It pays not to have all your eggs in one basket.'

'Is that a mantra that Helena used?' Konrad asked, deliberately leading the interview along a specific path.

'No, Mr Neale, it's a well-known saying, I believe.' Matthew gave a cold stare. 'What you want to know is what was my reward for completing the tightrope walk, and did Helena involve my son? She didn't give Josh any reward other than a proud kiss on the cheek for the publicity shots. She left Naomi to provide the rest.

'I was honoured with a "tight" rope, Mr Neale, a play on words you see. Helena loved a clever twist. She also loved the feel of a brand new silky climbing rope, not your rough hemp. Never that. Always silky to the touch with a bit of give in it. Have you ever been tied down to the bed and teased until you want to burst? It's blissful torture. With a blindfold on it's even more excruciating. You can feel but you can't touch and you can't see what's about to happen. It's a game of trust and reward, Mr Neale. You must try it some time.'

Konrad declined to give Matthew the satisfaction of a response, but he had to pause to gather his thoughts, before taking him further toward the core of the matter. 'How did the prosecution in your court case determine that Josh had been rewarded sexually by Helena?'

He could not mistake the furious look in Matthew's eyes. He sat back in his chair.

'What they concluded in the investigation of my wife's murder was incorrect. You are attempting to follow suit. I did not murder my wife in a fit of jealous rage because I believed she was having sex with my son, because she did not. I cannot recall killing my wife, none of it, and I can't say anything else because that is the truth. That's what I have always said.'

'Then why did you want to kill Helena?'

'I didn't want to kill Helena, Mr Neale.' Matthew was unyielding.

'Then why *did* you kill her? Was it jealousy? Was it envy? Your assertions make no sense. Perhaps you could talk me through what did happen leading to her death, if it weren't about jealousy.'

Matthew was frowning. 'I'm certain that Josh didn't have sex with my wife because I saw for myself that he declined her offer. It was on the CCTV.'

'So she offered him sex?'

'Helena was indulging in one of her painful psychological tortures and she told me what she was going to do. Emotional torture you see. She strolled into the gym where Josh was working out, and she was dressed in her bikini ready for a swim, full cleavage on show as usual. She shamelessly flirted with him. He looked at her, who wouldn't, but he shook his head and I watched him put both hands up, swear at her, and walk angrily out of the gym. She looked at the camera, waved and laughed at me. When she came back into the small office she said, "You see, I'm all yours, and he is a loyal boy to his father. Full trust."'

'Did Josh tell Naomi?'

'Now you're using that brain of yours, Mr Neale. You have to work this out, I cannot tell you, you have to ask me the right questions and we will reveal the truth.'

*

Annette paused the recording. 'Bloody hell, this is good stuff. We must persuade Josh and Naomi to be interviewed, I have to learn the inside story.'

'I could try the personal approach and phone Hawley Recruitment Solutions myself,' Konrad suggested pulling his mobile from his trouser pocket. 'Can you Google the details for me. I might as well do it now while we're thinking about it.'

Annette paused. 'There she is, Naomi Woods Co-Director, a neat portrait photograph and one of Co-Director Josh. They're awfully young to be company directors, don't you think? Still, if that's what you get left dealing with when your dad kills your stepmum, it's preferable to being homeless and destitute, I suppose.'

Konrad glanced across to see the computer screen, keen to remind himself what Naomi looked like. 'I'm still disappointed. I thought she'd be voluptuous like Helena, but she's like a little elf.'

'That's called the gamine look. Short hair, boyish, smart office clothes, neat, slim and all the things I'll never be. Now, do you want this number or not?'

The phone rang four times before being answered, 'Hawley Recruitment Solutions, how can I help you?'

'Is it possible to speak to Josh Hawley please?'

'May I ask who's calling?'

'Yes, this is Konrad Neale. It's a personal matter.'

'Mr Neale, this is Naomi Woods speaking. Josh is out of the office today but I'm sure he will *not* want to speak to you. Your team have been pestering us for interviews and we have declined, several times. Please leave us to get on with our lives, unless you have something new to add.' Naomi had a caramel voice, which Konrad found very enchanting, and the confidence with which she spoke unnerved him slightly.

'I do appreciate that our approaches have been insistent, but I've spent several hours with Josh's father in recent weeks and it would be unfair of me not to give both you and Josh an opportunity to give your version of events. You see, despite everything, Matthew Hawley remains adamant that he has no recall of his actions on the night he murdered Helena, and I'm merely seeking ways to support his assertions, or to find out whether it's at all possible that someone else killed her.'

'Most admirable, I'm sure, but the police investigation proved that he did kill her. Look, I'll speak to Josh. He may want to help his father in whatever way he can, but I'm not keen to involve myself. We have a business to run. Mr Neale, if by some miracle you can clear Matthew's name it would be amazing. I'm sure you already know this, but Josh can't face seeing his father. He hasn't visited once. You see, Josh can't believe what he did, and he's angry and hurt, so it's his call whether he agrees to an interview or not.'

Konrad gave Annette a wide grin with eyebrows raised.

'Do you have a mobile number that Josh can reach you on? A personal number?' Naomi asked.

'Yes of course.'

He ended the call and turned to Annette. 'There's a possibility Josh may agree to see me. Now, it's lunchtime. Let's get out of here for a while.'

Gorgeous George had been excited to see Konrad that Monday morning, but had been on the telephone when the subject of his crush had walked through the revolving door and acknowledged him. This was not enough for George. Determined to snatch a few words with his idol, he had made sure he was covering the reception desk at lunchtime. He had a letter. 'Mr Neale, I have important correspondence for your immediate attention,' George sang as he wafted an envelope like a fan. He held onto the letter tightly, forcing Konrad to step closer than he was inclined to. 'Nice aftershave. Paco Rabanne, if I'm not mistaken. Mmmm… it's simply divine on you, Mr Neale. Lillian, smell this!' Lillian stepped shyly towards Konrad, who magnanimously allowed her to sniff near his left cheek.

'That's lovely, Mr Neale.'

'Have you all quite finished?' demanded Annette. 'He's delicious, I'm sure, but I want to smell my dinner on a plate, so if you don't mind…'

George reluctantly released the letter he was still holding and having given Annette a filthy stare behind her back, he swooned at Konrad. 'Anytime, Mr Neale.'

Over lunch at a small café nearby, Konrad opened the letter, taking a few minutes to read it through. 'Strange, isn't it. When people have a shameful personal secret to disclose they put it in a letter, not an email, not a text message and most definitely not posted in comments on social media. This it seems is from a mother of one of Tessa Carlton's school friends.

'From what she is saying, Tessa and her daughter went to nursery school together before Tessa went to live with her grandparents. Listen to this.' He moved forward in his chair to whisper loudly to Annette, who carried on shovelling lasagne into her mouth.

"We were really worried about the behaviour of Tessa at nursery. I sometimes helped out with supervision at the morning sessions. Tessa did some spiteful things but always appeared upset at what she had done. At first, we didn't understand what was going on. For example, she once pulled the gold fish out of their glass bowl and left them to die on the sideboard in the classroom, but she was crying and distraught when we found her, watching the two, small fish gasping. Each time this sort of thing happened, her mother would be asked to discuss it. She always had Tessa's older sister, Helena, with her. There were questions asked about injuries to Tessa. Small stab marks, burns, and in one instance a cut on her eyebrow. Little Tessa said Helena had punished her for not doing dares. That was the word she used. Dares. Mrs Carlton denied any problem. She said Tessa was accident prone and told tall tales to get attention."

'Blimey,' Annette said, between mouthfuls of salad.

'And it's signed "Mary Walters". I don't think it gives us anything new, but if there was a requirement for Tessa to live with her grandparents because of abuse from her own sister, then social services must have been involved. Joe and Mike may have more luck trying to get hold of records from there. I'm sure social services have to follow up on these cases. You'd think so anyway.'

A catchy tune rang out from Annette's handbag on the floor, signalling her turn take a phone call. 'Yes, he's with me. We're having lunch together. It sounds like something juicy… can you email it over to me and we'll pick it up when we get back. What was the next thing? What today? Already? Okay, I'll ask him to call her. Thanks, Raj.'

Konrad had stopped eating his meagre salmon salad, waiting for the explanations.

'Your new friend Raj, in the PR department or whatever they call it these days, has received an interesting message on the dedicated email following your appeal for information on Tessa Carlton. He's going to forward it through to you. It sounds as if it's from an old boyfriend of Helena's. Could be interesting. The other message was regarding your wife contacting Raj about announcing your separation and pending you-know-what.' Annette mouthed the last part of the sentence to avoid being overheard. 'Delia wanted to forewarn the film company in case of negative publicity, and has asked to work together with Raj to devise the best wording for the formal announcement next week.'

'Oh shit.'

'Shit, indeed. If this leaks out early, and the papers get hold of it, no amount of positive PR could be put in place quickly enough. I suggest you phone home, and talk to Delia about bringing the announcement forward. Do Freddie and Eliza know?'

'Yes. I can't say they were surprised. In fact, Eliza seemed relieved. We had a very surreal adult chat and then planned the barbecue for Thursday to tell our friends and neighbours. We think it's only fair to give them the heads-up in case the press were to rock up unannounced.'

Konrad was perturbed by his wife's rash decision to talk to his colleagues before he'd had time to meet with them himself. He sighed. 'Let's get back to the office and do some damage limitation before the silly bitch does anything else to make me look like a coward.'

Chapter 16

No time to get out the tripod. The small video camera was placed on the corner of a shelf, and she stood closer than usual to make a brief visual diary entry. She was frowning.

'You're not very talkative. I consider it rude that you didn't reply to my text today. Nothing offensive was said, I merely asked if you were missing me, and yet you ignored me again. I have feelings. I can be hurt. Let's face it, Konrad, it's not as if you're that busy.

'Lunch with the fat Annette again. I noticed she had a bit of salad with her pile of pasta to make out she's dieting, I suppose. What a sad case.

'You always seem to have a lot to talk about, and I couldn't hear what the hot topic of the day was, even though you read part of that letter out loud to your chunky companion. The noise from the other customers drowned out the words and I missed the whole thing. Very annoying.

'Then, after a phone call, you left without warning. It must have been important. I need to get much closer to you somehow, so I think I'll come along to your family barbecue, and see what useful snippets of information your neighbours and friends have to disclose. You see, the plan forming in my mind needs refining before next weekend, which has put me under pressure.

'Being honest, Konrad, you deserve to be punished for what you've done by interfering in the lives of other people. We were almost there before you came along and ruined the final chapter with your nosy questions and social media searches. No one was bothered until then.'

She pushed her face within inches of the lens as the last few bitter words spewed forth. 'Why couldn't you just accept what Matthew told you and leave well alone? He killed Helena and he doesn't know why, any more than the judge or jury did at the trial. So why couldn't you do as you were asked? You really should have fucked off back to your boring life instead of screwing up mine.'

Chapter 17

The gathering was in full swing when Konrad decided to take a moment to observe the people in his garden drinking his beer and slurping wine he had paid for. They fell into three distinct camps: Delia's mindless sycophants, Freddie and Eliza's mates, and the real friends of Konrad himself. Barney was in charge of the barbecue, cooking up a storm and ogling at the flesh on show; young or old it didn't matter. Watching his good friend from a distance, Konrad laughed to himself when Barney was approached by a predatory golf club cougar who had imbibed rather too much of the fizzy stuff. She was rubbing herself against him in a most unseemly way, and had placed a hand on the front pocket of Barney's blue and white striped apron. Barney used the grubby tongs in his hand to remove it. *Quite right. Not your type, old pal. Stay well clear. She'd barbecue your sausage for you, and then leave without so much as a thank you.*

Delia approached her soon-to-be ex-husband. 'Are you going to make the announcement or am I to be left to tell everyone the truth?'

'I'll do it now. I wouldn't want innocent friends and family to hear what our marriage has really been like. It would put them off their burgers.'

Delia smiled with her mouth and wounded with her eyes.

Konrad had to remember not to look pleased with what he was about to say in a loud voice to the garden filled with people. He'd had time to think about it, and stayed right on message, as instructed. He even made them chuckle.

'I have to say a huge thank you to Delia, to whom I owe a debt of gratitude for her willingness to tolerate my antics over the years, especially on return home from The Valiant.' The neighbours had heard the story and laughed. He clarified for those not in the know.

'The rumours are true I'm afraid, I did mistake Delia's best vase for a urinal only last week. It seems this was the final straw, and we have chosen to separate with a view to divorce. Seriously though, working together so closely for decades can take its toll on a marriage, and this has been a difficult decision for us. Having said that, I'm relieved to confirm that we remain business partners and friends. Please don't feel sorry for either of us.

'We wanted you all to be aware before the press gets hold of the news, and before the official announcement tomorrow morning. There may be press hanging around the village for a while, but once things settle down we shall see you as usual at the golf club, or the pub where I shall be hanging my hat for a few weeks.' He noticed one or two friends taking photos on their smartphones.

'Delia and I would very much appreciate your discretion. No posting on social media until after the formal announcement, please. In the meantime, eat drink and be merry.' Raising his glass, he winked theatrically at Delia who smiled convincingly back at him and clinked her glass against his. They gave each other a kiss on the cheek to the sound of a few aaaahs.

Good God, that was really quite nauseating. I only hope they all fell for it.

He saw that Freddie's new squeeze, Chloe, had travelled down from North Wales. They had wedged themselves up against a tree to explore each other's mouths with tongues before Freddie would share her by introducing her to his old school friends. It had been mentioned that Chloe might arrive, but Konrad was impressed that she'd actually journeyed so far – just to have to go back the next morning by train to give an afternoon presentation at The Management Centre.

He must have scored a hit there, but I wonder what Delia's going to think of her. She'll probably hate the sight of Chloe. No one is ever good enough for her Freddie, especially one as pretty as that, and one who is going to spend the night... Excellent.

Handing Barney a cold beer, he sat down away from the throng.

'That went well, mate. No one would ever suspect what went on behind those prison walls,' Barney said pointing to the house. 'I must say The Camp Commandant has some nice smelling friends but they're all up their own arses. Posh load of twats. I do approve of Freddie's young lady, though. What a fabulous set she has.'

'Barney. You're a dear friend but that's my son's girlfriend you're perving over. She's way out of your league. In fact, I thought she was out of Freddie's, but I must have been wrong. Anyway, keep your voice down or they'll hear us.' Freddie and two of his friends had gathered to stand in front of where Barney and Konrad had perched on a low bench under a silver birch tree. The young men didn't seem to notice them and carried on talking loudly, sending up a few supportive cheers when Chloe had been taken by Eliza to be introduced to Delia. In the absence of the two girls, Freddie couldn't resist boasting to his friends about his conquest.

'I could easily have stayed in bed with her all day on Saturday and Sunday. She has the most amazing ways of... I won't say. You could use your imaginations, but you won't come close. Neither of you.' Freddie's old school mates were staring after Chloe and Eliza as they made their way through the crowds to where Delia was holding court with the hairspray brigade.

'Chloe has to be the horniest woman I've ever met. Ever. We must have been making a hell of a racket because someone was listening outside our hotel room. We heard them during a brief pause in the proceedings, if you know what I mean.' Before continuing, Freddie made a back and forth pumping motion with his forearm several times. 'We heard the floor creak really loudly right outside the door. Chloe freaked and made me wrap a towel round myself and have a look. I checked the corridor twice but there wasn't a sign of anyone. Having lost the passion of the moment, we had to start all over again. It was worth it for round two.'

Konrad experienced a repeat of the private shame from the Peeping Tom moment in the hotel the weekend before. Barney, however, was finding the conversation highly illuminating. With eyes as wide as they would stretch, and his mouth agape, he required a long swig of beer to regain self-control.

'I've heard older women are less inhibited and like to bring a vibrator into the mix. Did you get that lucky?' one of Freddie's admiring friends asked.

'And the rest!' Freddie took great delight in listing a number of sex toys that had been used. '… the works. I can't get enough of her. I could barely walk afterwards. I'm struggling now. Get yourselves an older woman, boys; it's the only way to die. Come on, I need to get her away from my mother.'

As the small group moved off to find Chloe and rescue her from death by Delia, Barney showered the grass in front of him with his mouthful of beer at the shock of what he had overheard. Konrad and Barney then sat in silence for a while until Barney finally spoke. 'Do me a favour, me old mate. Get us another cold beer. I'd go myself, but the front of my chef's apron is throbbing and I don't want people to think I've stolen one of your expensive sausages.'

*

During a lull in the party, when his attention was not being sought, Konrad managed to find time to contact Lorna. He was thoughtful enough to shut himself in his small home office to call her, away from flapping ears. He kept the facts simple. 'Yeah, it's going better than I expected. The friends and neighbours seem to have accepted the "amicable split" line, and Delia is keeping to her word. She makes a good actress, but then I suppose she always has.'

'That's good,' said Lorna. 'And I meant to ask, what was the upshot of your reply to that email? The one from the bloke who said he was Helena's ex-boyfriend?'

'Didn't I tell you? Sorry, I thought I had. He sounds as if he might be legitimate. He says he left his wife and child, and moved in with Helena for a while until she forced his hand. There were no charity challenges for him. Straight-up kinky stuff. The top ten of sadomasochism by the sounds of it. She wanted to try everything she'd read about or seen on films. The poor bloke had to leave the country in the end because she threatened to blackmail him by selling everything to the newspapers. She filmed what they did, ostensibly for them to be able to watch again and again.'

'Yes, but why did she turn on him? Why blackmail him?'

'According to Mr Bondage – that's my nickname for him, he's anonymous of course and used a throwaway email account – she had set twenty sex challenges and he failed to complete them. He stopped at thirteen and she was furious. She demanded his attention and that he fulfil her wish and she saw his refusal as rejection. He called her bluff and ended the affair. A bad move on his part as it turns out, because she unleashed her vengeance and he never worked in this country again. He was a plastic surgeon. Guess what? He made her look beautiful on the outside and the inside. He remodelled her girly bits.'

'What, outside girly bits, or inside girly bits?' Lorna asked, mocking Konrad for his inability to use the correct anatomical terminology.

'Both.'

'My word, what a sheltered existence I've led.'

'The poor man has been relegated to turning boys into girls in Thailand.' He decided to be brave and told Lorna about what he and Barney had overheard in the garden.

'Oh, God, so not only did you behave like a dirty old man, but you were nearly caught eavesdropping by your own son. Imagine if you'd been a bit slower getting back to your room that morning. Run the other stuff past me again, what did you say they were using? I got "vibrator" but I'm not sure about the other two or three things you mentioned.'

Konrad muttered and stuttered until Lorna laughed at him. 'Good grief, you old prude. Try online at Ann Summers, the website will have pictures you and Barney can look at.'

'Please don't tease, Lorna. It's been one hell of a long time and I think we should change the subject before I get on the train this minute and ravage you.'

'That's the beer talking… Change of subject coming right up. When has Josh agreed to see you and more importantly where?'

There was knock at the door.

'I'll have to phone you back… I've been rumbled.' He whispered before ending the call to Lorna.

It was Freddie and Eliza. They had been sent by Delia, who was demanding her husband's presence to say farewell to guests, many of whom were leaving the worse for wear, and regretting their decision to drink on a school night, as Barney called it. Most of the men had work the next day.

Konrad was dutiful and respected Delia's wishes, before heading back to his comfortable room at The Valiant Soldier. Freddie left him a brief text message to say he was going to catch the early train with Chloe and that they could meet up at the weekend.

Fair play, son. Fair play.

He hadn't felt sad or shame-faced at the thought of making the short walk from home to The Valiant Soldier with another bag full of his belongings. In fact, he had experienced an overwhelming sense of excitement at the possibility of new beginnings and a simpler life. With her parting salvo, Delia had made sure his optimism was moderated.

'Goodnight, Kon. I'll see you tomorrow evening when you collect Eliza, but after that you'll need to find somewhere else to park your possessions, including the hideous green monster-of-a-car. We'll be keeping our relationship on a business footing from now on, and I'll only see you at meetings, awards and so forth. The rest of the time we'll liaise by email or on the phone. Got it? I don't want you in my social circles and most importantly,

Kon, you are not to rub my nose in it with that whore. I know you. You'll be creeping off to see her at the earliest opportunity. I've news on that score. She's left the area, moved away and isn't interested in you any more.'

'Thanks for that, Delia. At least I know where I stand. The golf club is all yours. I'll stick to the pub for now. Goodnight.'

Although Delia was obviously trying her best to appear strong, Konrad was only too aware of how vindictive she could be if she felt she was being belittled or made a fool of. She could soon turn the affections of the media in her favour if she had good reason to. Lorna was reassuring when Konrad called her before retiring to bed. She had always been the voice of reason for as long as they had known each other.

'She's right, of course, we will have to be discreet, so bring your best baseball caps for the weekend. With any luck, you might not need them, I think it's going to be chucking it down so that'll keep any nosy individuals at bay.'

'Good. I want to spend time with you without having to be on constant alert. The even better news is that I'm booked in at the hotel until Tuesday. Josh Hawley and I are meeting a couple of times to sound each other out and we were going to meet in Chester, but he loves your part of the world, apparently, and has made a reservation at The Management Centre from Sunday night onwards. Naomi and the rest of their team will be holding the fort at their office, so he was quite flexible with the arrangements.

'I tell you what though, he sounded an awful lot like his father, which was odd at first, but he came across as being very open to discussion. I'm looking forward to it.'

'I'm sure you are. You'd better decide exactly what it is you need to know from him. Kon, listen, I'm sorry, I'd love to chat all night but it's late and I'm tired, time for bed now.'

The next day would be challenging, and he had decided to avoid the train for his journey to work that Friday. He had been offered use of a driver many times, and generally turned it down apart from journeys to gala dinners and award ceremonies. He much preferred a first-class carriage and a trip in a taxi to being chauffeured everywhere. However, common sense dictated that he should avoid being seen in public for a while, unless it was by design.

He was collected the next morning in an expensive-looking Lexus driven by a cheerful Jamaican man.

'Good morning, Zachary. How are the wife and children? I can't think how long ago it was that we last had one of our chats.'

'A very good morning to you, Mr Neale. It must be nearly three months since I've seen you. Settle back and enjoy the ride. When we get there do you want to be dropped at the front entrance or somewhere less obvious?' Konrad knew Zachary had been briefed.

'The front door is fine. Nothing to hide. As far as the public is concerned, it's business as usual, and a personal issue being dealt with sensibly and calmly.'

'Right you are, Mr Neale. Well said.'

Konrad settled back into the comfortable seats and checked his phone. There were messages appearing in rapid succession. He looked up at Zachary, catching his eye in the rear-view mirror. 'Here we go, Zachary. Stand by for the press interest before we get as far as the office.'

The first message was from Hit Grit Films and Channel 7, his employers for "The Truth Behind the Lies".

"The announcement on social media has been well received so far. There is a request for you to give a formal press statement. Are you still happy for us to proceed with the one we prepared yesterday? Raj."

No problems with that one.

Next was a supportive message from Annette in her own style.

'Well done for growing balls and using them. See you soon. George and Lillian have been advised to manage reception like a fortress. Netty."

He smiled at the thought of George and Lillian frisking those who dared to enter the revolving doors at Marriot and Weston's office block.

God help them all.

He then scrolled to the next message and froze.

"Getting divorced. You kept that quiet. How brave of you. I suppose you think this gives me less ammunition with which to persuade you to end your search. You're wrong. I have matters in hand and can shatter your dreams within days if you force me to. The lovely Lorna, your children, your new life, your career, and your reputation can all be taken from you. Delia will do the hard work. Withdraw your requests for information on social media, now!"

A cold sensation swept over Konrad as Tessa's words sank in. She was right, he was incredibly exposed.

A tactical withdrawal is perhaps wise. Let's see if we can calm her down a bit.

'Raj, It's Konrad Neale here. I'm not too bad in the circumstances, thanks for asking. Happy to go with the agreed wording for the formal press statement, but I'm also calling on another matter. I seem to have caused an upset regarding our appeal for information on Tessa Carlton. Can you put out on social media something along the lines of, "Thanks for all your help, but we are no longer looking for information regarding this person… blah blah blah"? You know how it goes. Also, it might be prudent to add an apology.'

'Are we about to get sued?'

'No, I don't think so. There's been a text message or two from her and she's upset that we're trying to find her. I've assured her we'll end our search but I'll find another way to get the information I want.'

He thanked Raj and turned his attention to wording a reply to Tessa's text.

"Hello Tessa,

I am sorry to have caused you so much upset. I can confirm that I have put in a request for the social media search to be discontinued. I hope this reassures you that no harm was intended.

Konrad Neale"

The reply was unsettling.

"Coward and a liar. Remember, I'll be watching."

What does she mean? Isn't she happy now?
'Everything all right, Mr Neale? You've gone a bit pale. Mrs Neale already turning the screws, is she?'

Konrad nodded. 'Something like that, Zachary.'

Chapter 18

'You are a disappointment to me, Konrad. This was supposed to be fun, but now you've ruined it by making things too easy. You plan to get divorced and predictably your wife has thought about the long-term benefits of your professional relationship. She thinks that if you behave like a thoughtful couple the public will continue to embrace you, and you each reap the financial rewards. Delia can stay as a business partner. How touching.

'Come off it, Konrad. You can't expect the public to fall for that load of old tosh. Delia doesn't know you've met with Lorna again, does she? She'll be outraged when she does, and then all bets are off.

'You are infuriating. In the same way that you've convinced Delia that you care enough not to embarrass her, you have the gall to try to placate me by telling me that you have called off your media search, and yet I don't believe you. This goes against your journalistic instincts, Konrad. All you have done is go underground. You shouldn't take me for an idiot.'

Chapter 19

Konrad stepped through the revolving doors at the main entrance to Marriot and Weston's and was almost engulfed in the outstretched arms of Gorgeous George, who had taken it upon himself to herd the subject of his affections into the lift and to the door of the editing suite rented by Hit Grit Films.

'Thanks, George, that's good of you, but unnecessary. As you could plainly see, hordes of press photographers were not waiting to hound me, but they should be arriving any moment, so please keep vigilant in reception. See you later.' He had again lacked thought in his choice of words.

'Later? What time will you be going for lunch? I could always fetch something for you. Call me?' George looked like a child does at a party when the arrival of jelly and ice cream is announced. He skipped back into the lift singing. "When will I, will I be famous?" This moment of joy gave Konrad the most wicked of ideas. 'George. How would you like to join Annette and me for a spot of lunch? We'll pick you up from reception at twelve thirty. You can help me to deal with the paparazzi if you like.'

The screams of ecstatic delight could be heard from the top of the lift shaft.

'What have you done now?' Annette asked.

'I have a cunning plan. Until then it's business as per usual, so let's have a quick meeting. I understand Joe and Mike have some earthshattering details to thrill us with.'

'They do indeed. Coffee and a Danish await you, my lord.'

After listening to the facts and leafing through the papers printed off for him, Konrad let out a slow whistle. 'I'm surprised it was Matthew Hawley who killed Helena and not her own sister.

What an appalling story of child abuse, care system inadequacies and parental fuck ups.'

'Sickening, isn't it? Can we use this?' asked Mike.

'We might have to check with the legal beagles first. Tessa has warned us off and declined to be interviewed. She's been bullying me with threatening texts, so I've pulled the plug on our social media searches for informants. What else have you got for me?'

'We've had no luck in finding her current pseudonym. Her health records stop when she was in care, as if she doesn't exist,' Joe explained. 'Mike and I did manage to find out why she ended up having to leave her grandparents' home. There's a record which dates back to when Tessa was about fifteen, when she was hospitalised with injuries that required reconstructive surgery; lacerations to her genitalia, cuts to her breasts, horrific stuff. No one was charged and there was never a court case or inquiry, nothing. It's detailed in the reports we printed off. Mike and I felt it had Helena written all over it.'

'Christ, does it ever.' Konrad confirmed his agreement with their hypothesis. He suspected as much when Joe described Tessa's injuries.

Joe continued. 'She ended up in local authority care but was ultimately admitted to an adolescent mental health unit for a period of over twelve months under a Section.'

Mike picked up the story. 'We had a hell of a job locating any of this information, and mostly its sketchy because the social services child care records were almost impossible to access, but the snippets from the healthcare system helped us to piece together a rough chronology. It's not perfect by any means. If the local authority covered up this assault, and she ended up sectioned, then it's no wonder she doesn't want you to find her. Helena is dead and, therefore, Tessa can finally get on with her own life.'

'If I were Tessa I'm sure I would either have hidden from my past or found a way to take revenge,' Joe said, sounding confident. He seemed to have grasped the intricacies of the situation. 'Maybe both.'

'This may explain what Matthew Hawley was trying to hint at,' said Konrad. 'But he didn't have enough of his own evidence. He killed Helena, but what if it was Tessa who put him in an impossible position, and to protect Josh, Matthew had to do as he was ordered?

'Take a look at the most recent text from Tessa that I received this morning. She's furious with me for trying to expose her existence. See what she has threatened to do. Imagine what she may have threatened Matthew with.'

'Bloody hell, we may be getting nearer the truth at last.' Annette was clearly delighted with the progress and already considering how the abuse history could be woven into the documentary. 'We're limited on time, boys, so let's keep digging. Oh, and avoid the press, they're going to be fishing for information on why Konrad is getting divorced. It should blow over soon, but no idle gossip please. Not a peep.'

Konrad took the paperwork from Joe with a mind to create a narration piece over the weekend. 'It shouldn't take too long. By the way, before you go back to your skulduggery with computers, did we get any other photos of Naomi and Josh?'

'Not yet, sorry, we got side tracked with this stuff.' Mike wafted sheets of scribbled notes in the air.

'Not the court photos, they're useless. Dressed in black and looking understandably distraught. I'd like natural ones if we can get them.'

That morning, Konrad was keen to revisit a certain part of his interview with Matthew. He asked Annette for her patience. 'I'm certain he gave us a clue, even if he didn't know it himself... Can we pick up where I bring Naomi into the equation?' He said looking again at himself and Matthew Hawley on the screens in front of them, psychological horns locked.

*

'Did Josh tell Naomi that your wife had propositioned him?'

'Apparently so, Mr Neale, and he also had a long discussion with me about it.'

Konrad couldn't help the surprised look on his face. 'That must have been extremely awkward. What did you learn?'

'More than I wanted to, if I'm honest. Helena had always appeared to appreciate having Naomi on the team and she'd spent the previous two years training her up to take more responsibility, just as she had done with Richard. It was jealousy that changed the dynamics. Helena saw Josh as hers. She had assumed ownership as part of the package that came with me, I think. On one hand, she watched as the relationship with Naomi and Josh grew, and she was fascinated by every detail of it, while on the other, she showed signs of envy; dreadful, damaging envy. Her way of hurting Naomi was through Josh.'

'Yes, I understand that, but it backfired.'

'To a degree it did. When Josh broached the subject he was angry with me for not believing him. This put me in a difficult position, as I had to tell him that Helena had done it as a dare, to test his loyalty to me. He was furious at that suggestion and called Helena all the names under the sun. During out discussions, he tried to make me believe that she had led him on more than once. Josh was citing sexual harassment. I was told to get control of Helena before it ruined his relationship with Naomi and his future.'

'How did Naomi react to this? And more importantly, how did you deal with Helena?' None of this information had been revealed during the court case and Konrad was now blindly seeking out fresh facts. The script had not been written for this section, nor had the research revealed anything of the hidden dynamics.

'Naomi is the calmest most rational young lady I have ever met, Mr Neale. She did nothing to rile Helena. She carried on as if nothing had happened. But because what Helena had done drove Josh away from her and towards Naomi, the result was a fascinating crescendo of suspense. Do you know the most interesting part of all this?'

'Let me guess. Helena didn't fire Naomi in order to split them up that way, she found more painful methods?' Konrad was getting the measure of Matthew and thus, vicariously, an understanding of Helena's twisted mind.

'You are the man I'd hoped you to be, Mr Neale. Helena tried to find information to discredit Naomi. She even attempted to set her up by making it look as if she was defrauding the business, but Naomi was too clever for that. She had the backbone to speak up in front of Richard and myself to announce that she'd found unusual discrepancies in the accounts, and wanted to bring it to Helena's attention before the accountant arrived that same day.

'The trouble was, the longer Naomi survived Helena's deviousness, the tighter the relationship between Naomi and Josh became. It came to an explosive conclusion when they moved in together.

'Helena could not be reasoned with. Josh had betrayed her and all hell broke loose. Naomi was sacked instantly, Josh resigned, and they set up in direct competition with Chawston Recruitment. Guess what name Josh and Naomi went for…? Hawley Recruitment Solutions and then they lit the blue touch paper before retiring to their own lives. They sent my wife a birthday message via a DVD recording. It featured them having the most outrageous orgy of sex with toys and gizmos that you will ever see. They spoke to the camera and waved at the end, saying something about having the freedom to have sex without it being filmed by her and that they hoped she found the final show a turn-on.'

To Konrad's astonishment, Matthew was smiling and wore pride as he recounted this episode.

'A bold move on Josh's part. How did you fair in all of this? You were piggy in the middle of course.' He wanted to push the storyline along.

'Helena used me against my own son at every opportunity.'

*

Annette was rubbing her hands together. 'There's the motive for everyone to see. How poetic. Is that what you were getting at?'

Konrad was deep in thought as he let out a long breath. 'No, but I now understand what's been niggling at me since we filmed this. Naomi. How did she survive when Helena eats people like her for breakfast? She ruins them with blackmail or sexual enticements or both. She gets what she wants.'

'Helena didn't want to ruin her relationship with Josh though, so maybe she kept her hands off Naomi because she thought she could still have her cake and eat it. Or in her case, father and son in the same bed. Filthy cow.'

'Do you think that was her goal?'

'Don't you?'

He was stunned. 'I've been so thick. It never occurred to me that she would stoop so low. That's sick, isn't it? Is it Annette? Please help me with this one...' Konrad was bewildered by Annette's revelation. He had not understood what Matthew had been trying to tell him all along. Matthew Hawley had acted to save his son, by killing his wife, the woman who wanted him and his son for sex and to do her bidding and play her endless games.

'Josh knew though, didn't he?' Annette said quietly to Konrad who was now sitting with his head in his hands, rubbing his fingers back and forth through his hair. 'I did mention that you'd been away with the fairies since you and Lorna split.'

'Yes, I appreciate I'm not at the top of my game. What you said makes sense, but why does Matthew insist that he cannot remember killing Helena? That doesn't fit. He says he was in the police station and they told him what he had done.' Konrad sighed. 'At least I know what to talk to Josh Hawley about on Monday.'

'According to the transcript, the next discussion is about Tessa Carlton and her letters, which ties in with Josh leaving to live with Naomi. Shall we look at that quickly before lunch?' Annette asked as she helped herself to a handful of peanuts. She caught her colleague looking at her and tried to justify her need for more calories. 'I only had one Danish earlier and I like peanuts, they help me to think.'

*

Konrad was staring intently at Matthew Hawley, waiting for him to expand on the details of how Helena used him against his son. 'How do you mean?'

'Our exposure in the press increased when they got hold of the story of the rival company and were keen to see pistols at dawn. "Stepmother and stepson in bitter business feud," that sort of headline.

'As a result, I left my job to join Helena's recruitment company. In other words, I was forced to take sides and had committed myself to Helena and to try to keep her reined-in, for Josh's sake.

'Her strategies and tactics for undermining Hawley Recruitment Solutions were not unexpected. First, she tried the legal route to force them into changing their company name. When that was unsuccessful, she used more devious tactics. If a new customer happened to be a man she was likely to win the contract. I didn't ask too many questions.'

'Why didn't Helena use the films of Josh and Naomi to blackmail them?'

Matthew tutted and frowned. 'Disappointing, Mr Neale. Think about it. If Helena published those pictures it would be revealed that she had recorded them and saved them, and let's face it, they're of her stepson and his girlfriend doing what comes naturally. No leverage there. She would have been labelled as a voyeur, nothing more.'

'I see,' Konrad paused.

Pay attention, Konrad. That was obvious and you looked stupid. You must listen to what he says. Watch his body language and stay focussed. There has to be more.

*

Konrad stood up. 'Right that's enough, let's collect George and have some fun and games with the press.'

Annette was happy to play along with his jolly jape. She walked with him to reception and gave her apologies for not being able to join Konrad and George for lunch after all.

'I've been called to a meeting with the big bosses at Channel 7 but you go ahead. Lillian, I'll take you next week, how about that?' Lillian looked thrilled and accepted the unexpected offer.

George had slapped on fresh aftershave for the occasion and powerful fumes were left in his wake as he walked from behind the reception desk. Konrad took him by the shoulders to prepare him for what to expect while they were out. George stood, back straight and eyes shut.

'No, George, open your eyes, I'm not about to kiss you. Not here, not anywhere, not ever. Right, pay attention. Remember, we are going for a business lunch and representing the company so be on your best behaviour. If we are approached by anyone they could be a reporter and might want a comment. I would really appreciate it if you could step in and ask them to respect our privacy. We'll go to the pretty Italian place up from Poncho's Deli. I think it's run by the same family. They're very thoughtful and the food is great. Ready to go?' George scampered along next to Konrad as if he was the happiest boy in town, beaming with pride, as Konrad held the door open for him when they arrived at the restaurant. Franco, the owner, showed them to a booth in the far corner away from the front window, and produced a menu before awaiting their drink order.

'Just a jug of water, Franco. I have a long drive ahead of me later. George what would you like?'

'Water will be fine. I'm on duty. Thanks, Mr Neale.'

'I tell you what. How about you call me Konrad, just while we eat lunch, it sounds too formal having you say "Mr Neale" all the time while I'm eating. Franco, we'll have two bowls of your finest Spaghetti Alla Puttanesca, please. There's nothing like a bit of prostitute's pasta to fill you up.'

'Is that what it means? I hope it tastes better than it sounds.' George giggled, visibly swelling with pride that he was being paid attention to. Being distracted, he had failed to notice two men who had asked to be seated diagonally across the room. The two were joined by a casually dressed young lady and it was no time at all before the three of them were pretending to take selfies, obtaining as many photos of Konrad and George as they could get away with.

George, meanwhile, was chatting in an animated fashion, telling Konrad about his pets. 'There's Fluffy the tortoise, and Lulu-May, my black pussy – she's a sweetie.' All of a sudden, he stopped talking and sprung into action when the girl, who Konrad strongly suspected was a journalist, approached the table.

'Excuse me, Mr Neale. I just wanted to say how sorry I was to read about you and your wife separating. It must be hard for you.'

Konrad shot a meaningful glance at George before pretending to be embarrassed, looking sheepish. George raised his hand and announced in his campest voice, 'Thank you for your concerns, but this is a private matter and we don't wish to be disturbed at this difficult time, isn't that right, Konrad?'

Konrad forced himself to keep a straight face by looking down at the table, ignoring the girl and trying half-heartedly to hide his features. He had spied the two men taking more photos, as did Franco who moved them to another table, asking them to stop interrupting the private lunches of his customers.

'Well done, George. Excellent job. Now shall we finish our pasta and get back to the offices before too many more people find us?' He knew from bitter experience that photographers with long lenses would be waiting outside and he kept up a light-hearted banter with George so that when they stepped into the street the photographers would capture a joyful scene.

*

'Well?' Annette asked. 'How did it go?'

Konrad was still chuckling to himself. 'It was the finest performance of my career. George was being his natural self and the media will have a field day. He swears on his black pussy's life that he will not say a word to the press. I did suggest that he could brush off their questions by telling the truth and confirming that he and I are work colleagues.'

'Do you think it will make Saturday's paper? Or will they dig about for more and turn it into a Sunday saga? I think you'd better warn Delia about your smoke screen just in case the silly cow takes it seriously.'

'Good plan.'

Fortunately for Konrad, Delia found the whole idea of deceiving the press quite amusing. 'It's a brilliant plan. Once they've been made to look foolish they'll give up on our divorce story as soon as we've announced how disgusted we are with their assumptions and false accusations. Well done, Kon. You must have learnt something from me after all our years together. I can't wait to read what they say. And while you're on the phone, I've told Barney I want our old car back, so you owe him money.'

She giveth and she taketh away.

Chapter 20

Konrad had never been driven so speedily by Zachary before, but the man had been given a special task to get him out of the city and back home in record time, and was rising to the challenge. 'Watch out for the average speed cameras,' Konrad advised, trying to read his emails and messages as the car weaved its way through the traffic and onto the motorway.

Eliza had phoned to confirm that she was packed and ready to go whenever he was, and was cheering him on, 'C'mon, Dad, the faster you get here the more likely we'll miss the Friday motorway chaos.'

He had given up concentrating at work. The demands from the press had increased throughout the day and although this was dealt with through the Channel 7 PR machine, it resulted in endless interruptions to his concentration and to the work in the editing suite. He was determined to ignore the requests for interviews and arranged for Zachary to collect him from outside a fire exit at the side of the building shortly after two o'clock.

'Thanks for this Zachary, I hope I haven't messed up your timetable for the day.'

'No problem, Mr Neale, it's what I'm here for. You seem to have hit a few of the national radio stations with news of your divorce. I'm sorry. It must be a dreadful day for you.'

'I expect the media will be full of wild speculation,' Konrad said, smiling to himself. 'I'm like anyone else, Zachary. My marriage is at an end and that's how it is. No great scandal, no shameful traumatic scenes. Life goes on.'

'You're so right, Mr Neale, it'll be yesterday's news before tomorrow.' Konrad smiled in response. He had trouble working out what the last sentence actually meant, but nevertheless Zachary's philosophical moment had made him chortle.

A trip to Wales would seem to be the perfect response to the announcement of his divorce, and he would be expected to disappear for a few days in the circumstances. No doubt the press would park outside his house, but their stay would be unwelcome, and Konrad was sure they would seek better and more exciting news elsewhere by Monday, at the latest.

Delia had returned to her frosty self by the time he called to collect Eliza, and he didn't have to make more than a perfunctory effort to be polite. He couldn't be bothered with the game of "keep Delia happy". He'd had years of that.

'I've just dropped in to see Barney and he's bringing the car back for you in a few minutes with the paperwork. You might have to get a replacement registration document. We signed the current one, but luckily Barney hasn't sent it off.'

'Can't you do that for me?' Delia asked, testily.

'I thought you wanted the car as part of the divorce settlement, dear. If you do, then as the current registered keeper and owner of the vehicle, I'll have to sign it over to you. The least you can do is organise the paperwork. Oh, and don't forget to tax it.' Konrad picked up Eliza's bags and boxes, and loaded them into the back of the Discovery.

That'll piss her off. She never deals with basic everyday life, like taxing vehicles, organising plumbers, having the central heating boiler serviced or clearing out the gutters. It's almost a shame I'll miss the entertainment when this dawns on her.

'Eliza, are you ready?' he shouted up the stairs as Delia found her voice.

'You may be enjoying this at the moment, Kon, but my solicitor will be in touch very shortly. I shall be citing unreasonable behaviour as grounds.'

Getting pissed up and piddling in her vase was worth it after all. Excellent.

'As you like, dear.'

'Please stop calling me "dear",' Delia hissed, just before Eliza appeared to kiss her on the cheek and spring into the car, full of enthusiasm for life.

'Okay, let's get The Green Mean Machine going! Yeeha!' She laughed and waved goodbye to her mother who stood stiffly at the door for a matter of seconds before trotting back inside. 'She didn't hang around long. I guess she's off to the golf club to swoon over Rolf, the new golf professional.'

'Rolf teaches golf?' Konrad teased. 'Does he look like a wolf?'

Eliza was amused by her father's cheerful banter and joined in. 'Yes, Rolf the wolf teaches golf and likes the odd milf.'

'What's a milf?'

'Dad, where have you been? It's an acronym. M.I.L.F. "Mothers I'd Like to F…" You know.'

'No, I don't know. Lately I'm finding out a variety of things I didn't know and I think I'm not as worldly wise as I pretend to be.'

Eliza gave him the sort of pitying look that most adult children give their parents at one time or another. A look of despair. 'For a man with your reputation you are dangerously out of touch with the milieu.'

'Christ, "milieu" is it now? I'm glad the money your university fees are costing me is being put to good use. Now then, prove yourself worthy and tell me what you really make of Freddie's girlfriend.'

Eliza raised one eyebrow and turned her head away towards the window. 'You're not too impressed with her, I gather from that expression. She's Freddie's type, but not my idea of a potential friend.'

'Because…?'

Eliza sighed. Her father was in interview mode. 'Because she's a bit false: Fake eyelashes, not a hair out of place, sweetness and light, with a "hee, hee, hee," and an "oh, please forgive me for being so forward, I'm not usually like this", bollocks.'

That sounds like a description of Delia when she's had a few, and flirts with the movers and shakers of the television world. Awful.

Konrad drove as fast as he dared until they reached the M6 and Birmingham, when they slowed dramatically to chug slowly with the flow of the traffic.

By the time they had picked up speed again, he was somewhat wiser about Chloe.

'I thought she was quite bright and career minded.'

Eliza shook her head. 'I'm not too sure about that either. She was tight lipped on the specifics, but she works as an event organiser for career conventions and shows. I thought we might have something in common, but we don't. Mum seemed to take to her though.'

'That's a bad sign.'

'Yeah, I might be wrong but I think Chloe is toying with our Freddie. There are no facts, as such, but I think she may have a more permanent boyfriend in the background somewhere. Just a hunch.'

'Poor old Freddie. He's going to get burnt playing with fire. Anyway, enough about him, how's your love life these days? You don't seem to have a significant other, at the moment, if that's the right expression. No one good enough for my Eliza?'

'I work at a slower pace than my brother, that's all. I am seeing someone but I have this underlying fear of being labelled a slut. It's always different for boys; they're Casanovas, playboys, seducers or wolves. Terms which seem to have acceptable connotations. If I behaved like Freddie, I'd be a slapper, loose, a trollop or a tart, and I don't want to be seen in that way. Besides which, the media keep an eye on Freddie and me from a distance and we can't afford any scandal.'

'You wait till tomorrow,' Konrad warned with a wicked grin appearing. 'The press were at my offices today, within hours of the social media announcement and I've been a very naughty boy.'

'Go on.'

'I took Gorgeous George to lunch as a deliberate set up, and the press fell for it. Photos as well. I can't wait for tomorrow when they wrongly accuse me of being a closet gay.'

'I understand the intention, Dad, but did you have to?'

He acknowledged his daughter's disapproval of his use of underhand tactics. He tried to reason with her.

'It'll help to settle them down quicker about the divorce, especially if they make assumptions and get it wrong. It was fun, George enjoyed himself, and no harm was done.' Konrad chuckled at the memory of George's performance, then he and Eliza settled into an easy conversation, with comfortable silences. He savoured his daughter's welcome company.

'I'll give Freddie a ring, while I think of it. I hope he's not entertaining Chloe at the flat, I'll be furious. We've got so much to sort out and he has a dreadful habit of disappearing when there's work to be done. I'm glad you're around to help me put up shelves and stuff. He's a dead loss.'

'I never could work that one out. You would always be the child in the garage with me, asking which tool did what, and helping to paint, while your brother was daydreaming elsewhere or playing with his mates on a computer.'

'Some things don't change. Oh, hello, Freddie... We're about an hour away, probably more. Are you around for when we get there? I've got some stuff from home to cart up to the flat... Right... Oh dear. See you later tomorrow, maybe, or maybe not. Do what you like, you usually do.'

Konrad could tell by the irritation on Eliza's face and in her voice that her brother was being true to form.

'As I said, some things don't change. He's out and probably won't be coming back to the flat tonight. Great, so I'm on my own for the evening.'

'I'll have dinner with you and keep you company. Don't worry, at least you can have the place to yourself, whereas I will no doubt have to suffer the indignity of seeing my son at breakfast in the hotel, eating his new girlfriend. It's not that pleasant.' He tried to physically shake the image from his head, making Eliza laugh at him.

'You won't have to put up with it after that. Freddie's in a foul mood. Apparently little miss perfect has been ordered to cover an event in Hertfordshire and must go home tomorrow. What a shame.'

Konrad pulled off the A55 into some services for a short comfort break.

'Just say you need a pee, Dad. I'll grab a pint of milk, it's the one thing I forgot to pack.'

He made sure he raced back to the car, giving him enough time to call Lorna, while Eliza shopped for a few more essentials. 'I'm spending the rest of the evening with Eliza at the flat, but we'll meet tomorrow, at the Warren, the usual car park down by the beach, you remember. If the weather is foul we could hightail it up to South Stack. Sounds good. See you after lunch then. Yes, I'll wear one of my most attractive hats and an all-encompassing waterproof jacket. See you then. Bye, Lorna,' he said, ending the conversation a little awkwardly. He wanted to call her darling, or at least another term of endearment, but he felt that she wouldn't take it well until he had finished his probationary period of trust building.

Barney must have been reading his mind.

"Are you there yet and have you got your hand down Lorna's bra?"

Bloody idiot.

"No to both. Now bugger off. I'll see you in The Valiant on Wednesday for a pint."

Eliza was climbing back into the passenger seat, as Konrad was finishing his reply to Barney. 'New girlfriend already?' she asked cheekily.

'Barney's not really my type, besides he takes up too much room in the bed.'

'You slept with him?' Eliza wrinkled up her nose.

'We've shared a bed many a time, me and Barney. Nothing wrong with two drunken bums in a bed when the need arises. Or when your mother locked me out. Where do you think I slept when I wasn't at home?' Konrad was grinning at the memories of the inebriated exploits he and Barney had engaged in over the years.

Eliza managed to unhinge his smile. 'I always thought you were at your girlfriend's house. You did have one, didn't you?'

God, why did you create such a bloody bright girl with the inquisitive mind of a detective?

His face answered her question.

'I thought as much,' she said. 'You've been so down the last few months. I assume mother found out and you had to do as you were told.'

Konrad was lost for words. He had wanted to tell Eliza and Freddie about Lorna, but not yet. Not until he was certain that she would have him back in her life permanently.

'Look, Dad, we're adults. You and Mum have been at each other's throats for years and, quite frankly, it's a relief that you're getting divorced. At least you stand a chance of being happy. Get a girlfriend, live a little, and do it soon. I don't suppose the old one will have you back?'

'I'm working on it.'

Eliza looked across at her father. 'God, you are, aren't you? That's a serious expression on your face. I'd like to meet the woman who has that impact on my dad. When you're ready of course.'

'How old are you again? I must have been stuck in a time warp because all of a sudden my daughter has become a mature, confident, assured and capable lady.'

'Thanks, and yes you must have been in a time warp to use the expression "comfort break" instead of pee, and not to know what a milf is.'

Chapter 21

Oh, no. Here they come.

'Good morning, Freddie, and good morning, Chloe. It seems we're destined to see each other at breakfast whenever I'm staying here.' Konrad tried to be polite, but he wasn't feeling it. He had deliberately found a table for two where he could be alone in the restaurant, and had spread the Daily Albion out, propping the top-half on the crockery and condiments. Much to his irritation, Freddie and Chloe deliberately sat at the adjacent table and engaged him in conversation.

'I might be along later this morning, Dad, or maybe this afternoon.'

'Don't tell me, talk to your sister. I'm putting up a few shelves in your flat this morning and that's about it. I'm not around this afternoon, so you'll have to apologise to Eliza for leaving her to do the work, Freddie. She's sorted out the kitchen, bathroom, the lounge, and is not impressed with your contribution.' He gave his son the disapproving Dad look.

'There's nothing much left for me to do then, by the sounds of it.' Freddie laughed.

This dismissive response from his son irritated Konrad who scowled. 'Really?'

'I'll help her as soon as I can. You see, Chloe has to leave tonight, so I was hoping to spend time with her today.'

'Perhaps we could help at the flat for an hour or two, Freddie,' Chloe offered sweetly.

I see what Eliza means. That's all a bit false nicey nicey... and so is she.

He took a furtive closer look at Chloe, noting the heavy make-up accentuating her brown eyes and her long wavy auburn hair, neatly tied with a hairband at the nape of her neck. She had sculpted eyebrows that seemed to be the fashion, but she didn't have any great long talons for fingernails. Instead, Chloe had neatly manicured hands, shiny nails but not painted. No wedding ring. Freddie seemed to hang on her every word, which for some reason that morning Konrad found sickening.

'Do you have any particular plans for this afternoon, Mr Neale?' Chloe asked, smiling broadly.

She sounds like a bloody hairdresser. "Going anywhere nice on holiday this year?"

'I'm meeting a friend, and we're going to Anglesey to revisit some old haunts. I'm looking forward to it.' Konrad made it clear that his plans were not for changing.

'So we may see you before I have to leave then.'

'Perhaps. I'm not sure what my timetable is. Probably dinner in my room. I have a business meeting on Monday and possibly Tuesday and I'll be keeping my face away from public places over the weekend.'

'Dad doesn't usually wear a baseball cap to breakfast,' Freddie explained unnecessarily.

'It's been nice meeting you. I hope we bump into each other again sometime.'

'Thanks.' He looked down at the newspaper in front of him, trying to ignore Freddie and Chloe. Their very presence was annoying him and it took a few moments to work out why. When it came to him, it was simple; Freddie had become a male version of Delia. He wanted to look good, swan around with beautiful people, take advantage of what he could, and not want to get his hands dirty. Eliza, on the other hand was a female version of himself, only braver. Konrad loved them both, but he wanted to shake Freddie and then give him a swift kick up the arse.

'On the subject of money, Freddie, have you secured a job for the summer? Because I'm letting you know now, that with an expensive divorce pending, my income isn't going to stretch to supporting you kids at uni, as well as paying for your mother's lavish lifestyle. I'll pay for the fees and the rent on your flat but the rest is down to you.'

'Actually, Dad, I wanted to speak to you about that. Chloe is based not too far from London, so I was wondering if there were any jobs going at Channel 7 for a few weeks or so.'

He looked his son square in the eye and after a short meaningful pause said, 'I think it's time you found your own work, Freddie. As your mother is about to strip me bare, there will be no coat tails for you to hang on to. Step up now, sunshine. Perhaps Chloe could help.' Konrad looked across at the girl and caught a glimpse of a furious expression, before hammering his point home. 'I'm sorry if you were expecting me to invent a job for you. It doesn't work like that anymore, but Eliza seemed to think she could offer bar work for the summer…'

Come on, Freddie, I've had enough of your mother taking me for a ride with nothing in return, and I'm not doing the same for you. Time to grow up, my boy.

'I don't want to do bloody bar work,' an indignant Freddie protested.

Having heard enough, Konrad stood up, folded the newspaper and tucked it under his arm. 'I'm sure you'll find something. Good morning.' With that, he left the dining room.

He turned to look back when he reached the exit and saw his son with hands held in the air as if unable to explain where he had gone wrong. Chloe's mouth was a thin slit.

Well, Freddie, she doesn't look too impressed with you now.

*

The rain had held off during the morning of DIY, and after a bite to eat, courtesy of Eliza, it was time to head over to Anglesey and to the beach car park to meet up with Lorna. She had already arrived, so Konrad parked The Green Machine next to her car.

Lorna had her walking boots on ready to go by the time Konrad had retrieved his from the back of his car, and she chatted as he did up his laces. 'It's a bit chilly for nearly summer, never mind, we've hit the tide times right, it's still going out, so we can have a good wander around the island.'

'I'm nearly ready. Hat on, phone off,' he said as he went to press the button to switch off his mobile. However, he thought better of it when he saw notification of three messages. 'Shall we look at these first? I'm dying to know what the fall-out is from my early lunch with George yesterday. There was only a hint in the Daily Albion that I may have been "out with a gay friend trying to cope with the agony of my pending divorce", and all that crap, but the photos were funny.'

'Yes, let's have a look, then we can ignore the phone after that for a few hours.'

'Right. The first message is from Annette. Usual piss-take. Sends her love. Then the next one is from Barney.'

"I'll never sleep with you again. You got me into your bed under false pretences you bastard. See you for a pint on Wednesday."

Konrad and Lorna laughed while looking at each other in appreciation of Barney's sense of humour. 'Looks like some of the papers have fallen for it. That's good news. Delia will be sending the "slap on the wrist" to the editors and the job will be done.'

He moved on to the third message.

"You say one thing and do another. I warned you I would be watching. You must cancel your meeting, back off and stop trying to find me. I gave you a chance. I deserve to live my life without fear, and so do you, but now we will both have to deal with it."

'What the hell does that mean exactly, do you think?' Konrad looked at Lorna for her help with an answer.

'How does your stalker know about your meeting with Josh Hawley?'

Lorna and Konrad were facing each other, worried expressions on their faces. 'I'm not sure. It'll be on my movements' calendar at the office, Annette and the boys in editing know, possibly reception. The Management Centre has a small meeting room booked for us for Monday and Tuesday, and Josh is booked in for two nights. I'm in the same room as last time, and Tessa seemed to know where that was. Is she getting information from the hotel?'

'What's she got that she can use against you, Kon? Nothing. Your divorce is announced. Delia knows about me, so as long as we're careful she'll get used to the idea. You're not really gay, so the papers have nothing. What can she do?'

'I don't know. I can take pretty much anything as long as it doesn't involve hurting my kids or manufacturing ways to undo our bid to have a life together. If my divorce is more painful, or my career takes a nosedive, then so be it.' Konrad shrugged, switched off his phone, and grabbed Lorna's hand. 'Shall we go for a stroll by the sea on the way to the island and through the pines on the way back?'

'Why not,' Lorna said, beaming at him and striding towards the gap in the sand dunes and the sound of the waves.

The view across to Snowdonia was marred by the ominous low grey clouds that obscured the peaks, but the walk was exhilarating, and productive. As they always used to, he and Lorna discussed his work. She loved hearing the intricacies of the recent interview he had held and the raw details from him when they discussed the subtle themes and nuances of what was disclosed by Matthew Hawley. For Konrad, having Lorna's ear and wise observations was confirmation.

'Bloody Annette,' he announced. 'She was right.'

'What about?'

'You and me. She said I was off my game, away with the fairies and basically a loss without you. She was right.'

'Yes, well, I'm here now so let's make the most of it shall we and see if we can figure out what your stalker, Tessa, is capable of?'

'Is it too soon to talk about where we are going to live?'

'Yes, Kon, it's too soon,' Lorna said giving a look of mock despair. 'Tell me what you actually know about Tessa.'

They made it back to the car park through the pines nearly two hours later, glowing and windswept. 'A cup of tea is called for,' Konrad announced as he unlaced his boots. Both cars had to be moved so they headed in convoy to the café at South Stack near the lighthouse, arriving half an hour before it closed. They treated themselves to a pot of tea and a couple of fruit scones with butter as the rain lashed down outside.

'I love this place, even in the rain. Shall we come back tomorrow and visit the lighthouse and maybe have lunch here?' Lorna suggested.

Konrad was nearly unable to reply. This was an irrefutable sign that his probation was going well. 'Yes, let's do that. It helps to clear my head. If the weather eases up we might even see the puffins.'

'Speaking of birds, I've been thinking about your Tessa.' Lorna put down her teaspoon having livened up the tea in the pot by adding more hot water and giving it a quick stir.

'Not too deeply I hope.'

'Deep enough… I think she wants to be found.'

Konrad took a slurp from his freshly poured cuppa. He placed the cup down to pay attention to what she had to say next. 'How so?'

'If she had kept quiet, it's likely that no one would have found her, but she hasn't and she's making a proper fuss. She seems to have disappeared from society after the age of fifteen maybe sixteen and even her own parents didn't have a clue where she was; therefore, she had no reason to worry that her new identity would be disclosed. So, my thinking is this: Tessa as a small child showed remorse for the bad things Helena made her do. She also tried to warn Matthew about Helena, so she must care about other people. So maybe she wants to confess something.'

'Like what? Do you mean our hypothesis about Tessa forcing Matthew to kill Helena to protect Josh? It's possible, but how does that affect what happens next?'

'I'm not certain, but I think it makes her more unpredictable. If she wants to be caught, will she go so far as to act again?'

'To kill someone?'

'I don't think so. She couldn't do it last time, remember… Kon, you must have been close to revealing the truth when you interviewed Matthew, otherwise why is she making these threats?'

'I'm convinced I was close to something, but the pieces of the puzzle won't fit together, which is why I have to keep trying to understand what he said and how it explains why he killed Helena. Josh has to be the key. I've got the transcript on my laptop. I keep reading the last few pages, but it's not there, whatever it is. I'm getting fed up with thinking about it.'

Konrad changed the subject, eventually plucking up the courage to suggest that he and Lorna could have dinner at the hotel together. 'I don't want to eat alone, and we can't risk going anywhere too public. Please?'

Lorna smiled and agreed without any protest. 'Just dinner. Nothing else, and no sneaky attempts to get me to look at your etchings, okay?'

'I agree to your terms and conditions. Seven thirty? I'm in room 110. Reception can let me know when you've arrived and I'll meet you there.

'It's a date.'

Chapter 22

Konrad had some work to do replying to emails and messages as a result of the speculation in the press that he was gay and that his wife had found out, thus the need for divorce. Social media had gone into meltdown, but Delia seemed to be enjoying herself with her replies on Konrad's Facebook. According to her email, retractions were ready to be printed in the guilty papers the next day, and George had become a minor Facebook sensation.

Good grief, he'll be unbearable on Monday.

In another email, Mike and Joe had sent him through some scanned pages of an article containing photos of Naomi and Josh during a gala dinner for Business Entrepreneurs of the Year, which had taken place several months before the murder.

'Handsome couple. She's so tiny,' he said aloud. Naomi Woods was described in the blurb alongside the magazine article as "a formidable business woman in a dynamic package". Looking more closely at the photos, Konrad changed his mind. He figured out that Naomi appeared petite because Josh Hawley stood head and shoulders above most of the men that he was pictured with, making Naomi seem minute in stature. She was in fact eye-to-eye with most of the other women at the same event. She was slim, but not scrawny, and had a good figure.

'I can see the attraction there, Josh.' Konrad scrutinised the picture of Naomi with her bright blue eyes staring into the camera lens. She wore a wide smile creating dimples in each cheek, had a short elfin haircut and athletic build, all of which contributed to a good-looking, confident woman with all the assets in the right place. The photos also contained poses from

Helena and Matthew, and the four of them made a marketing manager's dream. They were photogenic and magnetic. There was even a group shot of the whole team in posh frocks and penguin suits. 'Aha, there's Richard, getting a small glimmer of the limelight.'

He knew that Richard had been asked to give evidence at the murder trial of Matthew Hawley and wondered if he would have had anything to add to the documentary.

He raised this with Lorna over dinner, in the precious hours spent with her, which seemed to last for a frustratingly short time.

'What do you know about Richard? He seems to take up space in the periphery of the story but I can't get any sense of who he was or how he fitted in with the dynamics,' Lorna said.

'He was a mystery man, our Richard, and I take your point. He can't have been a spectator. If you imagine working for someone like Helena and in recruitment, you'd have to be a strong personality. I could kick myself for not asking Matthew about him. I think I've missed a significant character in the whole charade.'

'That's an interesting choice of words, Kon. Do you think what you've been led to believe by Matthew Hawley was a façade, a masquerade for something else?'

'I'm sure it is. Having said that, I don't think Matthew lied. I think he was duped by Helena.'

'Maybe he found out and that's why he killed her.'

'Perhaps Richard told him. We'll never know, because whatever that man knew will never be revealed. I wish I understood why Richard killed himself so soon after Helena's murder.'

'Was he having an affair with Helena?'

Before long the meal was over and despite dragging out the coffee afterwards, it was all too soon that Konrad was escorting Lorna back to her car.

'Look at that,' he whispered. 'Love's young dreamers don't seem too happy.' Konrad had spied Freddie loading a suitcase into Chloe's flashy BMW. He and Lorna had to hide in the dark shadows away from the lights that served the car park area, witnessing a forlorn Freddie plod off into the distance, head bowed as if he had been dismissed. He gave a short wave as Chloe drove past him out of the driveway and down the road.

'Good. I can have a relaxed breakfast tomorrow. Bloody yippee,' Konrad said. Lorna grinned at him and slid her arm through his as they continued through the main car park to where her car sat, outside the BBC building. When they reached it, he took a risk and kissed Lorna hastily on the lips, to test his progress. He was rewarded with a sensual lingering response in kind. 'You'd better go now, while the going's good.' Then there was a teenage moment, when neither of them wanted to leave. 'Goodnight then.'

'Yeah, goodnight. I'll see you tomorrow.'

'Okay, see you tomorrow.'

'Text me when you get in, so I know you're safe. Got your phone?'

Lorna checked her pockets and then rummaged around in her bag for a few moments before declaring that she must have left her phone at home. 'I'll text you. I promise.'

Once Lorna had dragged herself away from another emotion-laden kiss, Konrad stood against the building in the dark and watched as she pulled out of the BBC car park.

He was still deep in thought when he saw Chloe drive back in and park her BMW in the shadows.

She must have forgotten something. Dippy cow.

He didn't want to bump into her, so walked the long way around the building to get to his room through the entrance in the courtyard.

Within fifteen minutes of closing the door and switching on the TV in his room, he was in the shower and looking forward to a good night's sleep after his successful day with Lorna.

Things are going to work out. As long as I don't rush her, and don't do anything stupid.

Wrapping himself in a clean cotton-towelling robe, he lay on the bed to watch the late news. There was a knock at the door. Konrad hesitated and called out, 'Who is it?'

'It's me. Are you all right? Reception said it was urgent and that you're sick.'

He opened the door and sure enough, there was Lorna.

'What do you mean? What are you doing here?' he asked, letting her into the room, but before he could close the door a foot appeared, jamming it, followed forcefully by the owner of the foot. Lorna turned to face the intruder but, enraged, Konrad pulled the door towards him.

'Right, you little bastard, what's your game? Oi, what are you playing at?' Konrad made a grab for the dark clothing, pushing Lorna out of his way and as he did so he was showered in a cloud of fine white powder.

Chapter 23

He became aware of Lorna's voice next to him on the bed. She sounded distressed, but he was struggling to reach full consciousness and there was a fearful searing pain from his right eye. Lorna was holding something onto his head, covering most of the right side of his face. He couldn't make sense of this.

'Both. Ambulance and police. Please hurry, he's bleeding a lot and I don't know what else to do. Hang on, I think he's coming around. Konrad! Kon! Can you hear me?'

Lorna was kneeling at his side, sobbing and distraught, alerting him to the seriousness of a predicament that he could not yet comprehend. The towel Lorna pressed to his face was sticky with his blood and he was in his hotel room, lying face up but the wrong way round in the bed, half wrapped in the duvet.

'God, Kon, please talk to me,' Lorna begged.

'Lorna? What's happened?' Konrad asked groggily, slurring the few words that he managed to formulate.

'I don't know, Kon, I think we were assaulted, but I don't know.'

He wanted to shake loose the cotton wool from inside his head that was preventing him from thinking straight. He couldn't work out what had occurred to make Lorna sound so overwrought, almost hysterical. But he did know it was daylight; early morning light was filtering through from behind the curtains barely enabling him to see that the room around him was strewn with clothes, some of them bloodied.

What the fuck's happened to me?

There was an urgent knock on the door as a voice cried out, 'It's Martin, the duty manager, the ambulance and police are on their way. Can you let me in to help you?'

Lorna leapt up wearing a towelling robe covered in blood.

'Lorna, you're injured,' Konrad mumbled. His body ached and it hurt when he tried to move, although the agonising pain in his temples, which centred on his right eye, masked much of his discomfort. He held the towel in place, and kept his head as still as he could, subconsciously recognising the need to keep the pressure on his wound. Martin entered but stood immobilised by the scene.

'Holy hell, what happened?' Martin trembled, clearly uncertain how to proceed.

Konrad saw Lorna's face as she too looked back at the devastation in the room, utterly bewildered and frightened. 'I don't know what happened, I woke up a few minutes ago and we were covered in blood. Konrad's hurt really badly and I don't know what to do.' Her voice quaked with fear as she looked to Martin for strength and assistance, but he stepped back into the doorway.

'I don't think I should come in any further. I'll wait for the police and ambulance and direct them to the back here.' As he said this, sirens could be heard wailing through the streets of Bangor. Martin looked at his watch.

'What time is it?' Lorna asked.

'Just after five.'

'Five in the morning? How can it be the morning?' Lorna queried while she looked towards the window for proof. 'Why didn't I wake up?' she asked, turning to attend to Konrad. 'What the hell has happened to us? I don't understand.' Lorna brushed her hair out of her eyes and wiped the tears that were blurring her vision. As she did so she smeared more blood across her face.

Martin, rushing to escape the scene of carnage, ran outside to meet the emergency services who in turn arrived within seconds at the door to the hotel room. The police entered first followed by the ambulance crew who examined the wounds to Konrad's head causing him to scream in agony. One of the crew members called in via radio to the hospital with the relevant details.

'We are on scene with a forty-four-year-old IC1 male, Konrad Neale, and his female partner, Lorna Yates.' The ambulance man looked at Lorna for confirmation that he had taken in the facts correctly. She had sat trembling on the bottom corner of the bed next to Konrad; adrenalin overload was showing its hand. She managed a slow inclination of her head as the lady ambulance crew member wrapped her in a blanket.

'Mr Neale has deep lacerations across his left forehead and diagonally towards his right ear. There is severe damage to his right eye. The globe is traumatised and deeply lacerated. We have evidence of bruising elsewhere and unusual marks about the body.'

There was an unspoken acknowledgement between the ambulance crew as this specific information was shared.

'The head wound is of primary concern. The viability of the eye is questionable. GCS fourteen, a little confused, and was unconscious until just prior to our arrival. Pulse ninety, BP ninety over seventy-two, ETA ten minutes. We will be bringing his partner, Lorna Yates. Treatment for shock and other soft tissue damage.'

Lorna put her hands up to her own face and, feeling with her fingertips, winced as she felt the swelling and grazes to her cheekbones and brow.

The police introduced themselves and were asking questions.

'Miss Yates. Lorna. Is it all right if we call you Lorna?'

'Yes, of course,' she replied, her voice shaking.

'I'm Detective Sergeant Ffion Jenkins and this is Officer Lyons. We were just about to finish an uneventful night shift.'

'Sorry.'

'Goodness, don't be sorry. We're just glad we happened to be available to attend so rapidly. Can you tell us exactly what happened, in your own words? Don't worry, we know this is difficult but it's important.' DS Jenkins had a calming manner, helping Lorna to focus on answering her questions, despite the distraction of Konrad's distressing cries.

'I don't know. Really, I have no idea.' Lorna was turning her head looking around at the scene and then she placed her hands on her chest above her heart, one on top of the other. 'I had a call from the hotel reception just as I got home. They said it was urgent and that Kon needed to see me straight away in his room and had asked them to call me. It was a private matter and they said he was feeling unwell, something like that. So, I drove back and came through via reception to let them know I was here. I ran to the room, knocked on the door and Kon let me in. That's it. That's all I remember until I woke up. I can't believe it's the morning.'

DS Jenkins tried to calm Lorna down who was now on her feet pacing the carpet at the end of the bed.

'I know this is difficult, but can you tell me, what do you know about the knife?' she said, pointing to the dressing table area, which was blood spattered and where among other items, a long kitchen knife lay next to some rope and a blood-soaked hand towel.

'Nothing. I can't tell you anything. I have no idea what happened to us. Please, they have to help Kon.' Konrad was being transferred to a trolley for transport to the hospital and was in agonising pain every time he had to move his head. He reached out to Lorna.

'Mr Neale, we'll talk later but can you remember anything about who assaulted you?' asked DS Jenkins.

'All I can remember is Lorna coming through the door and then something happening after that, but I don't know what it is. Please help us.'

Lorna went with Konrad in the ambulance accompanied by Officer Lyons, a quiet young police officer who had been sent to take any further details. He knew who Konrad was, and keen to ensure that the media was kept away from the hospital.

Lyons made it his business to alert the ambulance staff to the requirement for absolute confidentiality and privacy. He watched in silence as Konrad spoke with Lorna during the short journey to the hospital.

'Kon, do you think this is her? Tessa?'

'I don't know… Lorna, your lovely face is battered and covered in blood. Are you hurt anywhere else?'

'I'm not sure, I hurt all over, but I'm more scared about not remembering anything and not waking up when they did this. How can that be possible, Kon? I think I must be going mad.' Konrad held out his hand to give Lorna some reassurance as best he could, saying, 'I'm as mad as you then, because for the life of me I can't work out how this could've happened to us, and where did the night go?'

'I'm sorry to interrupt,' Officer Lyons said quietly, 'but who is Tessa?'

After a short explanation from Lorna, Officer Lyons contacted DS Jenkins who had put the wheels in motion for a detailed investigation. She was still at the hotel and the room was secured as a crime scene. 'There may be evidence on Mr Neale's mobile phone and laptop.'

Konrad began to feel very lightheaded and vague. The voices of Lorna and Officer Lyons faded away as he gave in to semi-consciousness.

Chapter 24

Konrad awoke to the noise of gentle chatter in the distance and a trolley being wheeled across a floor. He was propped up at a gentle angle in a single bed, a hospital bed, and could only open his left eye. Automatically he put his hands up to feel his face and noticed the cannula puncturing the back of his hand, attached to a drip. Feeling around, he realised that most of his head was heavily bandaged. The excruciating pain of the day before had been replaced by an aching, throbbing pressure.

'Dad?' came a sweet voice from his right. He tried to turn his head enough to see Eliza, but this made him groan with pain, and realising her mistake, she moved to stand at the bottom of the bed. 'Dad, can you hear me? Can you see me?'

'Eliza. What are you doing here?'

'That's a bloody daft question for a man of your intelligence,' she said, crying but at the same time looking relieved that he had managed to speak.

'You got here quickly. How did they find you?' He was aware that he sounded drunk and that he was decidedly groggy, however he thought his questions sounded reasonable enough. Eliza, however, didn't seem to react in the way he would have expected her to. 'I know I'm in hospital but I haven't a clue what the time is. Did they catch the bastard?' he asked.

'Pardon?' Eliza stared at her father in disbelief.

'What have I said? What's going on?'

A nurse entered the side room where Konrad had been admitted after lengthy surgery. 'Awake at last. Welcome back. I'm Sheila, one of the staff nurses,' she said with a smile and an efficient assessment of her patient's mood. 'I expect you're wondering where you are.' Konrad gave a hesitant half-nod. He thought he was in hospital in Bangor where he had been taken by ambulance, but he was wrong.

'Mr Neale, welcome to Manchester's Royal Eye Hospital. You were brought here rather hastily yesterday morning. There are a number of things we need to tell you about, and the police have asked to speak to you as soon as you are able and conscious. I'll contact them and also bleep Mr Wells. He's your surgeon. He'll talk you through what procedure has been carried out. I expect your daughter and your wife will fill in some of the blanks for you.'

'Thanks,' Konrad replied, rather weakly. 'I can't quite believe I'm in Manchester… Where is Lorna?' He had assumed the nurse was referring to Lorna and had believed her to be his wife.

Sheila the nurse merely smiled and looked across at Eliza, raising both eyebrows before leaving her to explain.

'Dad, Lorna's been arrested.'

'What do you mean, arrested? What for?' Konrad tried unsuccessfully to sit up by rocking on his elbows.

'For that.' Eliza pointed at the bandage on her father's head.

'Come off it. That's not remotely possible.'

'She's in custody and the police say they have evidence that indicates she did it. I'll let them explain, I don't know all the details. Mum's here as well and she is the angriest I've ever seen her. You'd better protect your good eye because she's likely to spit in it.' As Eliza had just finished giving her father fair warning, Delia bustled in to the hospital side room. She was stiff with hatred.

'You absolute bastard.' The words came out of her thin lips like a series of bitter bullets. 'I'm glad you're alive, but only because I want to make you suffer like you never imagined possible. I've waited here to tell you in person. Now I can go home. The gloves are off, Kon, and you are on the fucking ropes. See you in court.' Delia's venomous tirade shocked Konrad into silence. He watched her storm out before looking to his daughter for an explanation.

'I suppose she found out that I was with Lorna?'

'And the rest…!'

'The rest of what? Will somebody please tell me what's been going on?' he shouted in anger and was almost close to tears with frustration. Staff Nurse Sheila heard his cries and came rushing back in, asking Eliza to leave.

'Mr Neale, you have had very delicate surgery and it's important that you remain calm and still for several hours. Mr Wells is on his way and he'll discuss everything with you. However, the police will best explain the other matters. They're on their way from Bangor; a Detective Chief Inspector Anwell and a Detective Sergeant Jenkins will be here in the next hour or so. Please try to be patient. We know it's difficult.'

'Do you?' Konrad was beside himself with annoyance at the true facts of his situation being hidden from him. 'I have no idea what has happened to me, my soon-to-be-ex-wife vents her spleen at me for something, I know not what, and my girlfriend has apparently been arrested for assaulting me, when she can't possibly have done it! Do you really have any fucking idea what this feels like?'

Sheila took a deep breath. 'You're probably right. I don't. But I do know that shouting at me won't help. Now, are you up to having something to eat or drink?'

He felt suitably ashamed for having taken his anger out on someone who was trying to help and he apologised profusely.

Sheila gave a ready smile forgiving his outburst. 'Apology accepted. I've witnessed much worse in my career, if I'm honest. I'll see what I can rustle up for you in the way of a small snack. In the meantime, here's Mr Wells.'

Through the door strode a slim bespectacled surgeon who shook hands warmly as he made his formal introduction. He moved a chair to the left side of the bed and broke the news to Konrad that he no longer had use of his right eye. 'In fact, we had to remove your eye altogether.'

Konrad's mind could not absorb the information. He stared past Mr Wells, trying to focus on the wall instead. The words spoken by the surgeon drifted by him, failing to register a meaning or a memory, barely lingering long enough to be heard.

'It is something that many people find hard to come to terms with. I'll give you some simple facts for now, and we can talk again later on when you've had time to let this news sink in.

'Your eyelid has been stitched shut to protect the surgery thus far. What we have tried to do is salvage the muscles, and we hope the blood vessels will grow through the round implant and allow some eye movement eventually. This helps cosmetically and with the psychological hurdles of losing an eye.' Mr Wells used his hands to demonstrate the descriptions he was giving.

'On top of the implant we have placed a conformer, it's an almond-shaped plastic material, which sits underneath your eyelid, and once your ocular prosthesis is ready, the conformer can be removed. Mr Neale, do you have any questions at this stage? Mr Neale?'

He turned his head in the direction of the voice. He couldn't focus. A dark and ominous feeling had overwhelmed him, making it impossible to stay in the present moment. He stared with one eye at the surgeon, not acknowledging him. Konrad's face was a blank.

The doctor stood and left without saying anything more. Instead he raised his concerns about Konrad's mental state with Sheila, who was returning with a jug of water and a small plate of sandwiches.

She took them away again, untouched half an hour later, when the police arrived. The door to the side room was open and he could hear Sheila talking.

'I'm not sure you'll be able to question him thoroughly; he's quite shocked at the loss of his eye. He's only just been told. Do you have to question him now?'

'I see. How much else has he been told about what happened to him?' asked a mellow male voice.

'I'm not sure. You could ask his daughter. She went out for a while to try to pacify her mother. That wife of his was like a thing possessed and most unpleasant.'

'Yes, I believe DS Jenkins had the pleasure of her company on Sunday and wasn't too enamoured either. Can you make sure we're not interrupted, especially by Mrs Neale if she reappears, and please continue to avoid anyone talking to the press; they've caused us huge problems.'

Konrad's heart lurched in his chest when he heard that comment about the press. It would explain Delia's reaction.

DCI Gethin Anwell and DS Ffion Jenkins walked respectfully but confidently into the hospital room introducing themselves before taking seats either side of the bed. DS Jenkins was obscured from Konrad's view, which he was obliged to point out.

'I'm so sorry. I didn't realise,' she said as she moved her chair to the bottom end of the bed, allowing Konrad to see her properly.

'Yes, I remember meeting you now. I was in a lot of pain so I didn't register your name.' He was desperate to understand the full picture and was bursting with a dire need. 'Look, can we cut the niceties. How about you tell me why you've arrested Lorna.'

DCI Anwell sat, bent legs akimbo, resting his elbows on his knees and chin on his hands. This helped to bring his eyes level with Konrad's face. He was a tall athletic-looking man with a slim nose and intense eyes. 'Hmmm. Mr Neale, in police terms this is relatively straightforward. The knife we found on scene covered in your blood had her fingerprints on it. There was no sign of anyone else involved in the actual physical assaults, although Miss Yates appears to have had an accomplice who filmed the whole event. We have a copy of that film and we therefore saw Miss Yates carry out a number of assaults, during and after you and she had indulged in sexual activity. Can you tell us about what happened that night?'

There was a significant pause while Konrad tried desperately to gain some semblance of composure. He looked from one detective to the other, searching for clues. Each time he did so his head throbbed. 'I… This isn't right. I can't remember anything about having sex with Lorna. She didn't. We didn't. I remember kissing her in the car park earlier, then later, about half an hour or so later, she knocked at my hotel room door saying that reception had called her and that I had asked to see her urgently. I never made any call to reception. I let her in. Then something happened.'

'Can you tell us what that was, Mr Neale. It's really important.'

He closed his one good eye, and tried to bring to mind what he had seen as Lorna came into his hotel room. 'I pulled Lorna out of the way. There was someone trying to get into my room behind her. There was a foot in the door and I pulled or pushed Lorna backwards and yanked the door towards me. A small bloke, I think, in dark clothes was there and I grabbed at him. I said something to him, but that's where it stops. I can't remember anything until I came to; lying on the bed the wrong way up and Lorna was holding a towel to my head and was on the phone getting help. She was in a terrible state. That's it.'

DCI Anwell looked at his sergeant. 'DS Jenkins recorded what you told us at the time about the events that night and what she wrote corresponds very closely with what you've just said. We also picked up on what you and Lorna said about there being a stalker involved recently. We have your phone and we are following up on this important line of enquiry. You see, Mr Neale, we don't think Lorna did this deliberately. She did assault you and that's why we've charged her with GBH.'

Konrad gasped.

'However,' continued the inspector, 'we are carrying out an in-depth investigation into the possibility that neither you nor Miss Yates were in full control of your own free will at the time of the assaults.' DCI Anwell stopped talking and made eye contact with DS Jenkins who sat silently watching reactions. Konrad was crying. Huge sobs wracked his body as he lay on the hospital bed.

It was several minutes before the inspector could carry on with his explanation. 'Mr Neale, we can't release Lorna Yates because of the nature of the assault and the evidence which suggests that she carried out the crime. However, we have made one of the finest forensic searches of a crime scene I have had the privilege of being a part of. The film that was delivered on a USB stick to the press is being minutely examined also.'

'The press. Good God.' Konrad teetered on the edge of the pit of despair.

'I'm afraid so. They have been warned they may face prosecution and will probably incur fines and internal inquiries. Rather predictably the gutter press ran with the story and the headlines this morning have been messy I'm afraid, to the extent that we have an officer here in the hospital to ensure that reporters are kept well away.'

'Tessa Carlton.'

'Your stalker? We're following what leads we can. I'll keep you updated. What we did find at the scene was evidence of a mind-altering drug on the wall inside the door to your room, your towelling robe and some on Miss Yates clothes that she was wearing when she arrived in your room. We also have CCTV footage of someone following behind Miss Yates as she heads towards your room in the hotel. We thought at first they were acting together, and that this person was the accomplice who filmed the attacks. However, you and Miss Yates tell similar versions of events and each of you describe memory loss. Secondly, there were no defensive wounds to be found on you, but the main error that the person in question made was that they filmed themselves by accident in the mirror on the back of the door. This person appeared to be conducting proceedings. We are sure it's a female wearing a cap and dark clothing. No fingerprints were found, but we are on to something. Mr Neale, please be assured that we will follow this through. Try to rest.'

'Can I see Lorna?'

'I'm afraid not. We'll talk again before you're transferred back to Bangor unless you prefer to go to a hospital nearer home.'

'No. I have to stay here. We have to find Tessa Carlton, but listen, please keep it quiet that you're looking for her. If she finds out, she'll want us both dead. Me and Lorna. She has to believe she's succeeded.'

'Is she really that desperate?' DCI Anwell didn't need a reply. The tears in Konrad's remaining eye and the expression on his face told the whole story. The two detectives stood up as if to leave.

'I need to see the film,' Konrad said in a monotone voice.

'I don't think that's a good idea.'

'I do. Can you make arrangements for me to see a copy, please? I may be able to help. It's what I do for a living. Did for a living.'

'We'll be back when you're feeling better. We need to discuss Tessa Carlton. Everything you know.'

After they left, Konrad stared into nothing. His life had been flushed down a huge toilet and he was at a loss about how to react. Reaching out to the tray table that hovered above his neatly made bed, he found the TV remote control. He turned on the news for a distraction, and when he saw himself in the headlines he increased the volume and lay back to listen. Resting his good eye alleviated the pain from the surgery to his right eye. His eyes wanted to work in unison, so to rest one, he had to rest both.

Fuck and double fuck with some added bastards and bloody hells. What am I going to do?

Chapter 25

The early evening news was rammed full of information about his private life. Most of it was accurate.

"Konrad Neale recently announced divorce from his wife, Delia. They had been married for twenty-two years during which time Konrad became a household name in television and radio. When his career waned, Delia was his rock. She battled to help his reinvention and was by his side at recent awards ceremonies and events marking the success of his documentary series "The Truth Behind the Lies".

"A rather ironic title, as it now appears there were several lies hiding the truth behind the marriage of Delia and Konrad Neale.

"The woman charged with grievous bodily harm, the woman who viciously attacked Konrad Neale in his hotel room in North Wales in the early hours of Sunday morning, was his ex-mistress Lorna Yates who works for the BBC.

"She had been scorned by Konrad Neale nearly four months ago and now it seems she has sought revenge in the cruellest of ways. He lies disfigured and in pain in hospital and she has been arrested and charged.

"In a bitter twist, she filmed the whole event and an unedited version was sent to the Daily Herald national newspaper who have since been requested to hand over this film to the police as evidence. Our sources say the footage contains scenes of sexual depravity and sadomasochistic activities. It seems that sex was the bait laid by Miss Yates and falling into the honey trap, Konrad Neale was treated to much more than a night of erotic extremes. His readiness to submit to such activities will surely blight, if not destroy, Konrad Neale's future career, and his handsome silver fox good looks have been permanently damaged by a vengeful woman who preyed on his weakness for sex.

"Konrad Neale's wife, Delia, has made a statement in which she expresses her disgust at her husband's behaviour in the face of what looked to be an amicable divorce, our reporter..."

Click.

He opened his eye. 'Eliza?'

'You shouldn't be watching that.'

'I still can't believe what's happening.' Seeing Eliza again, Konrad felt uneasiness, and couldn't determine what was bothering him about her presence. As he grappled with this thought, it came to him. 'Where's Freddie?'

Eliza hesitated. 'He's at the police station. They're asking him questions. I'm not sure what about. Dad, I'm sorry, he doesn't want to see you.'

'Why not?'

'He says it's because you deliberately belittled him in front of Chloe, but I think there's more to it than that. What did you say to him?'

Konrad recalled every word, but gave his daughter the brief version. 'I told him that I was expecting him to find a job to help support himself at uni, and not to keep hanging on my coat tails.'

'He said you refused to find a job for him at Channel 7.'

'Yes, of course I refused. I can't create jobs or invent them. Anyway, he only wanted to work in London because he could be closer to Chloe's head office and see her more often.'

'He's moved in with Mum for the summer instead, so Chloe will be a regular visitor. She and Mum can swap tips about fashion and make-up. How hideous.' Eliza sighed.

'Has your mother gone?' Konrad asked. He hoped Delia would calm down, whilst accepting that the likelihood of that happening was going to be slim. The well-publicised news about Lorna being his mistress and the wild reports of sexual deviancy would whip her up into a fearful frenzy.

'Yes, she has. I don't think she'll be visiting again soon.' Eliza tried to smile. 'Dad, is there anyone you would like me to contact for you? Barney has been trying to get hold of you on your mobile but the police have that. Can I tell him where you are?'

'Yes please, Eliza, I need a mate just now. He looks like a blithering idiot but he's not. Can you get hold of Annette Lichfield at Channel 7, my editor? I wonder if the police have spoken to her yet. Shit, I don't know where to start without Lorna being around with her sensible brain. Annette's the next best thing to common sense that I know.

'Finally, can you reach John Brace my solicitor, I'd better tie up with him about the divorce before it gets too messy.' Konrad felt pleased with himself for being able to think through his most pressing requirements, despite his fuzzy head and the pounding pain.

'Sorry, Dad, you can't use him. Mum got there first.'

'Christ. She likes to make things harder than strictly necessary.'

'However,' Eliza interjected, 'your bosses at Channel 7 have engaged the services of a big gun: Rupert Van Dahl. He's a barrister, apparently, and he's already dealing with the backlash in the press. The bosses must really want to support you through this.'

'Oh, Eliza.' He sighed at his daughter's naïve, optimistic view of the world. 'That's not for me. Employing a top-notch barrister is to help preserve the reputation of the company. He'll be doing their bidding, not mine. I'm not complaining mind you, he'll have a great deal of incentive to make me look like a poor innocent victim and gain the public's sympathy.' Following that train of thought, Konrad arrived at the appalling conclusion that in order for him to be made the innocent victim, Lorna would be labelled and treated as the evil perpetrator. There could be no mention of a stalker in the press otherwise the nightmare would only become worse for both of them. *Can I trust the police? I can trust Annette, she already knows about the stalker. She's the only other one apart from Lorna. Do Mike and Joe know? Did I tell them?* He couldn't remember.

'Dad?' Eliza had raised her voice.

'What?'

'You didn't answer my question.' Eliza looked concerned. 'I asked you if you needed anything else. I've asked for a phone to be put in here so we can call you, but is there anything else? I have to go, it's getting late and I have work tomorrow. I'll phone you.' She leant forward and kissed her father on the cheek.

'Eliza, you're amazing. I love you. Please don't think too badly of me. You'll see, "the truth will out". I'm not a sex pervert.'

'Dad, I'm not an idiot. You're so naïve at times; how could you be a pervert if your life has been filled with vanilla sex? Let's face it, you didn't even know what a milf was, let alone what some of things are they've talked about in the press, so I know it can't be true. Hang on in there.' She smiled down at her dad who had been holding his breath waiting for the rejection to come, and when it didn't he let out a sigh and a stream of tears. 'You can stop that nonsense, it'll make your bandage soggy.' With a gentle touch of her hand on his, Eliza left.

Still don't understand what she meant by vanilla sex. Sounds like ice cream.

Konrad had only himself for company for the rest of the evening, interrupted by the occasional visit from a staff nurse who would carry out vital-sign checks and administer antibiotics and steroids. His spirits had slowly and inexorably plummeted as the consequences of Tessa Carlton's actions became more apparent. The damage she had incurred was irreversible and catastrophic. Konrad managed to persuade himself that he could handle the condemnation for having been caught with his mistress in a hotel room, and he was convinced that he would recover his own public image, somehow, and be able to deal with the divorce.

What he could not accept, however, were the deeper and more painful losses. The loss of his eye, the loss of Lorna, and knowing that their reunion had been shattered into disgusting pieces and lowered to the level of cheap tacky pornography. He couldn't even picture it in his head. *What did they mean when they said on the news about sadomasochistic activities? What does that mean exactly?*

Chapter 26

She took a seat in front of the camera.

'I've been watching the news again today, Konrad, listening out for the latest updates on your story. It's the most exciting real-life television drama you've ever been involved in, and I'm sure the world must look entirely different for you now with one eye, your mistress in prison, your son disowning you, a wife beside herself with rage at your betrayal and your future career in tatters. It's what you deserve for poking your nose into private matters. Perhaps Lorna should have been ordered to cut that off while she was slashing at your face.

'Have you seen yourself on film yet, I wonder? You and Lorna were magnificent.

'I did think that taking on two of you would be a risk, but whatever those clever Chinese chemists have done to that powder is nothing short of genius. The Columbians have the raw stuff, the Devil's Breath, but the Chinese have finesse and the know-how to turn it into a much better product. I only wish I could get hold of more, but the stupid bastards got themselves caught in Paris. So, Konrad, you had the last of my supplies. I made good use of it though, don't you think?

'You and Lorna. What a performance and I must say you were the easiest cast members to direct. Everything I asked of you, down to the facial expressions, you carried out without question. I honestly thought I was going to run out of battery in the camera before the pair of you had reached the final climax. Konrad, if only you knew how tempted I was to join in with you and Lorna. It was such a turn-on watching you. Alas, it was not to be. I had a plan in mind, and despite your distracting cock, I had to make sure I followed it.

The police will be looking for Tessa Carlton by now I'm sure. I wish them luck. I'll be in touch soon, Konrad. Maybe, a get-well card would be in order.

Chapter 27

'Good morning, Mr Neale. I hope you managed to get some sleep last night.' Staff Nurse Sheila had woken him as she entered his hospital room carrying a tray. 'I know it isn't your usual standard of breakfast, but I'm reliably informed that the scrambled eggs taste much better than they look, although the toast underneath is probably a little on the soggy side it adds a certain… je ne sais quoi… to the dish,' she said as she placed the morning's offering onto the adjustable table, which she then manoeuvred expertly into place.

Helping Konrad to sit up, she changed the angle of the backrest and plumped up his pillows. On waking, he had felt disorientated for a few seconds mostly because, during the time asleep, he'd forgotten about the loss of his eye. The sad reality crashed back into his head as soon as he recognised Sheila and the clinical room he had woken up to find. He couldn't speak for a while as he readjusted.

'Your daughter has phoned already to see how you are. She's a lovely girl. Now then, eat what you can, and after breakfast you and I are going to get up close and personal behind these curtains – for a wash.' Sheila caught the expression on Konrad's face. 'Not me. You. Yes, Mr Neale, I know the thought is embarrassing but I'm a nurse and it's one of my specialities. You will feel so much better afterwards. Just think of it as a free spa treatment.'

'I'd rather not. You'll be getting out the hose for a colonic next.'

Sheila grinned and ignored the inference. 'Hopefully by tomorrow you'll be able to get up and about a bit more, but for now you have to keep that pressure bandage dry for a good five days in total.'

'When can I get rid of this catheter bag? It's embarrassing. I feel so incredibly weak and useless.'

'Let's see how you get on today. Eat up. I'll return to scrub your back in half an hour or so.'

'No rush, I'm not going anywhere. And Sheila... thanks for putting up with me. I don't usually swear at nurses. I'm sorry.'

'Mr Neale, you apologised yesterday. It's forgotten about. See you later.' Sheila waved briefly as she headed back out into the busy breakfast rush-hour traffic on the main ward corridor.

It was only when he started to eat his eggs did he appreciate what an impact having one eye would have on his life. He found judging the distance between the plate, cutlery, and mouth quite tricky. He had to concentrate hard not to miss the food altogether. Several times he misjudged where the fork was in relation to his mouth and stabbed his lips and clattered his teeth as a result. Without both eyes, his spatial awareness at close range was badly affected, the loss of one eye meant breakfast was out of focus and lacking dimension.

Looking around him at the far corners of his small room he realised that judgement over longer distances didn't seem to be as difficult, but in doing so confirmed that his peripheral vision would be problematical in the future. He had to move his head more than was natural to fully scan around him, and this still hurt.

His next trial was heralded by the return of Sheila wearing a thin plastic apron and surgical gloves. She moved the table and cleared space to work in. Raising the bed using the electric controls, she also pulled the concertina blue curtains around the area, providing privacy.

Her expert routine for carrying out a bed bath had been finely honed. Towels were moved to maintain dignity when possible, and each area of Konrad's body from top to bottom was treated to a thorough wash and dry. To his amazement there were other injuries to his body that he hadn't known about. He might have missed them altogether if it hadn't been for the running commentary provided by Sheila as she worked. She had sat him up and leant him forward to enable her to wash his back and shoulders. 'This might sting a little, there are some abrasions across your back.'

'Are there? Like what?'

'Like long straight red marks.'

'What are they from?'

'I don't know, Mr Neale. You really can't remember, can you?'

'No, I bloody can't.' He could feel Sheila's experienced hands move across his back as she outlined for him where his injuries were. She kept her voice down as she described what she saw. 'There are few of the same on your buttocks. They look a bit sore, so we'll have to keep an eye on those. Luckily the skin isn't broken like the ones on your back.' When he was dried, she sat him up to rest while she helped him to wash the front of his body. He was encouraged to do what he could for himself, but Sheila took over again by washing his lower legs and finally his feet.

With a fresh hospital gown on, he felt slightly more human, although the unwelcome sight of white surgical stockings being put on again offended him somewhat.

'Are those absolutely necessary?'

'Better than thrombosis, Mr Neale. When you're up and about, they can come off.'

'For Christ's sake don't let anyone take a photo. Can you imagine what the bloody press would make of it?' Sheila laughed.

Konrad told her how impressed he was at the way she had managed to change the sheets on his bed as she worked. 'We often do this in pairs because it's easier, but you're pretty mobile so it's not hard on my own. You just have to be organised,' she said as she neatened the bedclothes. 'I'm old school, so I'm sure my methods are probably out-dated, but they work for me and my back.'

'They've made sure you and Christine are the only two nurses who tend to me, haven't they? You're trustworthy, dependable and bloody good nurses, but even I know that staff nurses don't usually carry out such menial tasks as washing a patient and putting on his damned stockings for him.'

'No flies on you, Mr Neale, are there?' Sheila said, confirming his observation that he was being given special treatment. Not because of celebrity status but because of a scandal and a crime. The hospital couldn't afford any leaks to the media, and neither could the police.

Putting the tray table back in front of her patient, Sheila provided the means for him to brush his own teeth using a cheap brush, toothpaste, a small bowl to spit into and clean water in a large tumbler.

'At least I can brush my own bloody teeth.' Konrad's embarrassment at his level of disability had not gone unnoticed by Sheila. 'You let me know when your bowels call for attention and we'll see if you can manage to wipe your own bottom, shall we?' She had a wicked grin. He managed a smile and a small snort of a laugh. 'Thank God for a sense of humour, Mr Neale. Thank God.'

'Thank God,' Konrad said looking up at the ceiling. He wasn't entirely sure he meant what he said, but the sentiment was a good one. Sheila busied herself tidying up and finally asked if he wanted to watch the television before she left him alone again.

'Yes please. I'm not brilliant company for myself right now. I'll try to avoid the news channels.' He gave Sheila a half-hearted wave as she departed and switched on to BBC news straight away. He couldn't help his enquiring mind.

'Oh my giddy aunt,' he exclaimed. There on the screen was Gorgeous George. Konrad turned up the volume and prepared to be dismayed. George was being interviewed outside the offices of Marriot and Weston's, immaculately kempt, George was clearly emotional as he said his piece to camera in response to questioning from the roving reporter for BBC Breakfast.

'We are all still in a terrible state of shock. We can't believe it's true. He's such a wonderful man, so polite, so friendly and generous.

What the papers have said is outrageous and they should get their facts straight before firing off. Look what happened last week when they made allegations that Mr Neale was gay, just because he took me out to lunch. He looks after his work colleagues and his friends because he is a genuinely kind person and we wish him a speedy recovery. I have to go now, I'm too upset to say anything more.' Konrad watched the screen in amusement as George swiped the back of this hand across his forehead and sashayed dramatically through the revolving doors into the reception area.

The news reporter was reaching the summing up stage and ended her short piece by saying, 'We understand that Mr Neale is seeing his barrister today to begin the preparations for the high-profile court case that will be heard in the not too distant future.'

I'm seeing my barrister today? That's news to me.

He toyed with the idea of pressing the call bell to ask Sheila, but he didn't want to take her away from her other patients to answer a stupid selfish question. The phone rang, breaking into his ponderings.

'Hello?'

'Hello, Mr Neale, this is Jan the ward clerk, I have a call for you from a Mr Rupert Van Dahl. He says he's your barrister but that you may not actually be aware of that fact. I'm not sure if he's telling the truth, Mr Neale. Should I put him through to you?'

'Thanks for being so cautious, Jan. I really appreciate it. Yes, I do know of him. It's okay to put him through.'

'Good. I wasn't sure. I'll add his name to the list of approved contacts.'

Approved contacts. God, they are being tight with security.

There was a click and the line opened. 'Hello, Mr Van Dahl, Konrad Neale speaking.'

The conversation was brief. Konrad agreed to Rupert taking on the case and being his legal representative, because that choice had already been made for him, and they indulged in a bullet-point review. However, once Konrad had alluded to a more complex scenario than Rupert had been led to believe, he was cut short.

'Not on the phone. I'll come up to Manchester. Your case has been given priority by chambers. I'll be there later today. Can you give me the DCI's name… Gethin Anwell and he's at the Gwynedd police headquarters in Bangor itself? Right, I'll give him a call. Cheerio.'

He wasn't sure he liked Rupert. He reasoned that the plum in his barrister's mouth must have been huge to make him sound that ridiculously pompous. *Rupert Van Dahl. Typical posh boy from a top public school who's never seen real life, and the sort of wanker that I despise. Just my ruddy luck.*

He closed his eye to escape from the world for a minute or two.

When he opened his eye again, two people were sitting on chairs next to this bed. Annette had touched his hand to wake him.

'Hello, you pair. I'm so pleased it's you,' Konrad croaked.

'We're not supposed to be here. No visitors until after two p.m. apparently, but Barney sweet-talked the nurses who allowed us in because we're on your approved list. The policeman even had us checked out. This is a scary business, Kon.' It seemed to Konrad that Annette was trying hard not to show how shocked she had been at the sight of her friend wrapped in bandages, battered and bruised. Barney was less subtle.

'You look a fuckin' sight. Why are you in a nightdress?'

Konrad grinned and looked down at himself, which hurt, but having Barney with him made him feel more confident, more normal again. He loved that fact that Barney said what he thought; it was far better than everyone else's tentative approach.

'I'm wearing some net knickers as well.'

'And you reckon you're not gay?'

Annette sighed. 'Good grief, what are you two like together? It was bad enough having a lift in Barney's car all the way here, but the pair of you are worse. We've bought some goodies for you.' Annette unloaded a magnificent bunch of shiny red grapes and a large bag of yoghurt-covered raisins onto his table. 'There was more when we set out but we came over peckish after breakfast and we ate quite a lot of the biscuits and a couple of muffins before we got here. Anyway, enough of that; what's the news on your eye?'

'It's gone. The surgeon said it was too badly damaged to save, so they've removed it.'

With Annette and Barney silenced, Konrad tried to make light of the stunned pause and a bad state of affairs. 'Delia always said I had a wandering eye. Perhaps that was the one. Now it's gone I shall behave myself and Lorna will never have to worry about me being unfaithful.' As he said the word "Lorna" it caught in his throat. He had tried so hard not to get overwrought about how she was, where she was, and whether she would be coping, but his heart was literally aching with not knowing.

Barney gave his best friend a quizzical look. 'But the news said she did this to you out of bitter and twisted revenge for dumping her.' He shook his head. 'I don't get you.'

'I'll try to explain. You have to keep absolute secrecy on this. Total. One leak and we're dead. Annette knows about some of this but you don't. Lorna did injure me, apparently; although neither of us have any memory of Saturday night, and before you say anything, we hadn't been drinking. Not one glass. As Annette knows, I've been stalked for the last few weeks by a nutter, an unhinged woman who threatened me in no uncertain terms. It's to do with a documentary we filmed. I ignored the threats and this is the result. She made Lorna do this to me using some sort of drug.'

'They didn't say anything about this on the news. The police made a statement this morning and they never mentioned it either.' Barney said sounding sceptical of Konrad's disclosure.

'No, because they can't. She, the nutter, has to think she's got away with this otherwise the police may not catch her. I can't give you too many details 'cause I'm not even certain myself, but if it *is* Tessa Carlton and she used the same method on Matthew Hawley then…'

Annette looked visibly shaken. 'Then he is innocent too, like Lorna. Bloody hell, Kon, this is what he wanted us to prove.'

Chapter 28

According to Annette, Lorna was being held on remand at a women's prison facility in Gloucestershire. 'Two hundred miles of motorway between Bangor and Gloucester. There isn't one single women's prison in Wales, I found out. Isn't that a disgrace?' Konrad's face had crumpled as Annette said these words.

'How can we get to see her?'

'You can't I don't think. I've managed to contact her defence lawyers and once I explained who I was, they were really helpful. They'll ask her to put me on her list of visitors. I didn't tell them I was seeing you as well, that way I can be the go-between, as long as we keep quiet. Visitors get three one-hour slots per week, which is quite a lot. I'm going to go as soon as I can, it's only a couple of hours on the train from Paddington to Gloucester. I know you're desperate for news on how she is, Kon, but I was given platitudes, nothing more.'

'It's killing me not knowing how she is. Is she allowed to phone me?'

'I don't know. I doubt it. I'll take her any messages from you but they'll have to be verbal. In the meantime, Slow Joe and Mike have dug around for as much information as possible on Tessa to try to help you, but we've been contacted by the police to hand over everything, pretty much. The documentary film, the transcript, our notes, they even have the searches Joe and Mike did by hacking into the NHS spine thingy. Mike is shitting himself.'

'That sounds like a rapid response to me. Just be doubly sure who you're handing things over to.'

Annette scowled. 'I'm not an idiot.'

'What can I do to help?' Barney asked.

Konrad thought for a few moments before hitting on an ideal role for his friend and ally. 'I need you to spy on The Camp Commandant. I don't care what she does, but Freddie has decided to live with her to be closer to the sickly-sweet Chloe and there is something distinctly unpleasant about her. Which reminds me, I need to tell the police that I saw Chloe drive back into The Management Centre not long before I was attacked. I don't trust that girl and I don't know what she wants from Freddie, but it can't be love. Can you work on Freddie?'

'No problemo, compadre. I shall entice him into my workshop to look at expensive vehicles and my dirty calendars, and then I shall take him to the pub for a manly chat about sex and women. As you know, old mate, old chum, old mucka… that son of yours likes to show off and I am a pervert who likes to hear about slippy moments in the bedroom with a young woman who has a set of jugs I'd like to die in. Though she's a bit slim for me, that Chloe, I like a lot more meat on the bone…' Barney suddenly seemed to remember that Annette was sitting next to him and Konrad was thrilled to see how his friend's eyes were drawn like magnets to Annette's fulsome balcony of breast. He watched, entertained, as Barney blushed to a shade of crimson.

Annette took his words as an immense compliment. 'You are a man of discerning tastes after all, Mr Ribble. You and I will get on just fine. Shall I see if I can find us a coffee?' Annette rocked herself out of the chair and waddled towards the door. 'Back in a few minutes.'

Barney let out his pent-up tension. 'Konrad, me old mate. I'm in so much trouble.'

'No you're not. She took that as genuine flattery.'

'I don't mean that. I mean she's as horny as buggery and I can barely control myself. I want to stick my head in 'er tits and roll it from side to side in ecstasy. I've 'ad trouble driving, talking, and eating is the worst. She licks her lips at me and I get a hard-on. What am I going to do?'

Konrad hadn't had anything to smile about for what seemed like weeks. At first, he thought Barney was playing with him and messing about to cheer him up, until he heard the genuine agony in Barney's voice. 'It's true, you do like a big woman then?'

'Oh, dear me, do I ever. I wish Eliza had never made arrangements for me to give Annette a lift. I feel like a sodding teenager. She has a pretty face, shiny hair and a good brain, the whole package, and I want to unwrap it. What am I going to do?'

Konrad smiled, understanding his friend entirely. 'She likes a straight talker, so why don't you tell her what you think, and ask if she would like you to book into a local hotel tonight. That way you can test the water about the room arrangements and see me again tomorrow. I'll want an update. Have you got my hospital phone number? Keep me posted.'

Konrad had every confidence that Barney's wish would come true. He had worked with Annette for years and held close the secrets shared between them in the editing suite and over lunch. He was party to the inner workings of Annette's mind and secret sexual appetites.

He cast his mind back to the last half-pissed conversation they had after work in a local pub near the station, only a couple of weeks previously. Konrad had teased Annette about her love life, or rather lack of it.

'Don't tell me you'd rather spend it with your cats,' he'd said. She had been offended.

'No. As it happens I'm looking for a man of decent proportions, who is practical and knows how to enjoy life. I want a piece of rough. Someone who smells of hard work and who delights in a woman who has invested in her body.'

Konrad smiled at the memory of Annette indicating her own wholesome form, before she grabbed hold of her breasts and thrust them, fully clothed, in his direction. He had choked on his spinach and ricotta pie laughing at her wild indecent gesture, he recalled.

The day went by rapidly in the company of his two friends, but they finally made their move before three in the afternoon, having booked into a hotel nearby. Konrad, therefore, had time to doze off again between medication, drinks, and regular assessment by Sheila, and by Christine after three.

He liked Christine. She was a scatterbrain who often came in, looked at him, only to report that she'd forgotten what she was about to do.

'Vital signs?'

'No, done them. I know, empty your catheter bag. This is always a pleasure. Nice clear urine, Mr Neale.'

'That's good news at least I still have a pair of kidneys.'

'Yes, you do. But you could manage with one, just like you will with one eye. It's your mind that you have to cope with. The psychological barriers will be your test, but I have every faith in you and your good friends. What a fun couple they are. I saw them at lunch eyeing each other up over a plate of lasagne and chips. I take it they haven't been married long.'

Konrad was almost laughing. 'They haven't known each other long at all, but let's say there's enormous potential for them to be making children together very soon.'

'How lovely,' Christine replied, missing the nuances of the comment. 'Now then, your legal man is with the Welsh Police and I think they want to see you together. Are you comfortable? Need any pain relief? Right, I'll fetch them in and bring another chair. Press your call bell if you need to, but otherwise we'll ensure you're not interrupted.'

Konrad had been distracted from his dire circumstances by Annette and Barney, for which he thanked them. Now, however, he had to confront the horrors of what happened on Saturday night, but he equally knew that he couldn't cope with not knowing. There were things he had yet to be told and sights he had yet to see. One eye or two, it would scar him forever.

You're a bitch, Tessa Carlton, a fucking screwed-up psychopathic bitch.

DCI Anwell opened the door to allow a barrel of a man in a pinstriped suit to enter before him. He introduced himself, 'Hello there, Mr Neale, I'm Rupert Van Dahl.'

How can you be called Rupert and actually look like Rupert The Bear? I thought barristers were distinguished and lofty. Isn't Van Dahl a Dutch name? Aren't the Dutch tall people? Not short and round.

He sighed internally as he shook the proffered podgy hand and scanned the ruddy face of a man who liked a whiskey.

'Shall we get straight down to business? The police would like to take more detailed information from you on a few matters. They have also made the film evidence available to you. You don't have to watch this at all; in fact, you could see one or two still shots if you prefer, but if you insist then I suggest you watch it through before making any observations or comments. It could be a painful experience if you can't recall any of the events, so please state if you need to take a break at any time.'

'Mr Van Dahl, I have a chunk of time missing from my life during which, I'm told, I lost my eye and indulged in some sexual activities that are not in my usual repertoire. I'm not into sadomasochism, just so you know. I have to see for myself what happened.'

'I completely understand, Mr Neale.'

'Mr Van Dahl, I hope you never have to understand.' The expression on Rupert Van Dahl's face confirmed that this last statement had fallen on deaf ears.

Konrad was relieved to see DCI Anwell and DS Ffion Jenkins; he felt they had accepted his insistence that Tessa Carlton was implicated. What they had told him so far reassured him that they were determined to unravel the convoluted facts surrounding his assault and the conviction of Matthew Hawley; crimes that were linked and intertwined.

'You look a little better than when we last saw you,' DS Jenkins noted with a smile. 'Has there been anything else that you can recall to help us?'

'I know I gave you most of the details about Saturday night before it all goes blank, but I didn't mention about my son's girlfriend, Chloe. It's probably nothing, but–'

'It's never nothing in complex cases like these,' DCI Anwell interrupted. 'We are aware of your son's girlfriend, and we have spoken to Freddie. Please, tell us what you can.'

He was brief in his description of Chloe's return to the hotel after saying goodbye to Freddie. 'I have no idea whether that's relevant or not, but I felt I should mention it.'

'What do you know about her?' DS Jenkins asked.

'Not an awful lot. She met Freddie in the Tap and Spile pub the weekend before last and they hit it off straight away. He even spent the night with her at the hotel. She was something to do with organising an event there.' Konrad caught a look that passed fleetingly between the two detectives, but ignored it.

'Do you know who she works for?'

'No. I'm not sure she said. She was one of those airy-fairy girls, and I have a habit of switching off when I have to deal with people like her. They irritate me. I took more notice of her car; she had a blue BMW, a decent one, possibly a four series. Are you considering her as a suspect?'

'As I said, we're following up on all leads. Everything. Your work colleagues have been incredibly helpful on the issue of Tessa Carlton. I've had a team on it and they haven't managed to get much further than your two chaps did. They're good. We may have a use for them.' DCI Anwell kept the interview conversational, apparently appreciating Konrad's fragile grip on rationality and logical thought in the face of tremendous stress. 'I've updated Mr Van Dahl here with the details of our enquiry into Tessa Carlton, and the possibility that she had a hand in the events of Saturday night. That is, of course, just one theory.'

Rupert Van Dahl rolled forward in his chair to speak to his client. 'Yes, Mr Neale, this information puts a completely different slant on the case and I'm wondering how to proceed if evidence indicates that you and Miss Yates were both victims.'

DCI Anwell continued. 'We've transcribed the text messages from your phone and traced the relevant numbers to pay-as-you-go mobiles and a number of SIM cards. It's a non-productive trail at the moment. We're looking into a number of angles and so far, we've accounted for every one of the guests who were staying at The Management Centre as far back as two weeks ago. Having said that, your son's girlfriend is proving a challenge. She seems to have done a disappearing act and Freddie is not being as cooperative as we had expected him to be.'

This information, wrapped up in polite terms, struck Konrad as unacceptable. 'What do you mean Freddie has been uncooperative? I don't understand why he wouldn't tell you everything he knows.'

'We agree with you, Mr Neale, and we checked. He hasn't been to see you has he?'

'No. His sister tells me that I belittled him in front of his girlfriend and he's royally pissed off with me for how I behaved. I'm fairly sure that's not the whole story... Look, Detective Anwell, Freddie is besotted with this girl and she has him around her little finger.' He prayed he was wrong with his next question. 'Could she be Tessa Carlton?'

This time Konrad did acknowledge the look that passed between the two detectives. 'You think she might be, don't you?'

'It's one line of enquiry.'

DS Jenkins changed the subject. 'Are you sure you feel up to watching this film? You've had an awful lot to come to terms with in the space of two days. We can do this another time or in another way.' She bit her lip.

Konrad took a deep breath before daring to answer. 'I'm ready as I'll ever be, I suppose.'

DS Jenkins closed the vertical blinds on the windows into the hospital room, taking the time to alert the policeman on duty outside that strictly no one was to enter. She then hooked up the police laptop to the television set in the room. The detectives kept an eye on Konrad and his reactions. There was no sound track leaving only silence, creating a tense and unnerving atmosphere in the hospital side room.

*

The hotel room, number 110, was well lit from the main overhead lighting and from reading lamps on the wall above the capacious bed. Curtains were closed. Lorna and Konrad were kneeling on the bed facing each other, kissing passionately. He was seen unbuttoning her blouse to expose her bra, which she then removed for him, before taking his hands and placing them on her bare breasts, nipples tight. The towelling robe that he had worn that night had fallen open and from the angle of the camera Konrad's cock could be seen as it twitched and waved when he rocked back on his heels to disrobe. Then bizarrely he and Lorna turned to the camera as if taking instructions.

She kissed him again and moved his face into her breasts before he turned on all fours as she indicated for him to do. Reaching for a small length of rope, which had been placed on the pillow to her right, Lorna gently flicked it onto his buttocks allowing one frayed end to fall onto his balls. She gradually drew it upwards to tickle him, repeating this move several times. Konrad writhed in ecstasy, mouthing something. Before she pulled back her hand with the rope in it, she smiled at the camera and whipped Konrad hard on the back and on the buttocks, ten times in all. Konrad barely flinched; his expression was one of bliss. He turned back to face Lorna and she lovingly touched his face. He swung his legs round to sit on the edge of the bed where she stood in front of him caressing herself. He sucked at her nipples while she pleasured herself. She stopped, looked towards the camera and then walked around to the other side of the bed. As she passed by the dressing table, she picked up a long knife. Konrad stood up and followed her.

It was at this moment that a reflection could be seen in a long mirror on the back of the hotel bedroom door. A figure could be seen holding a video camera. Not a mobile phone. A digital video camera. The person behind the camera turned slowly to their right, following Konrad as he lay with his head dangling backwards, lying across the bed. Lorna stood over him, this time with a knife held in her right hand. She lowered herself onto his face as he explored her with his tongue and held onto her buttocks moving her back and forth. They both stopped again. Konrad sat up sweating and panting, talking to Lorna who crawled across the bed to face him. She struck first, slapping Konrad on his face and soundlessly shouting at him, he retaliated by holding her shoulders before punching her with a solid right hook to her jaw. He repeated this twice, with such force that she fell sideways on the bed, each time dragging herself up to fondle him and kiss him – the knife still gripped in her hand. Then sliding across to stand beside the right-hand side of the bed, Lorna beckoned to Konrad and he crawled towards her…

*

Propped up in his hospital bed, Konrad lay in a pool of sweat from the cold terror that had gripped him as he watched the TV. Remaining transfixed on the screen in front of him, he didn't speak or utter a sound until he forced himself to roll and heave over the side of his hospital bed as an unstoppable wave of nausea overtook him. DS Jenkins rushed to alert the allocated nursing staff who crashed through the door, demanding that Konrad's visitors leave immediately.

Konrad could hear what was going on as if the voices around him were in the distance. His mind detached itself from the trauma of what he had seen, and took him away to another place.

Chapter 29

A warm wet cloth was being rubbed gently across his chest and under his armpits, accompanied by whispered chatter between two female voices. Surgical-gloved hands were lifting his arm, as a towel dried his skin before slowly lowering it back to his side.

'His poor daughter is beside herself.'

'I know, but at least his other friends are here again today. She'd be in a real state without them. Why do you think his son doesn't come?'

'Don't know…'

Sheila lifted Konrad's left arm to wash its length, right to his fingertips. Another younger nurse, a healthcare assistant, had washed the other. They passed the towel between them.

'The psychiatrist is due to pop back in today. God knows what he thinks bloody sedatives will do, what this man needs is a bucket load of psychology and his girlfriend back. Did you overhear any more from the police, Leah?'

'Only that they're looking for the son's girlfriend. They think someone else is involved. Even I worked that out. Somebody had to be filming didn't they, unless they left a camera running themselves? Who would do that, and then send a copy to the papers with a pathetic request for money in return for destroying all copies? Poor man.' Leah looked down at Konrad's face and halted drying his hand. 'Mr Neale? Can you hear me? Sheila, his eyelid moved. Look.'

In a dreamlike state, he had listened to the two ladies and felt their hands on him, but there was a weight of fatigue as lethargy, like a cloak, held him down and prevented him from waking. He drifted away again.

'Come on, you stupid bastard. Wake up! We're late for the pub.'

Barney. Piss off I'm knackered.

'Kon, did you hear me, you silly bastard? Wake up.' Rough hands shook his shoulders, until he opened his eye.

My eyelid's stuck.

He focussed on the person standing at the end of the bed. He didn't recognise the man and momentarily had no idea where he was or what day of the week he was on, until Barney spoke again. 'About time. Fancy sleeping for three days, you lazy sod.'

Wondering why his friend would be saying this while wiping tears from his eyes, Konrad tried to sit up. He managed to raise his head slightly, before abandoning the whole idea. It was exhausting.

'Mr Neale, do you know where you are?' asked an unfamiliar voice, belonging to the unknown man at the end of the bed.

'No. Not really.' Konrad felt dopey. Doped up. Sedated. He wanted desperately to return to the cosy comfort of his dreamless sleep so he closed his eye and listened to others talking about him.

'Look, mate, can you ease up on the drugs? He'll never wake up if you keep him in that state.' Barney sounded irritated.

'Yes, we've lowered the dose, which seems to be working, so we'll drop it down more and see how he gets on.'

'Thanks, Doctor. He has to face reality again sometime.'

'He does, yes, but we need to be careful about how much he can manage. I have a psychologist waiting to see him when he's able to tolerate it. Paying private certainly has its advantages. The local NHS waiting list is a good six months if not longer. He needs support much sooner than that.'

The voices faded again for a while before other familiar voices replaced them, which for Konrad, felt like it had occurred in the same time frame.

'Fucking Freddie and that girl. What do they think they're playing at? Where exactly did you say you heard about that?'

Eliza.

'From the police, well, through the bat-like ears of Leah the assistant nurse. She picks up on some juicy snippets because her mother works in the police headquarters building in Bangor. She's a cleaner would you believe. Leah finds out the odd detail from her mother, or from us, and then chats to the officer outside here as if she knows a lot more and the one that's usually on duty seems a bit dim. He confirms or denies what she says and even adds a bit more information. Amazing.'

Annette. Where's Barney?

'I can't believe Freddie declined to give the police details about what he and Chloe discussed in the car park before she left on Saturday night. Also, why do the police believe it was Freddie, not Dad, who called reception asking them to get in touch with Lorna urgently? Why didn't the people on reception question why Dad didn't use his mobile phone, or call from his room by dialling for an outside line, like people usually do?'

'Who knows? But Freddie will get himself in hot water if he doesn't cooperate. He's still seeing her, that Chloe girl.'

'How do we know that?'

'Because your dad asked Barney to keep an eye on things, if you pardon the pun, so Barney has been phoning Freddie under the pretence of checking how he and Delia are coping with the adverse publicity. Freddie loves to boast about Chloe, and he tells Barney each and every revolting detail. Chloe visits him at your mother's, in secret. They use the summerhouse. Can't be seen, can't be heard, and your mother never goes in there. Only the cleaner sees the inside of the garden love palace, according to Barney.'

'Christ. We'd better tell the police. They're still trying to get hold of her for questioning. Little cow. What's her game?'

There were other noises, a door being pushed open, footsteps and a smell of coffee.

''Ere we go girls. This'll keep us going for an hour or so. Has the daft ha'porth woken up yet? Shall I give him another shake? It worked last time.'

Barney. There you are. Where's my coffee?

Konrad opened his one good eye and saw the cheering sight of Annette, Barney and Eliza standing together looking out of the window in his hospital room.

'I wonder what he's been dreaming about all this time,' mused Eliza as she gazed at the uninspiring car park beyond the hospital.

'Blue eyes,' came the mumbled reply from the bed.

'Dad!' Eliza rushed to her father's side and lay her head on his chest as she hugged him as tightly as she dared. He stroked her head.

'It can't be Chloe; she has brown eyes,' Konrad announced.

The sighs of relief from his friends indicated to Konrad that he had been the source of major consternation. 'I'm not dead then?'

Annette sat down with a solid plonk and reached for sustenance in the form of an enormous Chelsea bun, which filled the lower half of her face and deposited sugary cinnamon on to the tip of her nose. Without thinking she passed a second one to Barney. 'Thank God. We'd been so worried I lost my appetite.'

Good grief, it must have been serious.

Sheila came in through the doors having been alerted by Eliza pressing the call bell. 'Welcome back again, Mr Neale. I have missed you.'

'Hello, Sheila. I feel like shit.'

'That'll be the sedation. It's being tapered off so you'll gradually feel more with it. Try to relax if you can.'

'I can't. I don't even know what day I'm on. I don't know what happened.'

'Let's check you over first and get the doctor to have a look at you. We'll explain as we go along.'

Sheila looked at Konrad's three visitors who immediately understood she needed to spend some time with him, taking him through his circumstances step by step. They left nurse and patient alone.

Eliza was the first to be allowed back in. 'The police want to speak to you again when you're up to it. What did you mean about Chloe and her brown eyes?'

'I must have been rambling. I've no idea,' Konrad said, careful not to allow Eliza to find out about Tessa Carlton. He had to protect her for as long as he could. 'I'm more alert now, so I'll be fine to see the police tomorrow maybe. Why don't you go and get some rest, you look shattered, and all I've done is sleep, apparently. They said it was an adjustment reaction to finding out about my eye and what happened to Lorna.'

'Okay, Dad. I'll see you tomorrow. I've told the bosses that I'm not working this weekend. They're fine about it. Can Barney and Annette come in to see you? They want to give you a wee bit of good news.'

'I was right. They're made for each other.'

'Oh, that. Yes, you're quite right. It's lovely that they seem to have found each other. This is other news, about Lorna.'

His whole body reeled at the sound of her name and the dreadful emptiness of her absence caved in on him once more.

'Please, I need to know.'

Eliza's face crumpled as she cried in sympathy with her father's heartache.

Annette and Barney sat together to tell what little news they had.

'I've managed to get a visitor's permit for Tuesday next week, but I've also had a call from her solicitor with an update on how she's coping.'

Konrad held his breath.

'As I understand it, Lorna was overwhelmed to hear that you were desperate to see her and that you don't despise her. Her solicitor has also been made aware of the Tessa Carlton suspicions and the case is going to be a test for the legal minds of the judiciary, from what I can gather. The other women in the prison are wary of Lorna so she's managed to keep to herself. She sends you a message, which I wrote down. "We will see the puffins together."

I hope that means something to you, because frankly it sounds like a line from a spy film to me.'

There was silence from Konrad. He closed his eye.

'Shit. We've blown it big time. He's gone again.'

'No I haven't. Thank you, thank you, thank you. You have no idea how much those words mean. I can do this now. Me and Lorna, we can do this now.'

Barney and Annette made to leave, giving Konrad time to himself. 'Hang on, I need to speak to Barney for a moment. Would you mind?'

Barney sat with his friend, waiting for an inquisition. Sure enough Konrad had not lost his touch when it came to wheedling information out of a reticent interviewee. 'Annette seems remarkably comfortable in your company, Barney, my old pal. I take it you are sharing a room at the hotel?'

'Yes, matey, your advice was correct and I have surpassed her expectations apparently. We have a lot in common.'

'And? And what's the deal with the hanky-panky?'

'I'm not Freddie, I'm a gentleman and they don't tell.'

So, it is serious then...

'Well said, I consider myself duly reprimanded. Now tell me about Freddie and that bloody Chloe.' Konrad's tone of voice was commanding and Barney knew better than to fudge an answer. He confirmed what Konrad had heard in his semiconscious state and Konrad was furious with his son.

'Look, Kon, I've tried to reason with the lad, but he only listens to her. Even Delia is taken in by her. They borrowed The Camp Commandant's Range Rover – to go away for the night on Wednesday and haven't been seen since.'

'What day are we on again?'

'Friday. Friday evening, same week, same shit, different day.'

'Sorry, Barney, I think I left the planet for a while. I can't remember quite a lot. The last thing I recall is meeting Rupert the bear, my barrister, and then waiting to watch the film of what happened to me and Lorna, but then I come round and it's three days later. Head-fuck time.'

'Maybe it's best you don't remember. The doctor said it was such a shock your mind has wiped it from your memory. But he did say it could be temporary so we have to be careful not to make you try to remember it. That's why the TV has been replaced by a lovely brand-new iPod, which Eliza has filled with a selection of audio books, pod casts and music for your delight. No news and current affairs for you pal.'

After Barney left for a long trip down the motorway towards home, Konrad decided to give in to the request that he should relax, and with earphones on, drifted into a pleasant doze.

Chapter 30

The room was swaying as Konrad sat on the edge of the bed in a pair of striped pyjamas, taking instruction from Sheila and Leah who were at either hand in case he wobbled.

'Take a moment or two, you've been lying down for so long your brain needs time to adjust to the upright position for Homo sapiens and your legs haven't held you up for several days.'

'I'm dying to see what my en-suite looks like and have pee in my own toilet, and a poo. Won't that be a better prospect than a bedpan or being hoisted onto a sodding commode? You do realise this short walk is the most adventurous thing I've done in a whole week.' He prepared himself to stand. The last time he stood up properly and walked, he had been with Lorna.

'You move around safely enough today and we'll have the catheter removed tomorrow. For now, please just do as we ask and head for the chair. Mr Wells is on his way to take a peek at how you're healing.'

'Can I have the bloody bandage off?'

'Don't ask us. Ask him.'

'Can I have a leather eye patch? I reckon I'll look piratical and swashbuckling with one of them.'

'I'll swash your buckle if you don't concentrate,' Sheila scolded.

'Let's crack on then, I've got a busy day ahead.' Konrad enjoyed the banter between himself and the nursing staff; it kept him sane in an otherwise frustrating world. DCI Anwell was due to see him that day and Konrad wanted to know what progress had been made. 'Can I wear my own clothes? I'm sick of being a patient.'

Shortly after making an undignified landing into a chair, there was a knock at the door and Mr Wells entered with a set of patient notes in his hands. His bedside manner had been perfected over the years and Konrad was paying strict attention to the details that he outlined. The experienced surgeon had gauged Konrad's recovery well, in terms of acceptance and physical healing. 'Monocular vision has its challenges.'

'You're not kidding. I've had to relearn how to eat without injuring myself, and just now I misjudged the distance to a chair. Please tell me my brain will adjust.'

Mr Wells allowed himself a brief grin before confirming, 'Your brain will adjust, Mr Neale, given time.' Having removed the pressure bandage, Mr Wells was satisfied that the wounds were clean. 'Do you want to see? I can ask the nurse to fetch a small hand mirror.'

Doubt gnawed at Konrad. 'Is Eliza here yet? I think she should be with me.' He wasn't confident that he could tolerate his own reaction if he was massively disfigured and although he had an idea in his mind of how he thought he might look, the reality could be far wide of that.

'Yes, I think she's here already. She has presents and cards for you from fans and well-wishers. You're a popular man.'

I used to be. I thought no one would be sending anything since the press did their worst.

'Shall I invite her in and ask Sheila to find a mirror? We can sit together and I'll answer any of your questions as they arise.'

The man staring back at Konrad was a pale reflection of himself. A pasty bruised face with one perfect eye looked back at him. A deep reddish blue scar ran from his hairline above the middle of his left eyebrow in a diagonal line towards his right earlobe. Another more jagged line etched into his right brow and down to his cheek below. In the hollow, where his other eye used to live, was a swollen eyelid, bruised and lumpy in places where stitches held it shut.

I know it's me. But it's not me.

172

'Is it sore?' asked Eliza looking intently at her father's healing wounds.

Konrad was taken aback at her choice of question. He found it hard to comprehend that she was interested in pain. Not in how he looked, but in how he felt. 'Not too bad at all. It looks a bit of a mess.'

'That will improve,' Mr Wells assured. 'Please don't be tempted to keep touching it; you wouldn't want an infection. We'll arrange for you to see our specialist who'll make you a prosthetic from an acrylic polymer and match the colour exactly to your other eye, unless you want the David Bowie look. The prosthetic eyes themselves can be remarkably life-like, but the one area for concern is the scarring on your eyelid. That may be harder to resolve and difficult to make less obvious.'

'How does it stay in place?' Eliza asked.

'The prosthetic? In simple terms, we implanted a marble-shaped insert into the orbit, the socket. This was done at the time we removed the original eyeball. That implant has a small peg onto which the prosthetic eye will fit. We hope that the eye muscles will remain attached to the implant to give some movement and therefore the overall result will be more realistic.' Much to Konrad's relief, the doctor kept his information factual and straightforward.

'How long will it be before I can have my new eye?' Konrad asked continuing to stare in the mirror.

'That depends. Five to six weeks.'

'Can I have an eye patch?'

Eliza laughed at her father. She knew he wanted to be a pirate. She also had one last question. 'Why are surgeons in this country always referred to as mister and not doctor?'

*

After Mr Wells had left, Eliza produced a bag full of letters and cards that had been sent to Channel 7, and between them they waded through each, reading out the names of well-wishers. Some they knew, others from strangers.

'Look at this outrageous giant,' Eliza exclaimed. 'How is it possible to fit so much glitter and pink feathers onto a get-well card?' She showed Konrad the biggest card he'd ever seen.

'Let me guess,' he said, allowing Eliza to open it up. 'It's from George and Lillian.'

'Right first time.'

'If you'd ever met George you'd understand how easy that was.'

'I feel I've missed out. He was so bloody funny when the press interviewed him. I think he could be on the next reality TV series. Whatever that is. Probably, "First Gay Naked Love Island Dates" or something.'

Eliza opened another card. 'This is a posh one. It's from Josh Hawley, Naomi Woods and all at HRS.'

'Shit. Can I see that one, Eliza? Bugger. I had a meeting with Josh Hawley lined up for last Monday. I'd forgotten all about it.'

'Dad, calm down. He knows why you weren't there to meet with him, obviously. Whatever it is will wait.'

Will it wait? 'Yes. I'll phone him later when you've gone. We can cover some of the interview questions without having to meet up.' The unexpected contact from Josh had diverted Konrad. He found his thoughts returning to Matthew Hawley languishing in prison trying to find ways to help his son to understand a vital fact that could not be proven. A slight change of tone in Eliza's voice redirected his attention.

'This one's a business letter from a private psychiatrist.' Eliza handed over the letter she had pulled from a long white envelope.

'Probably touting for business... Let's have a little look before I chuck it in the bin.' There was a momentary silence before he came to a conclusion. 'No, this one couldn't be more important.' Konrad's voice faded away as he started to read on. 'Shit. Sorry, Eliza, this won't wait. Can you see if you can get in touch with DCI Anwell and find out what time he's coming today?'

The phone in the room rang loudly enough to startle him. Eliza answered it, moving the phone nearer to where her father now sat in his chair. 'Spooky. It's DCI Anwell. Do you want to speak to him now?'

'Yes, definitely.'

Eliza handed over the hospital phone. 'I'll leave you to it then. I could do with a break.'

Konrad whispered his thanks to his thoughtful daughter, spoke to the DCI briefly, and then sat back to read, in full, the contents of the letter from a child and adolescent psychiatrist by the name of Sarah Tyrell, based in Suffolk.

Konrad had an overwhelming need to share this with Annette, so he called her.

'Kon, how are you doing?'

'All right for a Cyclops. They let me get up today and the big bandage is off. I look like Frankenstein's monster, so…' He didn't have the words to explain himself.

'You sound better. What can I do for you? I know you didn't phone for a polite chat.' Annette had the measure of Konrad as usual. With the letter propped up against a water jug, at the optimum distance for accurate reading, he enlightened his friend.

'The first paragraph is just an introduction, who she is, where she works and how she found out we were looking for information on Tessa Carlton and Helena Chawston. She then apologises for the delay in writing to us. She had wrestled with her conscience about confidentiality but decided that there may be a risk to the public by not disclosing information. From what she says, it seems she went to the local police some time ago about her fears regarding Tessa Carlton but they dismissed her as being over-anxious. In short, she has taken a professional risk by sending us the following. Now listen to this. It'll blow your socks off.'

'That's nice. I have a hell of a job getting them off myself these days.' Annette seemed cheered to hear Konrad being so enthusiastic about life again.

'Funny woman… Now be serious for a minute and listen because if we can prove that Tessa did this to me and Lorna, we can get the case dropped.'

'This doctor had Tessa under her care in an adolescent unit where she underwent intensive psychotherapy, caused havoc with the other patients, and eventually absconded with another girl. She was never found.'

'Now then, do you remember that when she was about fifteen, Tessa was assaulted and badly injured? According to this letter that was entirely wrong. The hospital found out that she had not been physically assaulted by anyone else. She had done it to herself and although she tried to blame her elder sister, she eventually changed her story and said she heard voices telling her to cut herself.' He was gabbling.

'Kon, you have to speak slower. I know you're wound up about this but I can barely grasp what you're saying. Slow down.'

'There's so much here. Sorry. It seems that Helena, who was an adult by then remember, had wanted to meet with her sister to confront her. It's a lot more complicated than that, but in a nutshell, Tessa's revenge was to blame Helena again for something terrible. The self-inflicted injuries, for which Helena was accused, were not as dramatic as they first appeared to be from local authority reports. However, Tessa had cut her own breasts and labia.

'Do you see? It wasn't Helena that attacked her. The assumption we made is wrong.'

Annette was quiet at the other end of the phone.

'Annette? Did you hear what I said?'

'Yes, Kon. Give me a minute, I'm in front of my laptop and I'm trying to find that letter from Mrs What's-'er-face. The mother of the girl Tessa was at school with, and the stuff Joe and Mike unearthed from Health and Social Services. Right, I'm with you now.'

'I really want to scan this and send it to you, but I'm stuck in here.'

'Will the hospital fax it for you?'

'They probably would but I don't want anyone else to see this apart from us and the police. What else can I do?'

'Can you take a photo with Eliza's mobile phone?'

'Funny and what's more a bloody genius. That's what you are. My close-range focus is a bit iffy, but I'll ask Eliza when she gets back, she's gone for a break.'

'Bless her. I expect she needs one. In the meantime, give me the general gist.'

Konrad took a steadying breath. 'This psychiatrist is saying that Helena was blamed all along by Tessa for things that Tessa actually did of her own volition. She killed the school goldfish, she hurt other children, she injured herself and made sure Helena was either blamed or under suspicion. Their parents, Mr and Mrs Carlton, were at a loss and thought they were protecting Tessa by sending her to her grandparents to live. They emotionally distanced themselves from Helena, viewing her as the reason their family had been torn apart. In fact, quite unwittingly, they helped to protect Helena for a few years. Now here is something that none of us knew before. Are you ready for this?'

'Yes. Get on with it.'

'Helena and Tessa had a younger brother.'

'No way.'

'Yes, way. It says it right here. Dr Sarah Tyrell was asked to assess the whole family. The reason Helena stayed with her parents is argued in depth during the child protection meetings that were held. As we know, the involvement from social services had been slow, but had eventually resulted in the two girls being split up. The younger child, a boy referred to as Dickie, was ten years younger than Helena, and the two of them remained at the home of their parents under child protection review for a year or so. No problems reported. However, when Helena left to go to university there was a re-referral to social services for Dickie under the category of emotional neglect. He was put into care.'

'So how old was Tessa when Dickie was born?'

'She would have been four. She wasn't sent to live with the grandparents until she was… eight. Blimey, that was four years after Dickie was born. God, this is amazing stuff. Listen to the next bit…

'Helena was eighteen when she went to university and little Dickie would have been ten. Tessa would have been fourteen and still living with her grandparents, just about. Dr Tyrell was asked to be involved in reassessment of the family regarding whether it was safe for Tessa to return to the parental home.'

'What? Just because Helena had left?'

'That's not made clear, but it seems to be the case. What we didn't know was that Tessa did return home and lived there until the time of her assault, which she blamed Helena for. This is where the facts have got muddled. In the time Tessa returned home and Helena left, Dickie seems to have suffered at the hands of Tessa and the parents failed to act, yet again.

'According to this letter, Helena visited the family home with her grandparents during a holiday from uni because she was worried about her brother.

'It was during this visit that Tessa cut herself. There was a vicious argument between the parents, the grandparents, Helena and Tessa, and it was Helena who reported concerns to Social Services about Dickie, which compounded recent reports from Dickie's school.' Konrad was silent, waiting for Annette's response, which took some time to arrive.

'This is a tragic story. What were those social workers thinking?'

'We don't have any information on their perspective; just what was known by this doctor. She says that by the age of fifteen, Tessa could have been assessed as being a high functioning psychopath. What Dr Tyrell is saying here is that Tessa was so manipulative and intelligent that as an adult she would be considered dangerous, and have the capacity for serious harm to others and especially to Helena.'

'Blimey, Kon. That's why Helena changed her name, disowned her parents, and had a massive fear of rejection and loss.'

'Exactly, my genius friend. All the police have to do is find Tessa and prove that she is at the bottom of this. Can you look again at the documentary transcript and see if Matthew Hawley alludes to this in any way.

'Annette, one last favour. Ask Mike and Joe to find out what happened to Dickie Carlton, please?'

Feeling that progress was about to be made, he rewarded himself with a cold drink before he picked up the phone again. His throat had dried with the anticipation of his next conversation and his adrenalin levels peaked as the call was answered.

'Josh Hawley. Who's speaking?'

'Hello Josh, this is Konrad Neale. I'm phoning to thank you for your card and to apologise for missing our appointment on Monday. Sorry you were inconvenienced and out of pocket.'

'You don't need to apologise. Not in the least. You're on the mend then?'

'Only just, but I'm better than I was.' Konrad drew breath and took an enormous gamble. 'Josh, I want to help your dad and I think what happened to me may be connected with him.'

There was such a long pause that Konrad started to doubt that the call was still live. He listened intently, picking up on Josh Hawley's breathing.

Don't hang up. Please don't hang up.

'How can that be? Is the woman who attacked you connected with my father?' Josh asked.

'No, she isn't, but it's possible that Helena's sister is involved in the attack on me.'

'Look, Mr Neale, no offence but this was raised in the court case. It's all rubbish. You can't keep dragging up the same debates about my father. He killed Helena, full stop.' The voice coming through the phone handset was angry.

Konrad tried his best to remain composed and factual. 'Yes, he did. He isn't denying that. But he still says he can't recall any of it. Nothing. I can't remember anything of what happened last weekend either and I've been stalked and threatened by a woman believed to be Helena's sister Tessa. That person filmed the whole attack on me.'

'Are you saying you believe my father?'

'Yes. Without a doubt. I'm living the same nightmare.'

There was a long pause again before Josh spoke. 'How can I help?'

Chapter 31

Gethin Anwell was alone when he arrived at the hospital ward after lunch. In his mind, Konrad believed that all detective chief inspectors were battle-weary individuals in scruffy overcoats who barely slept, thus rendering them fatigued and craggy. DCI Anwell was the antithesis of this imaginary DCI. He was an athletic man with determination and enthusiasm for the job in hand, which Konrad admired. Indeed, they seemed to have developed an unspoken mutual regard to the degree that Konrad perceived a certain procedural leeway in his favour.

'Good to see you're up and about, Mr Neale.' Relief was evident in Gethin Anwell's voice as the two men shook hands. 'I thought we'd sent you off to the local asylum last time we met.'

'I've no idea where I went, I don't really remember, which of course has left me in the dark again about what happened to me. It's an awful feeling knowing that other people have seen a part of your life that you have no memory of. On your own today?'

DCI Anwell moved a chair to sit opposite; the adjustable table remained between them. 'No, DS Jenkins is having a chat with Eliza. We saw her in the car park. She'll be here soon with coffee if we're lucky.

'About your reaction to the film evidence, I've been told not to take you down that road again, so perhaps we'd better park the idea for now, but I do need your help as part of the investigation to try to identify the intruder.

'The nurses thought it would be better if I could show you a still photograph of the alleged perpetrator in your room on Saturday night. The person behind the camera. One shot that's all. Do you think that would be manageable?'

Konrad didn't hesitate. 'Yes. Let's do it. Before that, I have something for you. A letter.' He handed over the correspondence from Dr Sarah Tyrell the psychiatrist.

'Right, you look at the photo, I'll read the letter.'

Konrad stared at the picture in his hands.

A dark blue baseball cap, a camera to your face. Wisps of hair against your pale skin. A neat nose. Female. Mouth open. A slight figure in a polo shirt and jeans. Hips. Tessa. Depraved, deviant and debased. You stood there filming me and Lorna having sex. You saw it and I can't even remember it.

'Any thoughts?' DCI Anwell looked up from the pages he was holding.

'Several, but I wouldn't care to say them aloud. I don't recognise her. I want to, and I wish to God I could say it was Chloe, but I can't.' Frustration made his words more clipped than he intended.

'Okay, not to worry. Here's something else for you to look at.' Konrad was shown a still photo from CCTV of the reception area at The Management Centre.

'That's Chloe.'

'Good. You said you thought Tessa had blue eyes, so we took this shot of Chloe and our clever techies have produced this.' Konrad looked at another picture of Chloe but with blue eyes.

'Right. How does this help?'

'Have you seen anyone who looks like that following you recently?' DCI Anwell asked. Konrad shook his head. He was not keeping pace with the detective's thinking. 'Maybe with different coloured hair, or clothing?' Anwell asked.

'I don't think so, no.'

'It was worth a shot. Maybe these will help. The team have produced a number of pictures, with alternative hairstyles; clothing and the like. When you have time between visitors, just have a look through. You never know what might nudge your memory.'

'Can we do it now?' Konrad asked, extending his arm and holding out a hand for the next picture. DCI Anwell handed him four more to look at and sat back patiently while Konrad took his time perusing each one.

As he reached the third in the series, a quizzical expression crossed Konrad's face. He lent forward, placed the photo down carefully and used another to cover up the lower part of the picture. 'This rings a bell,' he said staring at the detective. 'If it's who I think it reminds me of, then it would be an alarm bell.' His voice faltered. 'Maybe I'm clutching at straws but...'

'Say what you think.'

'I think it reminds me of Naomi Woods. The problem is I've never met Naomi, I've spoken to her on the phone, but this reminds me of the pictures I've seen of her.'

'And she is...' Anwell said, pen poised to take accurate notes.

'Naomi Woods is the partner and business partner of Josh Hawley. Josh is...'

'Matthew Hawley's son.'

'Yes.'

Konrad looked again at the photo-fit picture as Gethin reached for his mobile phone to call headquarters. 'I need anything we have on a Naomi Woods, company director of Hawley Recruitment Solutions. Anything. See if she can be linked into Chloe Jordan. It's highly likely they are one and the same person.'

He stared again at the images in front of him. 'Shit. It could be.'

'This might mean that she's been hiding in plain sight. Tessa Carlton has played the long game. What a clever woman. Now we need to tie her in to the scene of the incident, texts to you, Chloe Jordan...'

'The letters to Matthew Hawley,' Konrad added. 'And Helena's death.'

The two men stared at each other trying to grasp the convolutions of the task ahead. Coffee arrived in the hands of a smiling DS Ffion Jenkins. 'Eliza's going off to do some retail therapy. She seems brighter, and so do you, Mr Neale. It's lovely to see you sitting up.'

'I'm a bit battle scarred.'

'Maybe so, but by the time they've finished, you'll have the sort of rugged features that women find irresistible. Personally, I love a scar.' She moved closer to Konrad, placing the coffee on the table.

'I'd better move those photos,' he said. 'I'm ludicrously clumsy when it comes to coordinating at short range.'

DCI Anwell updated his junior officer on the results from the review of the pictures.

'DI Bevan will be furious. Due back from leave on Monday isn't he, sir?' she commented with a cheeky smile. DCI Anwell gave an approving smile in return.

'He'll have to hit the ground running, then, won't he, DI Jenkins? Now then back to matters in hand,' he said turning to Konrad. 'Have you heard from Freddie since I last saw you? We would like to speak to him again, but he seems to have changed his phone number, and is no longer at your wife's address. He has to know vital information that will tie Chloe to Naomi.'

Konrad felt saddened to hear that his son had gone to such lengths to avoid being found. It felt like a personal betrayal and now there was every chance that he had sided with the enemy.

'Sorry. I think I've been excommunicated. Eliza doesn't even know. Barney, my mate who's keeping an eye on Freddie for me, said that Delia lent Freddie and Chloe the car on Wednesday and they haven't been heard from since. Or you could try Delia directly, she won't speak to me I'm afraid.' DCI Anwell seemed to appreciate how awkward Konrad felt about his son and changed tack.

'We'll find him soon. I'm sure. Meanwhile, this letter is very interesting indeed. Can I keep it?' He paused, folding the letter neatly and tucking inside his suit jacket. 'We appreciate this is a frustrating time for you, but please be assured that we are being very thorough with this investigation, Mr Neale, because these matters are serious and your case will have to go to court, so we need all the evidence we can. What we have so far from the crime scene, including the film, indicates an assault carried out by Lorna Yates, and it could be argued as extreme domestic violence.

'However, with the information about Tessa Carlton stacking up, we're now racing to ensure we have enough proof to support the prosecution's case. The forensic evidence reinforces your report of memory loss, and the same for Miss Yates, so my team has to pull together information and, if possible, make another arrest.'

'Can't the charges against Lorna be dropped? If the evidence is that we were drugged, can't they be dropped?' Konrad was desperate to secure Lorna's release.

'Not at this stage. I'm afraid not.' DCI Anwell's mobile phone rang quietly. He answered and looked across with an apologetic expression. 'Sorry, I have to take this. It could be important news on Naomi Woods.' He stood and walked over to the window, nodding and giving grave affirming noises to the caller. 'Uh ha, mmm, yes, I see. Can you double check the details on that with Dorset immediately and call me back?' Anwell turned to Konrad. 'It seems Freddie may be in Dorset. Do you own a white Range Rover Evoque, Registration KON 1?'

'Yes. I'm due to sign it over to Delia as part of the divorce, but technically I still own it. Has the silly bugger crashed it?'

'I've asked for more details, but I wanted to check with you first. You knew he borrowed it?'

'Not personally, but as I said, Delia lent it to Freddie and Chloe. Are they okay do you know?'

'I'll let you know as soon as I can satisfy myself that the facts are correct. Bear with me.' With that DCI Anwell left the room. He could be seen talking quietly to the policeman on duty outside. Konrad also watched DS Jenkins speaking to a staff nurse at the nurses' station in the corridor who picked up a phone and sent another staff member on an errand of some urgency.

Now what? Another expensive repair bill to pay?

DCI Anwell popped his head back in to Konrad's room to apologise. 'I'm sorry, this may take quite some time. I'll come back when I have details.'

Konrad had no choice other than to wait. He tried to get hold of Barney for an update, and ended up leaving a message instead. He toyed with the idea of contacting Delia. She would know where Freddie was and what he was up to, but she would probably slam the phone down and he couldn't afford to rile her any more than she already was.

Chapter 32

Konrad decided to tune out for a while, so he plugged his headphones into his iPod and chose a compilation album of old blues tracks. He thought about Naomi Woods and tried in vain to imagine her with brown eyes and long auburn hair.

How long can you wear contact lenses for, I wonder? How securely are wigs fixed on?

He was thinking through the practicalities of Chloe Jordan having lively kinky sex with Freddie without her disguise slipping when Sheila and Leah interrupted his internal meanderings by arriving to carry out regular baseline physical health checks and to tidy his room. Konrad was glad of their company and took advantage of an amiable chat to engage them in a fact-finding mission.

'Ladies, I have a couple of important questions to ask you as part of some research. I'm rubbish at understanding things like make-up and fashion, and I was wondering why some women chose to change their eye colour using contact lenses? Do many people do that?'

Sheila looked at Leah before conceding to her younger colleague. 'You'll have to answer that one. I'm far too old to know whether that's what young people do. I tried it once for Halloween but the lenses played havoc, and having spent an age getting them in my eyes, I panicked and took even longer to take them out again. The result was the same; red eyes.'

Leah laughed. 'Lots of people do use coloured contacts lenses. You can get loads of different colours and some people give themselves cat eyes or black lenses and weird stuff like that.

You can get zombie lenses for Halloween now. All white with a pinprick dot of black as a pupil. My mum has green ones that she wears every day, I can't even remember what her real eye colour is.'

'How long can you keep them in for?' Konrad asked.

'You can get extended wear lenses. They last for a few weeks before you have to change them.'

'That's excellent. Thanks. Really helpful. Now, as that was an easy question for two members of staff at an eye hospital, I would like to test your knowledge about all things girlie by asking you to tell me what you know about wigs.'

'Are you planning to disguise yourself and escape from our evil clutches, Mr Neale? Can't you put a hat on instead?' Sheila asked as she wrapped the cuff of a blood pressure monitor around Konrad's upper arm.

'Sheila, this is serious research. If you were wearing a wig, or needed to wear one after chemotherapy for example, can you buy ones that attach firmly enough not to slip in a high wind, or if you jumped up and down on a trampoline?'

Sheila shot a puzzled glance in Leah's direction. 'His blood pressure is fine, so it can't be that sending him doolally.'

'I'm not bonkers. I just need to find out. It's important research. But if you don't know, then just say so. I can always find a nurse with more brains who's willing to help me,' he teased. This seemed to kick start an interesting exchange of anecdotes between the two ladies who each had stories to relate involving relatives and wigs.

'Who knew? Wig caps, adjustable wigs, wig tape and wig clips. Wigs made of real hair too,' Konrad said when they had exhausted their catalogue of wig tales.

So, it's perfectly possible. Draw your eyebrows on a bit thicker, add more war paint, different clothes and Naomi becomes Chloe.

Now then, let's see if I can educate myself about what vanilla sex is.

Sheila stopped what she was doing and stared, aghast. Leah found the question hilarious. 'I can't believe that neither of you have heard that expression before. Where have you been? Anyway, why are you asking questions about contact lenses, wigs and sex? Trying to solve your own mystery, Mr Neale, would be my guess. Ask away, I haven't had this much fun while emptying a catheter bag for ages.'

Konrad was past caring what they thought. He was desperate for information and cut off from the usual technology that would allow him to search for answers in private.

Having found to his disappointment that vanilla meant conventional, he was crestfallen. 'Is that it? So, it's the opposite to kinky.'

'There's sliding scale between the two extremes of each, Mr Neale, if you think about it. If you're a real prude and the missionary position with your nightie pulled up is all you're in receipt of, then that's about as vanilla as it gets, but if you're more adventurous, more fun, it could still be considered conventional sex. Where the line crosses into kinky would depend on the individual, I suppose.'

Sheila stepped in to change the subject but failed. 'That answers that question. Anything else?'

'Yes. How would I know what my line is if I'd never experienced kinky?'

'I once read in a magazine that kinky sex is good for relationships; it said that bondage, hot wax and use of sex aids improves trust between couples and increases self-esteem. Who knew?' Leah appeared unfazed by the content of the conversation, but Sheila was decidedly uncomfortable, shaking her head and muttering 'Oh dear' under her breath before managing to usher Leah towards the door.

'No more questions please. I'm sure this is highly inappropriate to be talking about, research or not, Mr Neale.'

'If you want more details I'll lend you my copy of Fifty Shades,' Leah offered.

'There you are, I'm not such an old stuffed shirt after all, I have heard of that,' he confirmed. 'Let me check my iPod and see if I have the audiobook version. If not, I'll take you up on your offer.' Leah left the room chuckling despite stern words from Sheila.

After being left alone again, with only his iPod for company, thoughts of Lorna crowded in and Konrad struggled to make sense of the chain of events that had taken place in the short space of a week. He experienced a sinking sensation as if he were being sucked under by suffocating quicksand and had no strength to keep his head above the surface. As gloomy shadows threatened to overwhelm him, he was glad of another interruption when Sheila came to break the spiral of negativity. Or so he assumed.

'I have a couple of visitors for you, but they have some difficult news to bring you, so if you don't mind I'll stay too.'

Konrad was bewildered, not knowing what to expect until he saw DCI Anwell and DS Jenkins. Their whole demeanour indicated that a dreadful announcement was about to be made.

'What is it? Is it Freddie?' A cold dread had swept through his body. His mouth dried.

'I'm afraid so, Mr Neale. Dorset police found your car in a secluded spot after a call from a local dog owner out for a walk. They found Freddie's body. He had been dead for an estimated two hours. A crime investigation has been initiated because the suspicion is that he was unlawfully killed.'

'How?' Konrad croaked.

'It was made to look like auto-erotic asphyxia. Self-strangulation for sexual pleasure, but this is being treated with a great deal of scepticism.'

'Fuck.' Konrad wiped his nose with the back of his right hand. 'Where's Chloe? Where's that bitch?'

'All forces have been alerted to detain her for questioning, but there's no sign of her. I'm so sorry, Mr Neale. I have no idea what to say.'

'I think I killed him.' Konrad slouched, head bowed.

DCI Anwell looked across at Sheila. 'Why would you say that, Mr Neale?' she asked gently.

Konrad ignored her, leant forward, and with his words aimed squarely at DCI Anwell said, 'I called Josh Hawley earlier. I told him we were looking for Tessa Carlton, I asked him for help. He must have spoken to Naomi. He said she was due back from a business trip later today. I didn't have a clue she was involved until I saw those pictures. What have I done?' Konrad's muddled thoughts were reflected in his despairing tones.

'You haven't killed Freddie.' DCI Anwell looked down at Konrad, who was pressing his fingernails into the tops of his thighs. 'This isn't your fault. Look, I've been working alongside the team who investigated the murder of Helena Chawston-Hawley and we've made significant progress. We will catch whoever did this.'

'You'd better catch the bitch before I do and fucking hurry up before she kills anyone else. Is Delia safe?' Konrad felt a switch turn on inside his head as he disconnected from his emotions.

'You don't really think Tessa Carlton will go after the rest of your family, do you?' DCI Anwell frowned. 'Try not to worry too much, local police have been asked to speak to your wife to inform her of your son's death, after which she may stay with a friend or perhaps your daughter will travel home to be with her mother. DS Jenkins will track Eliza down after we've spoken and we'll take her to wherever she wants to go. I know this is not going to be easy but we have to make a public statement if we're going to stand a chance of arresting Naomi Woods, or whatever she may choose to call herself.'

'Keep my family and Lorna safe.' Konrad said his words becoming increasingly bitter. 'Get the evidence and let's do a bastard press conference and tell that fucking Tessa bitch that the gloves are off.'

'We'll get whoever did this. But we have to do it by the book. I'm sorry to leave so soon, we have to go now, people to arrest and question – including Josh Hawley,' DCI Anwell repeated himself, 'I'm sorry.'

'You get her. Do you hear me? It's her turn to cry.'

Chapter 33

She checked the battery level before setting the camera on its tripod. The bland branded hotel room could have been anywhere in the country. They always looked the same; cheap and cheerless, clean and unfriendly. She sat poised for an earnest one-way conversation, with a self-satisfied smirk appearing gradually as she spoke.

'Lots of people are looking for Tessa. I don't know why they're wasting their time. She hasn't been seen or heard of since she left Willow Hall and abandoned the stupid Dr Sarah Tyrell to her own analyses. Silly cow. She was useless as a doctor. The do-good doctor, who was nothing more than an advert for Laura Ashley, made us sit in a circle and talk about our families for hours on end. I had nothing much to say, but Tessa Carlton talked endlessly about her bloody sister.

'For hours we endured the endless envious bitching about Helena, not to mention the uncaring disinterested parents. By the way she described them, I'm pretty sure her immediate family members would have died a long time ago if Tessa hadn't been locked up. She was capable of killing her family, I'm certain. But perhaps I should be grateful she didn't, because my life wouldn't have been so rich without Tessa. Thanks to her I knew practically every detail about Helena's upbringing.

'Let me explain, Konrad. You see, once Tessa and I had made good on our escape from Willow Hall, I had options for my life; a new one, a better one. Tessa always said she'd never have anything to do with her family ever again, which left an opportunity too tempting to ignore. So, slowly and deliberately, I worked my way into Tessa's family, which at first meant studying her sister Helena from a discreet distance.

'Helena had a life of wealth and respectability that I wanted to be a part of but you can't just barge in. I needed a legitimate reason to be in her life, so I studied her: her likes, dislikes, habits, reactions, wishes and weaknesses. These were revealed through her actions, as well as idle gossip from the brainless hairdresser, beer-soaked car mechanic, shallow beautician, and weak-willed accountant. Additional useful facts were gleaned from articles in newspapers and business journals. I confess, Konrad, to silently stalking her, unseen, undetected. As far as I could work out, Helena had done well in most things except for relationships.

'I know it sounds a bit mad, but once I got to know her I started to understand how much she'd irritated Tessa. She was so utterly tiresome in her pretend niceness that I became frustrated at how ordinary and horribly pleasant she appeared to be on the surface. Nice people irritate the hell out of me, and Helena turned out to be exactly the same saccharine individual that Tessa had spoken about when recalling her earliest childhood memories. Enough to make you vomit.

'When they were toddlers, Helena smothered little Tessa with adoration, treating her like a favourite doll by brushing her hair and trying to dress her up in whatever she thought looked pretty. Tessa would be dragged around, ordered to sit in the Wendy House and play "pretend" games. A pet to keep her sister amused and occupied while their parents ignored them.

'Some couples shouldn't have children in the first place if they can't be bothered with them. I only had Tessa's word for it, but those children, Tessa and Helena, must have been accidents because the lack of affection displayed in that household was astounding even by my standards. Tessa and her siblings were treated more like belongings than part of a family, from what I could understand.

'They had toys and a neat bedroom to share, but when visitors arrived the children were paraded in front of them and then sent back to their rooms to amuse themselves for hours. Mum and Dad would respond if ever they made too much noise. "Shut up or you'll live to regret it!" would come the shout from downstairs where they would be watching an inane programme on the telly. Helena did as she was told.

'Tessa didn't want to. She had a natural rebellious streak that had always existed inside her, and she soon discovered that by being naughty she could gain her parents' attention through that bad behaviour. It worked a treat. Let's face it, Konrad, some attention is better than none at all.

'One story Tessa told took place on Sunday afternoon, when she found her mum's make-up bag, and indulged in wild creative art by drawing on the bedroom wall with lipstick and eyebrow pencil. Her mother's screaming and rasping anger was apparently heard throughout the house when she found her. There was Helena, sitting on the floor covered in rouge and blue eye shadow, drawing on her sister's face with black eyeliner.

'Having worked so well, Tessa used a similar strategy to enrage her mother on endless occasions, always implicating Helena, who until then had preferential treatment as the well-behaved child. I think Tessa told me she was less than three when she worked out that blaming Helena was not only a satisfying form of entertainment but guaranteed attention from one or both parents. She hated her parents for their stupidity and they too became the target of her frustrations. Helena was the tool, the weapon she used towards their social destruction.

'Nobody cottoned on that Tessa was the one with the brains, Konrad. So, she carried on blaming Helena for the decimation caused. I know just how brilliant that feels. It's the ultimate power trip. Helena was assumed guilty because she was the oldest child and "should have known better..." She was held responsible for the fire in the shed and the death of their cat, Mr Tibbs; he was old, Konrad, and he smelt, so Tessa dispatched him with some garden wire while practicing how to set snares. She managed to convince her parents and teachers at nursery school that Helena would dare her to carry out these acts and had threatened Tessa or tortured her if she failed or refused.

'She made a bed of nails once. Actually, it was a short plank of wood and the nails were pointy end down, but the principle was the same. Waiting until her dad was on his way up the garden to find the two girls, Tessa lay on it wrapped in strips of bed sheet screaming at Helena to "stop" and "let me get up!" She had persuaded Helena to stand over her, hold a pair of garden sheers, whilst wearing a tea towel headdress. Tessa had told her that they were ancient Egyptian priests carrying out an important ritual. Helena was so stupid that she fell for it and had played along. Hearing the noise, their dad ran to open the door and dragged Tessa up from the nails, at the same time as swiping Helena with a vicious backhand. "It was a dare, Dad," Tessa told him. "We were playing Egyptians and I had to, she made me." Pretending to cry to her dad, he accepted that Helena was the instigator and that Tessa was nothing other than the poor victim of Helena's vicious assault. Those bloody ignorant psychologists and psychiatrists became fixated on the issue of sibling rivalry and Helena's sweet veneer was described as being part of a complex adjustment disorder. They may have had a point. It would explain why she was so eager to fit in and be liked. She clung onto friends like a strangulating ivy plant until they tired of her demanding ways and need for assurances.

'Tessa had counselling and lied her way through each session. When she was no more than eight, she became quite adept at giving herself rope burns, bruises and on the odd occasion she would cut herself. Nice little slashes or nicks. She wasn't one of those psycho self-harmers. This was planned. The reasons were purely practical, you understand.

'Did you know she had a younger brother, Konrad? Little Dickie. Tessa said he was a delightful child and so easy to influence. Wasn't it thoughtful of her to give Helena a break now and again and blame Dickie for so many wrongdoings? Helena was apparently a bloody nuisance, spending most of her waking hours protecting Dickie from Tessa and spoiling her entertainment. Bitch.

'Tessa hated Helena. She hated her parents and hated her grandparents. Nanny and Granddad Carlton were as uninteresting as her parents were, and as gullible. They tried to understand, even when Tessa raged at them, smashed up the house and ruined the seedlings in the greenhouse out of spite.

'At those endless social services meetings her grandmother would lie and say how well Tessa was coping with their house rules. The old bat must have been quite insane. Tessa made their life a misery and exhausted them until her granddad had a heart attack. Then social services sent her home to play with Dickie again because Helena had gone to university. Without Helena, he had no one to help him.

'Tessa was fucking furious when she caught him on the phone to Helena. He begged her for help... "please, Helly, come and get me. I could live with you," he whimpered. He was a pathetic excuse for a ten-year-old boy.

'If he hadn't created such a fuss then he wouldn't have been taken into care. Tessa wouldn't have tried to set-up Helena and, therefore, she wouldn't have been sectioned. It's his fault. He told the police that he'd seen Tessa cutting herself and, because they're stupid, they believed his word against hers. Still, Dickie probably had a miserable time in care. Good. I hope he was rogered by a pervert. Serves him right.

'Anyway, that's all in the past. I have to think about you now, Konrad. On one hand, you have annoyed me. You interfered. On the other, I have enjoyed the game we've played. It occurred to me as I was contemplating whether or not your wife should die, that after Helena's death I was missing the thrill of the chase.

'You haven't worked that bit out yet, have you? How Helena was killed...'

She paused. There was the sound of several pairs of boot-clad feet stomping down the corridor. Gruff voices of two men could be heard making arrangements to meet in reception after they had showered and changed. Doors closed with an inconsiderate bang. She relaxed back into the chair and continued.

'You'll be interested to know, the police have arrived at home to speak to Josh. They wanted a few words with me but I'm not back yet. He's just phoned me again to check how long it would be before I could join him at the police station to meet a Detective Inspector Bevan from Bangor. I would have been back with Josh much sooner, Konrad, but I took a detour.

'After I left Dorset, I stopped off at your house to see your wife, the stiff and starchy Delia. The stupid bint thought I was really worried about Freddie and she even tried to comfort me. I've been having so much fun. I told her that Freddie and I had arranged to meet but that he failed to show up and I couldn't get hold of him on his phone. Delia didn't question my version of events. "Never mind dear, we all have lovers' tiffs now and again. It's part of relationships. I'm sure he'll soon be begging for forgiveness," she said. How quaint.

'She phoned his friends while I had a good snoop around your house again. I didn't have much chance when I came to the barbecue, but this time I checked your office. You have been busy trying to find out about Tessa, haven't you?

'For an intelligent man you're remarkably slow to pick up the clues, but I have to assume you know that I'm Chloe by now. No one can be that thick.'

She brushed her hands through her hair and adjusted her position in the chair, leaning forwards, glowering in the direction of the video camera.

'A lot of hard work has gone into securing my future and you, Konrad, have screwed things up. Getting close to Helena took years to achieve and I prepared as thoroughly as I could for the task ahead.

'When the time was right, I applied for a job with Chawston Recruitment. My predecessor had disgraced herself by turning up for work under the influence of drugs. Despite swearing that she never touched illicit substances, she was dismissed for gross misconduct. Richard told me she was delightfully disinhibited and had said the most inappropriate things to Helena on the day of her instant sacking. I wish I could have witnessed her antics for myself. It took a fair while to plan that one.

'Anyway, to cut a long story short, Helena employed me because I was the best candidate. I excelled at recruitment, Konrad, and what's more I completed my apprenticeship and learnt everything about Helena. There wasn't that much to know. She was a success, a rich ambitious businesswoman who was desperately lonely, mostly because she frightened every single man away with her insecurities and her habit of attaching herself like a limpet to anyone who showed her some affection. Then she would predict that they would leave her, so she would push them away by testing their loyalty. In a series of self-fulfilling prophecies, they all left her one after the other, after the other.

'Then along comes Mr Fucking Teflon. Matthew Hawley. He tolerated everything she put him through. It was sickening to watch. He was even nicer than she was pretending to be. I tried to scare him off until I realised what an asset he could be. As for his son, Josh, he was my gold medal, my pinnacle, my reward.

'Helena loved that boy, so I took him.'

She switched off the camera and put it away, only to unpack it again as soon as she had the opportunity to complete the video diary of the day's events.

Breathless excitement arose in her voice and her eyes darted from the lens of the camera to a plain white door to her right.

'I'm back at home now with Josh and he's been in a good mood since you called him earlier. You shouldn't have done that, Konrad. He told me straight away. I was on a business trip at the time you see, assessing Freddie's potential. He had his uses, but you showed your hand, Konrad, and sentenced your son to an early departure. Don't worry, he was in a state of exceptional euphoria when he died. What a lovely way to go.

'I phoned Josh before I left your son gasping for breath in that fancy car of yours. "Hello Josh, it's me," I said. "I'm leaving for home in the next few minutes. Our potential new team member didn't work out, I'm afraid. He wasn't really up to the job. Not nearly enough experience and it showed during the interview. It doesn't matter, I have another candidate in mind."

'I was thinking about you, Konrad. I do that a lot lately, as you've probably guessed.

'Freddie was so useful to me for a time and out of respect for you and to him, I took great care in becoming Chloe. Now is the right time to tell you that I was saving my best wig and contact lenses for you originally, Konrad. Chloe was going to be *your* honey trap, but that would have been a poor performance in comparison to the one you and Lorna gave that Saturday night.

'Freddie helped me to get so much closer to you, to Delia and your lives. He served his purpose. However, Eliza has not been such a pushover, she was far more awkward and she didn't fall for my charms; in fact, I suspect she hated Chloe. No hard feelings, I like Eliza, she has a toughness I admire in a woman.

'Your Freddie, on the other hand, was so young and eager. He fell into my bed and never have I witnessed anyone so keen to learn about sex. I must say I found the lessons enjoyable myself. That's the beauty of youthful men; they assume to know so much and are shocked to find the opposite. I had him simply begging, Konrad. You'll be pleased to hear that I was with him teaching him how to avoid premature ejaculation when I sent those texts to you. He was blindfolded, with me astride him, so he couldn't see the phone in my hand. He couldn't restrain himself either and, unfortunately, he required punishment and a few more lessons before he obeyed me. When I say "don't come yet" I mean it.

'I'm a good teacher, Konrad. I taught Helena everything I know. She trusted me to show her how to ensnare a man, you see. Naomi Woods, friend and confidante, that's me. I had to because she had no idea how to pleasure a man and who else was going to help her? Did you know that, Konrad? She had not a clue until I showed her. I was invaluable. Without me, she couldn't have kept Matthew interested enough. I'm not boasting. It's a gift I have.

One shouldn't be selfish about sharing one's abilities to those less fortunate, I always say.

'That reminds me; the police arrived at your house as I was leaving in a taxi to get on a train. I was standing at the station, in one of your baseball caps. You won't mind that I borrowed it; in fact, you may never even notice that it's missing. You forgot to pack it. I was watching the crowds milling about, but I dithered a bit before buying a ticket because I couldn't decide whether to go home or to visit you in hospital. It was such a tempting thought to spend time sitting and chatting with you, and at least that way I could have admired Lorna's handiwork on your face. No doubt the police will be there guarding you, and I wouldn't have had much time alone, just the two of us, but it was worth considering the risk. I wanted to see your fear. Never mind.'

Naomi let out a long dramatic sigh.

'Thanks for this chat, Konrad. I've found it helpful to clear the air, and it's helped me to realise that rather than making the job of the police too easy by walking straight into their arms at the hospital. I was right to make my way home and convince Josh that there has been a dreadful error on your part. Mistaken identity in the face of trauma. He believes what I tell him, you see, because he's been conditioned to, like Helena was.

Chapter 34

He was beside himself with frustration. He had his catheter removed, he was mobile again and yet the doctors seemed reluctant to support his discharge. Sheila took the brunt of his foul mood as she and Leah were making his bed.

'When is Mr Wells coming to see me? I have to get out of here tomorrow at the latest and I either do that with his agreement or against medical advice. Either way, I am packing my meagre belongings and going to Eliza's flat.'

Sheila maintained a calming steady tone as she tried to placate a pacing Konrad. 'He's in surgery, Mr Neale, and you of all people should appreciate the priority he has to give to that. He'll be with you when he is able. Why don't you try phoning your friend Annette again and see how things have gone in Gloucestershire instead of taking your impatience out on the NHS staff.' Sheila gave him one of her scary teacher glares. Grunting, he walked out of his room, along a corridor and into a small empty office. He shut the door and prayed for privacy.

Annette answered almost immediately. 'I was about to call you.'

'Sorry, I couldn't wait. What's the news? How is she? Is she well? Has she remembered anything else? What's her lawyer like, did she say?'

'Kon, for goodness sake shut up and let me speak, then you might get an answer to the endless stream of questions.' Annette took a moment to compose herself. 'Lorna is a resilient woman and she's making the most of her time in the remand centre. She's been talking to some of the other detainees and has probably furnished us with enough documentary material to last a decade.'

'Not interested.' Konrad dismissed Annette's opening remarks.

'Well, she is. She's been speaking to a woman who was at Willow Hall with Tessa Carlton, so she's as up to date as we are on Tessa's family history. However, she has found out something that we didn't know. Are you sitting down?'

'Yes.'

'Good. Pin your ears right back and get ready to phone your pet detective chief inspector because this is a shocker.'

'I'm listening.'

'When Tessa Carlton absconded from Willow Hall, she was with another girl.'

'Yes, we know that.'

'The other girl was called Naomi Woods.'

Konrad took a moment to think about the information.

'Which means that either there are two Naomi Woods' floating about somewhere or Tessa Carlton took the other girl's identity knowing that she wouldn't be resurfacing.'

'Correct. If that is the case it explains why Tessa was never seen or heard of again. She became Naomi.'

'What did Lorna find out about the girl called Naomi when she was in Willow Hall. What sort of girl would run off with Tessa and become her first murder victim? That's what we are saying, isn't it? The real Naomi was murdered.'

'I think it is, Kon. It would explain how Tessa was able to live as someone else. The information that Lorna gleaned from her informant indicates that the real Naomi was a damaged child, easily influenced, mother had died of a drug overdose, father was in prison and not interested. It's a classic case of Tessa identifying who best to use for her escape plan from what I can gather. It sounds as if she groomed Naomi, befriended her, gained her trust, helped her and made herself an indispensable friend. With no family to bother about her and not being under a Section, the effort to recover both girls was minimal. They were sixteen at the time.'

'Bloody hell, Annette, the case against Tessa is stacking up. I'll contact DCI Anwell and let him know. What's Lorna's solicitor like? Any good?'

Annette was pleased to let Konrad know that Lorna's solicitor was on the ball. 'She rates him. He's planning to propose that a case is made to the CPS that both you and she were the victims in this case. If I'm right, that's what your snobby barrister suggested too.'

'Yes, he did.'

'In that case, if the police and CPS can produce enough evidence to put Tessa Carlton at the scene and as the perpetrator, then you're both in the clear. If the forensic evidence proves the two of you were drugged at the time of the incident, then Lorna cannot be said to have full intention to cause serious bodily harm. Without the presence of intent, she can't be held liable for the crime. Do you see?'

'Only out of one eye at the moment.'

'Very amusing. I'm glad your sense of humour is holding up because frankly I thought they would have carted you off to the funny farm by now.'

'I don't have time. I want Lorna out of there and I'm determined to see Tessa Carlton locked up permanently.'

'Where's Naomi Woods now, still at the nick?'

'I hope so. I haven't had an update. What else did Lorna say?'

'Don't sound so anxious. She misses you and is worried sick about how you'll cope with the psychological fall-out from the physical injury and public humiliation. She hasn't seen your face since the night of the assault, remember, so her imagination has run riot. I tried to tell her how dashing you look in your fetching eye patch but she thinks I'm appeasing her.'

'You are. Did you tell her about Freddie?' Konrad had difficulty in asking this without emotions getting in the way. He had almost succeeded in putting up psychological barriers to help him remain rational and focussed, but Freddie's death had produced seismic cracks in his protective armour. With only his own strength and that of his friends to call on, he was feeling vulnerable.

'Kon, she already knew. It was all over the news. She wanted confirmation of the funeral arrangements and she's desperate to be with you. I know she's a tough old stick but it's solely her strength of character that's getting her through each day. She's lost weight, you have too, but you haven't lost each other, so hang on in there. I'll be visiting her again when I can, and she has my number when she needs to talk or get messages to you.'

'Annette, I can't thank you enough for what you've done. I'd be lost without you and Barney.' Annette assured him it was 'no trouble', before ending the call.

Having satisfied himself that Lorna was in one piece, Konrad let out a long sigh of relief and sat down on a chair in the corner of the room.

For a while, the silence was welcome until he was unable to tolerate his thoughts. *What am I supposed to do with myself? I need to know what's going on out there.*

A firm knock heralded the arrival of Staff Nurse Christine who nosed around the door.

'Checking up on me, are you? Don't panic, I'm not about to kill myself, I've got family and responsibilities, and besides which I like life too much.' As Konrad said this he slowed the end of the sentence. 'Christine, have you got a pen and paper handy, by any chance? I need to scribble something down before the thought escapes.'

Richard, Naomi's colleague, and Helena's right-hand man in Chawston Recruitment. Why did he kill himself? When Helena died, why was life so intolerable that he wanted to die? Did he have any family responsibilities to consider which would have stopped him from committing suicide? Did he die by his own hand or was he killed because he knew about Naomi?

When he wrestled with the questions, he couldn't extricate his thoughts about Helena's death from his own assault.

How many people has Tessa killed?

The phone rang, interrupting his spiralling thoughts.

'Hello, Mr Neale, it's Jan on reception. I have your barrister for you again.'

'Rupert Van Dahl speaking. Hello, Mr Neale. I hesitate to ask how you are, so I'll steer clear of that question for now. I have news that you will want to hear regarding your case. The police have been doing a magnificent job and Naomi Woods has not only been arrested and questioned, but charged with the wilful murder of your son, Freddie. She has also been questioned and charged with conspiracy to cause grievous bodily harm to you because the forensic evidence has put her at both scenes. Now for the bad news: the charges against Lorna Yates have not been dropped. However, her legal counsel will argue on the common law test of criminal liability. Actus reus non facit reum nisi mens sit rea. Mens Rea, Mr Neale. It could be argued that you and Lorna could not have committed any wilful acts if there was an absence of free will, because if you were deliberately drugged with a substance that had an effect on your capacity and induced amnesia, then this would be determined as non-insane automatism. Do you see?'

'Yes, I understand completely and I can't tell you how immensely relieved I am.' Konrad was choking back more tears. 'When will Lorna be freed? Can I see her?'

'I don't think you understand. The court case is going ahead and it will be a judge and jury who decide whether Lorna acted wilfully or not. The evidence alone cannot determine this and it must be argued in court. The bottom line is that Lorna did assault you. Chloe Jordan, also known as Naomi Woods, was found to have been the other person present at the time but has been charged with conspiracy as if she were an accomplice. She didn't carry out the assault... Konrad, are you there?'

Sitting with the phone handset dangling limply by its flex between his fingers, the tinny voice of Rupert Van Dahl could be heard calling his name. 'Konrad? Are you still there?' After several more seconds, the phone went dead.

Sheila found her patient sitting in the small office, receiver in hand. 'Mr Neale, Mr Wells is here to see you.' She walked over to Konrad and gently touched him on the shoulder, followed by a firm shake. 'Mr Neale, can you hear me?' Konrad turned his head towards the sound of her voice but he barely registered who she was.

Mr Wells stepped forward into his field of vision and took an adjacent seat. 'My team tells me you wish to be discharged to the care of your daughter and that you are adamant about this.' Konrad could only reaffirm this with a crisp nod of the head. 'I'm confident that your wounds are healing well and that physically you are fit to leave our care. However, I am not at all certain that psychologically you are in a fit state of mind to cope with the pressure and stress of current events, your assault and the death of your son.'

After a lengthy pause the rasping response was said without inflection. 'What can you do about that? Nothing. So please let me go to be with my family.'

'I'd feel much happier if I could be given your promise to take up the psychology appointments made for you.'

'If that makes you happier, then I agree. Either way, Mr Wells, I have to get out of hospital today. Eliza is collecting me and I'll stay at her flat until we go home for the funeral.'

Konrad caught sight of his reflection in the glass window to his left. For a second, he was taken off guard by his own appearance.

Now I look like Matthew Hawley. Haggard and gaunt. This is what that bitch Tessa has done to us.

*

It had been a long journey from Manchester to Bangor in a taxi with Eliza making minimal small talk along the way – trying to appear normal and avoid any reference to her brother. He could see himself in the rear-view mirror and was reassured that his eye patch was in place, covering the worst of the damage to his face. The scars across his cheek and forehead remained inflamed but were nevertheless showing signs of healing well. On the phone during the taxi ride, Konrad had spoken to DCI Anwell who had been unable to dissuade him from making a personal visit to the station. Therefore, before stepping foot inside Eliza's flat, she was forced to take him to Gwyedd Police Headquarters to meet with DCI Anwell.

'I can understand that you want to be part of the investigation, Mr Neale, but this is our job. Look, our investigations so far do correlate with what you've told us. Dr Sarah Tyrell has been spoken to, we have followed up on missing persons' reports, and we're looking into Richard's apparent suicide, but none of that changes the case against Lorna Yates I'm afraid.'

Until that moment, when the last of his strength was sapped, Konrad hadn't appreciated how physically drained he had become. He sat digesting the detective's words and the enormity of the situation overwhelmed him. 'I feel incredibly powerless. Is there really nothing I can do except wait?'

Chapter 35

The pews in St Mary's village church were filled, requiring some mourners to take up standing room at the rear and in the side aisles. Konrad took Delia's hand in his left and Eliza's in his right as they sat pale and tremulous in the front row overlooking Freddie's coffin swathed in white lilies. Delia sat with her elderly mother, Grandma Lewis, to her left. Konrad was always astounded at the resemblance that his wife had to her mother, despite the fact that their characters couldn't be more different. Grandma Lewis was Eliza's and Freddie's favourite grandparent based on her ability to make mischief. Sitting on the pew, head bowed, Grandma Lewis looked every day of her seventy-nine years as she battled to maintain her own dignity and bring comfort to her daughter. Konrad's parents took their place to Eliza's right, where Granddad Neale provided a broad shoulder for Eliza to turn her face into when the emotions became unbearable. The redoubtable Grandma Neale knelt in prayer, seeking relief from the pain of loss by hanging onto her lifelong faith in God. As the vicar began her solemn task, Grandma Neale stood tall with an iron poker for a backbone, her gaze never wavering from the large cross hanging above the altar.

'I would like to welcome you to this celebration of the life of Frederick Charles Neale who passed all too soon to take his place with our Lord Jesus Christ. I feel very honoured to be here today as we remember his life because ever since I first came to St Mary's I have watched Freddie, and his twin sister Eliza, grow from gangling adolescents at upper school, to the delightful adults they became. Freddie was always the charming, athletic young man seen with his friends enjoying life to the full and breaking many a girl's heart...'

The words that the vicar spoke were well meaning and personal to a degree, but Konrad was numb to their impact. All he could think about was the last sight he'd had of his own son, walking away head bowed, into the dark night of Bangor's side streets near The Management Centre. The last time they had spoken together was over breakfast with Chloe there, gloating behind her false hair and contact lenses. The bitterness of the memories threatened to engulf Konrad before the tears of sadness could take hold. He wanted to turn around and stand up to face the friends and family gathered to mourn his son, and to tell them the harsh truth, but he knew better than to commit such a radical breach of cultural boundaries.

Eliza was sobbing inconsolably, although her efforts to hold her tears in check were plain to see, she failed. The young people that she and Freddie grew up with were standing together tears flowing freely down their young faces as, with immense courage, Freddie's best friend Lloyd walked to the front of the church and took his place behind the lectern. He had written a poem in honour of Freddie's smile and charm, which he proceeded to read with an unexpected confidence for one so young.

When he finished, there was a palpable hush throughout the congregation with only the sound of Eliza's heartrending sobs breaking the peace. Konrad rose from the pew and offered his hand to Lloyd, expressing his thanks and admiration. Lloyd stepped closer and gave him a man-hug reducing him, finally, to the stream of tears that had threatened to flow throughout the service.

Stepping outside and walking behind Freddie's coffin to stand at the graveside, Konrad felt himself slipping out of reality. He was there in his body, but he witnessed the events as if through someone else's eyes, far away.

'For as much as it hath pleased Almighty God of his great mercy to take unto himself the soul of our dear brother here departed, we therefore commit his body to the ground; earth to earth, ashes to ashes, dust to dust; in sure and certain hope of the Resurrection to eternal life, through our Lord Jesus Christ.'

Konrad watched the earth being scattered on the wooden coffin, but he didn't connect with his own actions as he reached down, took a fistful of earth and threw it on top of the shining walnut lid.

For the rest of the warm and sunny afternoon, the funeral became a blur of heartfelt commiserations from friends, colleagues and police who had attended the private service. Konrad didn't even register the reactions of his friends to his injuries. Throughout, he continued to hold Delia's hand for comfort although she barely spoke or acknowledged his existence. It was the only thing he could do.

'Kon, are you and Eliza going back to Wales or are you staying at home for a while?' Annette asked him, gently taking him aside in what used to be his lounge. She had found him trying to mingle politely with guests eating sandwiches with murmured reverence. Delia was coping by tidying up, wiping surfaces and plumping up cushions to keep her house in order.

'We'll stay for a few weeks, I think. Eliza might go back to Bangor she said, but I'll stay here until the trial. I've got my room at the Valiant and I'm nearer to Delia if she needs me, and to my real mates, so I'd rather be here. I'll come into work when I can.'

'You don't have to.'

'I know, but I want to. I'll go bonkers if I sit around for the court case. They don't tell me a bloody thing and the waiting is killing me. Did Mike and Joe manage to find out about Dickie Carlton, by any chance? If not, it'll give me something to do.'

Annette hesitated. 'Yes they did as a matter of fact. I'm not sure this is the place...' Barney sidled up to Konrad making him jump.

'Sorry, mate.'

'Bugger, I wondered who it was for a second.'

'I forgot you don't see so well from this side. My fault.' Barney was stuffing a large slice of gala pie into his mouth and handed Annette another. She beamed at him.

'You've got to hand it to The Camp Commandant, she knows how to put on a decent buffet.' Barney smiled. 'When can we make a dash for the perimeter fence and head for the pub? I have a couple of pints with my name on them and one or two for you, mate.'

'You can make a start without me if you like, I ought to help Delia clear up the mess.' Konrad conceded. Barney protested briefly at his friend's weak will, but was escorted by Annette in the direction of pudding, to fill more time before they could reasonably take their leave and head to The Valiant Soldier.

'Thanks for going to so much trouble.' Konrad touched Delia's elbow, which she withdrew immediately. They were alone in her clinical kitchen.

'Drop dead.'

'I thought we were being civil to each other now.'

'You thought wrong. If you hadn't run after that whore like a dog in heat, then none of this would have happened. I will never forgive you. Never. Not as long as I live. So please piss off to the pub. Oh, and just so you know, as soon as the divorce is settled I'm putting the house on the market and moving to town so we won't have to meet each other unless we have to. Until then stay away from me. Do I make myself clear?'

'Abundantly. You don't want my help to tidy up then?'

'No, I don't want your help so take your fat friends and piss off.' Delia hissed her final words of dismissal.

When he caught up with Barney and Annette they were on their second round of drinks and perched on high stools at the bar of The Valiant Soldier. The place was buzzing with chatter until Konrad stepped through the door, those inside saw him, and the volume of the hubbub rapidly reduced.

'Please, being quiet and sombre was never Freddie's way, so carry on and pretend I'm not here. Pint please, Rob.' He stood between his two friends and shrugged. 'I guess they were all talking about me. Hardly surprising in the circumstances.'

'Yes, old mate, you are the talk of the town and most of the cities I would think. Has Delia recovered from the indignity of having her photograph taken by the bloody paparazzi?'

'She wasn't really in the mood for a chat, Barney. In fact, she was close to poking my other eye out, which is why I left before her talons put in an appearance.'

'You'd think the papers would have been considerate enough to avoid press intrusion at your son's funeral, but no, there they were lurking in the graveyard, the bastards.' Barney shook his head in disgust. 'I must say Eliza was magnificent in the way she handled them. She's a credit to you, Kon.'

'I hope the court proceedings are going to be managed with more dignity,' Annette said. 'I've been called as a witness for the defence by the way. Did Barney tell you?'

'Yes. I'm relieved to be honest. Lorna needs the support.' Konrad tried to keep his voice low as he leant over the bar to pick up his glass of beer. 'Anyone else we know been called?'

'I've no idea. I've just been asked to give any dates that I'm unavailable to attend court. When is the pre-trial hearing thing? I thought that was soon.'

'It is. Next Thursday. I've been asked to attend a meeting with the CPS barrister. Rockin' Rupert will be there to outline what I'm to expect at the trial itself. To be fair to the chap, he's been keeping me as up to date as he can, but the police investigation has been so intensive that what I have to say as a witness will be minimal by the sounds of things. I presume Lorna will plead not guilty but I've no idea what Naomi Woods is likely to plead. I don't even know what name she's using legally.' Konrad paused to take a sip of his ale.

'Does it matter, so long as they get to the truth and she gets locked up. She's a psycho. Fancy using drugs to make people do what you want without them even knowing what's happening. That's the same as those date rape drugs but weirder.' Barney, realising that he had spoken too loudly, apologised by holding his hand up. 'Sorry.'

Annette filled the awkward moment. 'Did I tell you, Mike and Joe found an article in The Telegraph about the Chinese women in Paris using drugs to rob people? They used bunches of flowers which they invited elderly innocent victims to sniff after they stopped them to ask for directions. The drug was in the flowers and the victims didn't remember a thing afterwards. They gave themselves away because each time they asked for directions they said they were looking for a mysterious "Dr Wang". They targeted old people, isolated them, took advantage and robbed them blind. One poor couple had about seventy-five grand stolen from their apartment apparently. Clever buggers the Chinese. The French police say the three people they arrested were a small part of a much wider criminal network operating in the same way.' Annette slurped her gin and tonic as she looked for Konrad's reaction.

'That has to be the one. Did the article say anything about how long the memory loss lasted for?'

'I think so. It was quite detailed. Look it up, it's online.'

Chapter 36

The courtroom fell silent as Konrad took the stand as the opening witness for the prosecution. Rupert Van Dahl, in gown and wig, kept eye contact with his client who was approached by the court usher and asked if he preferred to swear on the bible or to affirm that he would tell the truth.

He tried to remain composed as he read from the card. 'I do solemnly, sincerely and truly declare and affirm that the evidence I shall give shall be the truth, the whole truth and nothing but the truth.' He was trembling as he handed the card back to the usher and, as he did so, raised his head towards the dock at the far end of the courtroom.

There, in a glass-fronted cubicle, sitting four or five feet apart, were Lorna and Naomi, flanked by prison escort staff. The two accused women were neatly dressed in business suits staring straight ahead, expressionless. Lorna's hair was scraped back in a severe ponytail. They looked out from behind their glass prison onto the modern windowless courtroom where the legal teams sat at long beechwood veneered desks, which mirrored those of the judge and the court reporter. The whole room was efficiently lit with spotlights atop the wooden clad walls, and natural light streaming through a large skylight. The number of public and press present in the courtroom was restricted, with the vast majority clamouring for news and photographs outside the square modern edifice of the Crown Court in Caernarfon.

Konrad had been advised by the witness support officer to address the judge and the members of the jury when answering questions from the stand. He didn't need reminding. The judge sat to his immediate right necessitating a forty-five degree turn in order to see the elderly man in glasses who would be guiding the jury and managing the trial.

Rupert Van Dahl commenced the case for the prosecution with a simple line of questioning. 'Mr Neale, could you tell the court, in your own words, what you recall of the evening of Saturday the thirteenth of May 2017. Your statement indicates that you had spent the day with your ex-girlfriend, the accused Lorna Yates, in an effort to patch up your relationship, which you had ended some four months previously. Is that correct?' Konrad was prepared for this.

'Yes, that's correct.'

'Would you mind telling the court how you met Lorna Yates?'

'We met through work. Lorna started as a researcher with Channel 7 a few months before I began on the first series of "The Truth Behind the Lies". She carried out much of the background information gathering for each of the documentaries and we met shortly before the filming of the first case in March 2016.'

'Did your wife know about your affair at that time?'

'No, she didn't.'

'You state that you fell in love with Lorna Yates during the time you were having an affair, so please can you explain to the members of the jury why you decided to end your relationship in February this year.'

Konrad had also been expecting this particular line of questioning. Even so, he found that his well-rehearsed lines had escaped his memory and he stumbled through the explanation. 'I was under considerable pressure from my wife. She had found out about Lorna. The TV series was a spectacular success, you see, and Delia, my wife, is also my business manager. She was furious that I had jeopardised our financial future and undermined the trust of the viewing public. I was weak. I should have followed my heart instead of worrying about my reputation.' He scanned the faces of the jury and saw only minor changes in the facial expressions of two women. The rest remained resolutely deadpan. Rupert had warned him not to try for any sympathy and now Konrad knew why.

'Realising your error, you pursued Lorna Yates, desperate to reignite your relationship. Isn't that so?'

'Yes, it is.'

'Did anyone encourage you to do this?'

'My colleague, Annette, gave me the confidence to at least try.'

'She informed you of where Lorna Yates had moved for work, and as you say in your statement, that happened to be Bangor, the very city where your children attended university. Did that ever strike you as more than a coincidence, Mr Neale?'

'No,' came a slightly hesitant response.

'What do you know about Lorna Yates' private life, and her history before she met you?'

'Well, as far as I am aware, her parents were originally from Cardiff and although she grew up in Herefordshire she always calls herself Welsh. She's an only child, good education. Went to university to study English literature, but I can't recall where. Her CV said she had worked in customer services and public relations in London before landing her job with Channel 7. I once met one of her previous partners, a chap called Daryl, who she lived with in Camden for several years. Apart from that we socialised in the same group. Her friends at work were my friends too. They still are.'

'I see. What can you tell us about Lorna's mental health? Has there ever been any indication of a vengeful nature in her behaviour towards others?'

'No. I don't know anything about that. She's always been sensible, balanced and caring, from my experience.' Konrad shifted his weight from one foot to another. He shot a puzzled look at Rupert Van Dahl.

'Take us back to the time of the assault, after dinner on Saturday the thirteenth of May this year, if you will. You and Lorna had a meal together in the restaurant at The Management Centre in Bangor, and after walking Lorna Yates back to her car, what did you see?'

Konrad produced the well-rehearsed chronology of events leading up to the moment that Lorna knocked on his hotel door that night.

'And that is the last thing you remember, Mr Neale? You pulled at Lorna Yates to get her out of harm's way and grabbed at the person wearing dark clothing who was forcing their way in through the door.'

'Yes. I have no recall of anything until the next morning.'

'When did you realise that it was Lorna Yates who had inflicted life changing injuries on your face, which resulted in the loss of your right eye?'

'I didn't ever realise. I was told that the attack on me had been filmed and that this showed Lorna deliberately cutting me with a knife.'

'My Lord, the film of this attack is central evidence, and my client is aware that the jury have seen this recording in private because of its disturbing nature. However, for the purposes of the public hearing, still photographs have been produced to demonstrate the specific act of harm undertaken by the defendant Lorna Yates and which, as evidence will prove, was filmed by Naomi Woods as a conspiracy of revenge against Mr Konrad Neale, the victim in this case.'

The usher ensured that each member of the jury had sight of the photographic evidence. 'Mr Neale, in the photograph labelled exhibit A1, can you confirm for the court who the two people are in that photograph.'

Konrad inhaled deeply to help steady his shaking hands as he held the photo in front of his left eye. 'That's me lying on the bed and Lorna is holding the knife.'

'For the record, Lorna Yates is holding a knife with two hands, cutting into your forehead as she kneels over you, lying on a hotel bed. Do you recall this happening at the time?'

'No.' Konrad shook his head, and looked to the judge. 'I can't remember this happening to me.' A small quaver in his voice prompted a comment from the judge.

'We appreciate how difficult this is, Mr Neale, but if you would, please continue to answer the questions as they are put to you.'

How could Lorna have done that?

The jury and Konrad were asked to examine three further photographs including one taken by the police of Konrad's injuries once he reached A & E on the Sunday morning.

'In the preceding weeks, you had received a number of threatening texts, Mr Neale. Can you tell the jury more about these, and who you thought these were from?'

'The first text arrived at about the same time that I tried to get back in touch with Lorna.'

'On the same day in fact. April ninth.'

'Yes. I believe it was. At first, I didn't know who it was from, but they must have been in the park watching me. After the first one or two, I also received a typed letter, unsigned. I thought then that the texts and letter were from Tessa Carlton.'

'If it pleases the court,' Rupert Van Dahl addressed the judge. 'It may be of help for me to put this reference into context. Tessa Carlton is the sister of Helena Chawston-Hawley who was murdered by her husband, Matthew Hawley, the subject of Mr Neale's documentary at the time this offence took place. It was presumed by my client that Tessa Carlton had written instructing him to desist from seeking to interview her. Whoever wrote the letter expressed a wish to remain out of the public eye. Is that correct, Mr Neale?'

'Yes.'

'Mr Neale, during the course of the police investigation you helped to identify the second accused, Naomi Woods, as the person behind the camera filming your assault at the hands of Lorna Yates. Is that also correct?'

'Yes. That's correct.'

'Is it not also the case that you believed Naomi Woods to be Tessa Carlton.'

'Objection!' The defence barrister for Naomi Woods, a formidable looking woman who bore an uncanny resemblance to Delia, jumped up from her seat. 'Leading question and irrelevant.'

Rupert addressed the bench. 'My Lord, I'm merely seeking to establish my client's knowledge of the identities of the accused.'

'You may continue, but make your reference clear.'

'Thank you, My Lord. Mr Neale, did you know that Lorna Yates does not have Welsh parents, and that she did not grow up in Herefordshire?'

'No.' Konrad stared hard into Rupert Van Dahl's eyes then beyond him, he focussed on Lorna's impassive face.

'No further questions at this time, My Lord.' Rupert Van Dahl took his seat.

What the fuck's going on? Rupert warned me to expect the unexpected but why did they keep this from me?

'Your witness, Mrs Steele.'

Chapter 37

Konrad swallowed hard as he faced the sharp-featured woman in gown and wig about to begin her cross-examination and a theatrical presentation of her argument. 'Thank you, My Lord. Mr Neale, my learned friend, Mr Van Dahl, would have us believe that you are a stable individual of sound mind and an upstanding pillar of society. I suggest that you are in fact unreliable as a witness in this case.

'Tell me, apart from your appalling memory of events at the hotel on the night of the thirteenth and into the early hours of the fourteenth of May this year, you also lost touch with reality a few weeks later whilst undergoing treatment at the Royal Manchester Eye Hospital. You were cared for and given medication by a psychiatrist for an adjustment reaction. Is that correct?'

'Yes.'

'What can you remember about that?'

'Nothing. I blacked out. I was watching the filmed evidence of my assault when I... when I... lost it.' He couldn't think what to say. In fact, he could barely concentrate on the words being spoken. He wanted to sit in the corner of the witness box and hug his knees to regain control over his racing thoughts.

'You say you "lost it". I see. When you took your discharge against medical advice, your eye surgeon states he had concerns about your mental state. That, we know to be true. Tell the court, have you attended the psychology appointments set up for you to help deal with your traumas?'

'I went to one.'

'I do hope that was of some help. Perhaps you didn't really require further psychological treatment if you only went to one appointment.' Mrs Steele's sarcasm was not lost on Konrad or on Rupert Van Dahl who objected. With a sickly grimace, Mrs Steele apologised and continued.

'Mr Neale, my learned friend suggested in his presentation to the court that you and Lorna Yates met last year and fell in love. I put it to you that you lied. You and Lorna Yates go back a lot further than that and indeed you first met her in 2010, seven years ago, Mr Neale.'

'No.' Konrad arched backwards and a deep frown appeared on his face. 'I have no recollection of meeting Lorna before she came to Channel 7.'

'Surely you must remember… No? Let me help your unreliable memory. You were a regular client at a club called La Maison in London, conveniently sited a short distance from the studios where Saturday Night Live took place. You hosted that particular show for five years, Mr Neale, and during that time you were a frequent visitor to La Maison, so much so that if there had been a La Maison loyalty card you would have reaped many benefits, I'm sure.'

A gentle ripple of amused interest was heard from those in the courtroom during which Konrad caught an exchange of looks between Naomi Woods and Lorna, but he couldn't read what was meant. Feeling a hollow coldness in his legs, as if the strength in his muscles was ebbing away, he was forced to lean against the front of the witness stand, gripping the smooth pale wood under each hand as Mrs Steele continued her rapier-like approach to undermining the prosecution's case.

'Your membership fee included "the personal services of an escort with additional costs incurred for individual choice from a menu of sexual pleasures". That's what it says right here in the membership information.' Mrs Steele waved a leaflet in the air. 'According to the membership information and invoices, your preference was for young flexible white females who specialised in oral sex. Is that right, Mr Neale? You paid for sex on a regular basis?'

Konrad saw his barrister turn to the prosecution team sitting immediately behind him to whisper questions and stab his forefinger at the papers in front of them. Infuriation was written on Rupert Van Dahl's face as he looked back up at the witness box.

That was years ago. Three of us went after the show on a Saturday night. Fame and fortune, sex and drink. It was normal back then.

'Mr Neale, please answer the question.'

'I did go there, yes, but I don't recall meeting Lorna.'

'You should remember, you went there week in and week out over a period of several years. I put it to you, Mr Neale, that when you met Lorna again you knew exactly who she was and used her past to force her into providing sexual services to you personally. I also put it to you that it was she, not you, that ended the relationship and she tried to break away from your charmless blackmail by securing another job, far away. You said just now that you pursued her, not the other way around. Was that a lie?'

'No, it wasn't a lie. I did go after her. But I swear I had no idea she had worked as an escort. That was years ago. She can't have been one of the girls. It doesn't make sense.'

'Do you deny that you were a member at a club called La Maison?'

'No.'

'Do you deny that you made use of the escort girls at La Maison?'

'No. I don't deny any of that. But I didn't know Lorna used to work there. I swear.'

Mrs Steele, the lead counsel for Naomi Woods' defence, paused as she arranged the papers on the desk in front of her.

'Mr Neale, can I ask you to confirm whether you have ever met the other defendant, Naomi Woods, in person before today.'

'I've met her before, but she said her name was Chloe Jordan. She was my son's girlfriend.'

'That's what you believe to be the truth?'

'Yes. I thought she was, at the time.'

'Did you ever meet my client Naomi Woods at La Maison?'

'No, I don't think so.'

'Thank you, Mr Neale. I would like to ask the jury to look again at the still photographs taken from the digital video film that the prosecution have presented as evidence in this case. My Lord, two of the photos presented to the court show Mr Neale preparing to strike and physically assault my learned friend's client whilst in a state of sexual arousal. There were a number of these assaults, which were viewed by My Lord and by the jury, during which Lorna Yates can be seen reeling from the force of the blows. Mr Neale, can you deny you assaulted my client?'

'No, of course I can't.'

'Objection! My Lord, my client has already made it abundantly clear that he has no recall of any of the events that took place in the hotel room that evening.'

'Sustained. Mrs Steele, please rephrase your question.'

'Yes, My Lord. Mr Neale, is this you in these photographs?'

Konrad stared, transfixed by the scene on the photo. Perplexed.

The judge coughed. 'Mr Neale, you must answer the question.'

'What was the question?'

'Is that you in the photographs?'

'Yes.'

'Thank you, Mr Neale. No further questions.'

Harry Drysdale, the barrister representing Lorna, stood for his cross-examination of Konrad, on behalf of his client. He had a kindlier disposition.

'Mr Neale, thank you for trying to answer my colleague's questions, and I'm sure the court appreciates the amount of time you've spent in the witness box. I have only one or two more questions for you. Firstly, do you believe Lorna Yates willingly assaulted you?'

'No. I do not.'

'Why not?'

'Because I believe we were both drugged by the intruder. Naomi Woods.'

'Can I make this clear for the jury, My Lord? The main prosecution witness and victim in this case does *not* support the view of the prosecution that my client, Lorna Yates, is guilty of the crime for which she has been charged. No further questions.'

Good cop. Bad cop. I get it.

'Thank you, Mr Neale, you may step down.'

He barely registered his walk from the witness stand to his seat in the courtroom next to Eliza where the usher offered him cold water. He tried not to spill the contents as he gratefully accepted the much-needed drink, trying to manage his jangling nerves and control his breathing.

Next to take the witness stand was DS Jenkins who was asked for her version of events. It was a factual account, spoken clearly and concisely. Rupert Van Dahl emphasised the extent of the injuries to Konrad's face, his client's interactions with Lorna, and DS Jenkins' observations relating to his amnesia.

When Mrs Steele cross-examined DS Jenkins, she took a direct aggressive approach to bolster her argument that the scene at the hotel was 'more reminiscent of a snuff movie than a romantic sexual encounter. Wouldn't you say?'

'I'm not qualified to comment,' Jenkins replied. A stern expression firmly fixed in place.

'When you examined the scene of the crime what struck you about the items in the room other than the clothing?'

'I'm sorry. I don't understand the question.'

'I do apologise Detective Sergeant Jenkins. Let me be more specific. Were there items in the room that related directly to the injuries sustained by Mr Neale, and if so what were they and why were they significant to the police investigation?'

DS Jenkins confirmed her understanding and paused for thought before answering. 'The items of particular interest were the knife used in the attack and a number of lengths of rope which had been placed neatly on the dressing table. The knife had not been wiped clean, and I repeat, there were no defensive wounds found on Mr Neale's forearms that would indicate self-defence. These types of wounds were significant by their absence. However, we also found a blindfold and some tie wraps, which led to an initial hypothesis that Mr Neale was unaware of the threat posed to him by the assailant. Other items of interest included a double-ended dildo, several other sex toys, and a number of condoms. Six, as I said in my statement.'

Really? Where the hell did they come from?

'Why would the rope and the sex toys be of interest in relation to injuries sustained by the alleged victim in this case?'

DS Jenkins hesitated. 'As well as the injurious cuts to his face, Mr Neale had lacerations or marks on his back and buttocks, which were found to match with the rope. According to the forensic reports, there was evidence of the sex aids having been used by both parties.'

'Yes. That is indeed the case. Thank you for clarifying that, DS Jenkins. Most helpful.'

Konrad was still trembling from his experience in the witness box and from the shock of being told that Lorna, the woman he'd left his wife for, the woman he loved for her common sense and humour, the woman he had planned to spend the rest of his life with, was being accused of behaving like a first-class sex-crazed psychopath. He was so caught up in the horror of the situation that he failed to listen in full to the details of the evidence being given by DS Ffion Jenkins, or to understand the implications.

'Call Detective Chief Inspector Anwell.'

Gethin Anwell, in pristine suit, shirt and tie, took the stand to be examined by Rupert Van Dahl, who continued to insist that the motive for assault had been that of revenge.

'DCI Anwell, you interviewed my client at length in the hospital and in the police station at Bangor when he was fit enough to attend. Did you at any time suspect that Mr Konrad Neale was not telling the truth about the events as he recalled them from the night of the thirteenth May?'

'No. Mr Neale was always cooperative and in fact he consistently tried to convince the investigating team that he and

Lorna Yates had been the victims of a revenge plot by a woman by the name of Tessa Carlton. During our interviews, Mr Neale identified Naomi Woods as the most likely person to be Tessa Carlton, based on photographic evidence, texts he'd received and the chronology of events.'

'Did he at any time say that he had met either Lorna Yates or Naomi Woods six years previously.'

'No. He reported that he had known Lorna Yates since February 2016, but that he'd never met Naomi Woods. However, once he had identified Chloe Jordan as possibly being the same person as Naomi Woods, it was obvious that he had met her face to face.'

'What did your investigation reveal about Ms Woods?'

'Naomi Woods had a legitimate job as a businesswoman, working with her partner, Joshua Hawley, running a recruitment service, Hawley Recruitment Solutions. She was well qualified and experienced in that role and respected in her industry. She had previously worked for Helena Chawston-Hawley who was murdered by her husband in 2014, but we know that Naomi Woods did not feature as a suspect in any way, although she gave evidence at the trial in that case.'

'On investigation of her past history, we found a connection between Naomi Woods, Tessa Carlton and Lorna Yates.'

'Can you clarify for the court what that connection was please.'

'Yes. All three had been patients at Willow Hall, an adolescent unit in Suffolk. We also identified that after disappearing from Willow Hall, Naomi Woods had worked as a chambermaid at a gentlemen's club in London where Lorna Yates had also been employed as a barmaid.'

'Do you have a record of the name of that club?'

'Yes. La Maison.' There were hushed mutterings from the public gallery.

'Did all three of these women meet or know each other at any given time?'

'Yes, we found records for Lorna Yates that confirmed her admission to Willow Hall coinciding with the time that Tessa Carlton and Naomi Woods were resident – albeit an overlap of merely two weeks.'

'What happened to Lorna Yates and Tessa Carlton after they left Willow Hall.'

'Tessa Carlton disappears from any records and we have reopened an investigation into her disappearance. According to formal records, Lorna Yates appears in stable employment in 2012 with a PR company in London. She was twenty-five by then, so we had a gap of eight years that were not fully accounted for. Miss Yates insisted that she was travelling through Europe and the UK, and being paid cash-in-hand for casual labour jobs in pubs and clubs whilst studying for an Open University Degree, and she also did some agency administrative work. We have been unable to corroborate every single one of her stories, however, we have confirmed the majority of her employment history. Our investigation also confirms that she lived in Camden for a period of twelve months between October 2013 and November 2014. After that she moved to a flat in Forest Hill. There are no records of any previous contacts with the judicial system or other health institutions.'

'Thank you, DCI Anwell. That's most illuminating. Taking you back to the assault on my client, can you outline for the jury why you believe that Konrad Neale could be unable to recall the events that took place in his hotel room on the night of thirteenth of May 2017?'

'Yes. Mr Neale's last recollection was of a powdery substance being blown into his face just before he grabbed hold of the alleged intruder who had forced their way in through the door to Mr Neale's hotel room. Room 110. Our forensic team found evidence of a powdered substance and had this analysed. It was found to be a refined synthesised version of a drug that has been used previously to render victims entirely suggestible and leaves them with no recollection of events. The original substance derives from a South American plant, the Borrachero tree.'

'Is this substance known to have been used before for criminal purposes?'

'Yes, but this version was more refined and more predictable in its effects. Our conclusion initially was that both Mr Neale and Miss Yates had been affected by this, but on examination of clothing, only minimal powder was found on the clothes Lorna Yates was wearing when she entered the hotel room. However, there was a significant pattern of powder still remaining in amongst the blood stains on the towelling robe worn by Mr Neale when he opened the hotel room door. Powder was also found on the door, the light switch and the wall immediately to the right of the doorway.'

'Your conclusion was, therefore, that only Mr Neale had been drugged.'

'Unfortunately, that proved difficult to ascertain. We found evidence of the powder, and our interviews with Mr Neale and Miss Yates indicated memory loss in each case, but it has not been possible to state categorically that either of them suffered from amnesia directly as a result of deliberate intoxication.'

'I see, but it is possible.'

'Yes. It's possible.'

Chapter 38

The heat from the central wood burning stove could not penetrate the chill of dread that had made its home in Konrad's knotted stomach. He sat at the kitchen table in a rented stone and slate cottage hidden away in Llanrug. The bleak November rain pelted down outside the windows, adding to the air of general grey gloom. Rupert Van Dahl took a sip of strong coffee before trying again to explain himself.

'Look, I know it was a shock, but if we had warned you beforehand then there would have been accusations flying around about coaching witnesses. The police have carried out an extensive investigation and the court will get to hear irrefutable evidence that will prove the guilt of the accused.'

'Fuck me, Rupert, you could have said something before I was hung out to dry. At this moment in proceedings, I look like a liar and a pervert. Christ, how am I supposed to deal with this mess? I've lost everything. Everything apart from Eliza and now she knows about La Maison she'll probably disown me. I don't even know what to believe about Lorna any more. How could she have kept her past *that* secret, and why?'

Rupert raised his eyebrows. 'You did the same. I don't suppose she knew about your habit of procuring sexual services, which you should have at least mentioned to me. You made us look as if we had deliberately withheld information. Please tell me there are no more surprises about your private life, and, while you're at it, you can give me chapter and verse on La Maison.'

Konrad heard the resignation in his barrister's tone. 'I never mentioned it because it wasn't relevant. It was years ago. If you'd been married to Delia, you'd have gone there too.'

'I doubt it.'

'No, really… the place was full of England's finest legal and medical minds and half the MPs of Westminster. It was a smart club for discerning professionals whose sex drives outweighed that of their wives and partners. It wasn't a seedy dive with scabby drug-fuelled prostitutes locked behind doors, quite the opposite. La Maison was a high-class establishment with a bar and piano music, where like-minded men could be sure of a warm welcome, attention, and a room for the night in the company of intelligent women who found sex enjoyable. Expensive but worth it.'

'Tell me whether you used the services of either of the two defendants at La Maison, before they take to the witness stand.'

'Lorna was never an escort there. I knew most of the girls intimately and it can't be possible that one of them was Lorna. No way. Not a chance. I've slept with Lorna, I know every inch of that woman. As for Naomi, who knows? It's possible.' He stood up from the table and paced the length of the stone flagged floor, a glass of red wine in his hand.

Rupert agreed. 'You have a good point. We can find no indication that Lorna ever worked as an escort at La Maison. I've had an investigator on the case since this morning's revelations in court, and two members of the staff at La Maison did remember her working behind the bar there during the time you were a regular customer, so you'll have to be patient until we have the chance to put the record straight on that fact.

'Look, Konrad, the trial is going to be a long one and you may have to hear information that you don't agree with, but please understand, we have a strategy in mind with which to undermine the defence's case. They are insisting on self-defence as an argument, and blackmail and revenge as the motives but that simply does not wash.'

'Too bloody right it doesn't. How many more witnesses are you calling?'

'Two more. Our strengths will come during the cross-examination, so try not to worry.'

Konrad snorted at Rupert. '"Try not to worry". Are you having a laugh at my expense? Can you imagine the headlines tomorrow? "Dirty pervert TV presenter has roving eye cut out by ex-prostitute lover..." or some such shit. God, what a mess! Who are our last witnesses?'

'Doctor Sarah Tyrell and then finally Delia.'

'Delia? My ex-wife Delia? You're either very clever or exceptionally stupid and I have no idea which.' Konrad knocked back the last of the wine in his glass, slammed it down on the table and walked away towards the open plan lounge. 'Shut the door on your way out. We're done.'

Rupert Van Dahl swiftly gathered the papers from the table and left the cottage under cover of darkness, leaving Konrad with his thoughts.

Slumped in a high-backed chair, which was in dire need of reupholstering, he held the phone to his ear, waiting for Eliza to say something in reply to his question. 'What do you want me to say, Dad? I understand about the extramarital affairs and I understand you wanted to divorce Mum, but do I understand why you made regular use of escorts for sex? No. Why couldn't you have a wank instead? Then we wouldn't have to wait for the next wave of sordid details to come out in the press and I wouldn't be made to feel tainted by your life choices. Some prude you turned out to be.'

'Sorry, Eliza, I never wanted any of this to happen. I don't know what else to say to you, other than sorry. Please don't come to the hearing. You stay out of it and keep yourself away from the press furore and public scrutiny as much as you can.'

'Dad, I'm still here for you. Call me every day. Okay? Anyway, like it or not I'm coming to court tomorrow to give you my support, but Mum says please don't try to speak to her as she can't guarantee she'll be civil.'

Konrad had to smile at his daughter's comment, and admire her family loyalty.

*

Delia's hair remained solidly in place although the card in her hands was vibrating rapidly as she read her affirmation out loud to the court in a quavering high-pitched voice. Rupert Van Dahl stood and gave her a transient grin of reassurance before asking his opening question.

'Mrs Neale, for how many years have you known my client, Mr Konrad Neale?'

'I've known Konrad for over twenty-five years.'

'In that time has he ever been physically violent towards you?'

'No. Never.'

'Has he ever raised a hand in anger and threatened to physically hurt you in any way?'

'No. Never.'

'Could you please describe to the court what level of intimacy you had in your marriage before you decided to divorce?'

'Konrad and I had drifted apart over the years and our physical relationship was minimal.'

'Were you aware of his use of escorts in the past?'

'Yes. He would make use of a club in London where he stayed at the weekend. I did know about it although we never discussed it openly.'

'Did you know about his affair with Miss Lorna Yates?'

'Yes. I asked him to stop seeing her in order to salvage his career. I'm his business manager and the public expected him to be seen with me, as his wife, at engagements. He was besotted with her, so they started seeing each other again in the weeks before he was attacked.'

'Did that make you angry?'

'Yes, but it also made us decide to divorce, which we probably should have done years ago. We stayed together for the children and for his career.'

Konrad couldn't quite comprehend what his wife was doing for him. He looked at the faces of the jury and saw their admiration for her honesty. Rupert Van Dahl completed his questioning, making way for the impressively cutting tongue of Mrs Steele.

Here comes old Iron Breeches. Watch out, Delia, the cow made mincemeat of Dr Tyrell, poor woman.

*

He had not been surprised when Dr Tyrell had immediately left the courtroom following her grilling by Lorna's brief, and then by Mrs Steele. Between them, they undermined the psychiatrist's statement and questioned her professional opinion about the three girls who had been in her care at Willow Hall. At least she had remembered the facts about who absconded when and with whom. 'Lorna had been treated for depression and discharged back into the local authority care system. Tessa Carlton and Naomi Woods had absconded together and never returned.' Mrs Steele had taken the opportunity to condemn the standards of care at Willow Hall and Dr Tyrell eventually crumpled under her cross-examination, confusing the details of each of the three girls and thus undermining her credibility as a witness.

'Any re-examination, Mr Van Dahl?'

'If I may, My Lord.' Rupert Van Dahl stood again. 'Dr Tyrell, you said to my learned colleague that Naomi Woods had strong psychopathic traits that were similar to those of Tessa Carlton. In your view was Naomi Woods, the defendant, capable of influencing Tessa Carlton?'

'Yes. Tessa was much more obvious in her manipulation of the other girls in the unit, she was boastful and a bully, but Naomi was more skilled, and more successful. She would watch and learn about her fellow patients. Once she had identified their strengths and their weaknesses, she would groom them, for want of a better expression. She was crafty and underhand.'

'Did you ever see Lorna Yates being targeted by either Tessa Carlton or Naomi Woods in an attempt to bully her in anyway?'

'No, not that I was aware of. As I said, Lorna kept to herself. She didn't mix with the others.'

'No further questions, My Lord.'

*

Mrs Steele now took aim at Delia Neale and played to the audience once more.

'It's very admirable of you to stand as a witness for your feckless, adulterous ex-husband, Mrs Neale. One can only assume he must be worth the maintenance money… Mrs Neale, you say you tolerated your husband's infidelity and that your sexual relationship with him had been minimal. How long was your marriage purely one of financial convenience, would you say?'

'Probably for the last ten years.'

'So, would it be fair to assume that you have no real idea of your husband's sexual preferences?'

'I don't understand what you mean.'

'Has your husband ever indulged in bondage, whipping, use of sex aids or sexual violence with you or anyone else?' Mrs Steele swivelled slowly as she shared the words with the court and the jury.

'He certainly never has with me. No.'

'But he could have with someone else.'

'He could have. I wouldn't know.'

'No. You wouldn't know. Thank you. No further questions.'

Mrs Steele sat down and had a whispered conference with Mr Harry Drysdale, the brief for Lorna Yates, who indicated that he didn't need to ask any additional questions on behalf of his client.

Delia appeared bewildered as she was escorted from the witness stand and seated on Eliza's right. 'What a bitch…' Delia cursed under her breath into her daughter's right ear.

The judge stirred. 'Does that conclude the case for the prosecution Mr Van Dahl?'

'Yes, My Lord.'

'Then we begin the case for the defence. Mrs Steele, you continue to lead on the case for Naomi Woods, with your learned colleague Mr Drysdale as the counsel for Miss Lorna Yates.'

'That is correct, My Lord,' confirmed a smiling Mrs Steele.

'I suggest we adjourn for lunch and then you may call your first witness when we reconvene at one thirty.'

*

Konrad sat next to Barney in the public gallery waiting for Annette who had just completed giving evidence as the first witness for the defence. She had been called to stand, and her role was to paint a positive picture of Lorna as a hard-working professional who had been led by Konrad to believe they would have a future together.

Annette answered in measured terms, confirming that Lorna was a resilient individual who had shown genuine affection for Konrad and who was not known to behave vindictively. 'She had her heart broken when he ended their relationship, but then again he was devastated too.'

Konrad exchanged a hopeful grin with Barney, relieved that there was a positive representation beginning to emerge of the relationship he and Lorna shared. His optimism was short-lived, for within moments of Rupert Van Dahl taking up the cross-examination for the prosecution Annette's contribution was all but nullified.

'You have known Lorna Yates for four years you say. Did she ever mention to you that she had worked in a brothel?'

'No.'

'Did she reveal to you that she'd spent time in an institution for mental health problems? Or been brought up in care?'

'No.' Annette's shoulders dropped.

'We can safely say then that your friendship was not as close as you have led us to believe. Did Lorna Yates talk to you about how she and Naomi Woods rekindled their friendship when they worked together at La Maison?'

'No.'

'Surely she must have mentioned that she had deliberately applied for a job in Bangor at BBC Wales to be close to where Konrad Neale's children were at university and therefore tantalisingly near to where he was likely to be seen?'

'No, I don't believe that was her intention at all. She moved from London once they split up in order not to see him again. She wasn't just based in Bangor, she worked for other studios and departments for BBC Wales.'

'The police investigation strongly indicates that Naomi Woods and Lorna Yates conspired to bring about the humiliation and personal destruction of Konrad Neale. The evidence suggests that they worked together to entice him into having a night of sexual extremes, they drugged him, filmed the action and then Lorna Yates, as the woman scorned, deliberately disfigured my client in an act of violent vengeance. You visited Lorna Yates in prison seven times in all. What did she tell you about the attack on my client?'

'Not much. She can't remember any of it. But she didn't set him up, I'm sure of it.'

'I put it to you that Lorna Yates used you as a friend of convenience and that you know little or nothing about her. My esteemed legal colleagues have sought to paint a rosy picture where in fact a darker truth resides. No further questions.'

Konrad was astounded by how swiftly and efficiently the barristers twisted words and facts to suit, but most of all he was dismayed at the misuse of facts to guide the jury into believing their argument.

My own barrister is condemning Lorna to being found guilty of something she didn't do. Is this the final twist of the knife from Tessa fucking Carlton?

He looked at Naomi Woods sitting placidly in the dock and saw her aim an almost imperceptible smirk at her brief. Whatever their scheme was, it was on course. From where he was sitting Mrs Steele was playing a game of double agents. She led for the defence but in favour of her own client, and was setting up Lorna to take the blame for grievous bodily harm and attempted blackmail. Mr Drysdale would have to up his game if Lorna were to stand any chance of a not guilty verdict.

Mr Harry Drysdale stood to re-examine Annette.

'You said just now that my client, Lorna Yates, failed to recall any of the events which occurred on the night of May thirteen this year. During your visits to see her in prison, at any time did she disclose knowledge of the events of that night, anything at all?'

'No. She really had no memory of it. Nothing. She remembered waking up and finding Konrad seriously injured. Lorna was convinced that an intruder had attacked them. She was devastated to be charged with assault. Lorna isn't capable of attacking anyone like that deliberately.'

Konrad let out a slow breath and Barney did the same sitting beside him, hands clasped between his knees.

Chapter 39

Naomi took out her mobile phone. These were considered contraband in prison, but inmates managed to smuggle them in without too much difficulty; mostly to order drug delivery by drone, or to stay in touch with the felonious outside world. She recorded her diary via the small camera as a video selfie. She couldn't imagine how she would cope inside the remand centre without her personal chat with Konrad. Once complete, she would simply upload it to her data cloud. She sat on her bed, leaning against the wall.

'I should have been a lawyer. They are among the most highly paid liars, short of world leaders and politicians. What a shame the opportunity never arose, I would have been a QC by now, I reckon. Still, there's no use in dwelling on fantasies. I had a simple mission in life to complete instead, which I would have done if you hadn't cocked it up for me, Konrad.

'I look at you across the courtroom, sitting with what's left of your sad pathetic family or with your fat friend, and I experience a certain satisfaction at what I've achieved of your demise so far. Your face is a mangled mess, your false eye was enough to frighten children, I hear, and that eye patch barely makes up for it. Your son is dead, Lorna's going to prison for years, your wife divorced you – more's the pity – your daughter despises you, and your once-adoring public are ridiculing you. Yet I could have done so much better. Yes, really, I could.

'As far as Delia is concerned I should have thought that through more thoroughly. You would have suffered to a much greater extent if I'd managed to keep you two incarcerated in holy matrimony and trapped inside that hideous house for the rest of your days. Pure torture. I would have put cameras everywhere and watched the destruction like a soap opera or death by nagging in the Big Brother house. "Konrad has entered the diary room, he can take no more of Delia's incessant bleating about money and he's hanging a rope from the rafters." What a missed opportunity.

'And, you know, I was too impulsive killing Freddie so early on in the script; I could kick myself for that error. I was sloppy and directionless probably because he was making too much emotional fuss. This is what happens when I become angry, Konrad. You made me so fucking infuriated by undoing years of my work that I become impulsive. Me and Josh had a respectable business, a house worth a million with no one any the wiser about Helena, or Tessa, their parents or Richard. Then you started asking your questions.

'This is a pattern that repeats itself, Konrad. When people don't do as I ask, or as I tell them, then I have to be rid of them. Helena was a good pupil but she should never have tried to come between my prize and me. I warned her, and like you she tried to take me on at my own game. Silly idea.

'Tessa made exactly the same basic error, stupid bitch. Her mouth was her downfall. Too full of her own self-importance, too keen to show off how evil she was. It's us quiet ones you have to watch, just like Dr Tyrell said.

'At least Freddie made it into one of the major scenes; Tessa didn't even make it through scene one, act one. She's somewhere in Elveden Forest, underneath a hump in one of the many cycle paths. I've no idea where, they all look the same to me. Decent of me to keep her memory alive by introducing her to you and to Matthew Hawley, don't you think? Letters from a dead woman, an email from an ex-boyfriend of Helena's that doesn't exist.

'You work it out.

'Mrs Steele is my heroine. She takes no prisoners that woman, and the jury are convinced that Lorna put me up to filming you both. Excellent skills of persuasion and a confident performance. Brava, Mrs Steele!

'I don't even remember your Lorna being at Willow Hall, she sounded like a proper goodie two shoes, the young Lorna Yates, but by the time I did see her at La Maison she wasn't so passive. If I'm right, she wasn't a bad barmaid actually. Nice figure, healthy looking, flirty with the clientele but efficient with her service. Don't despair, Konrad, she wasn't escort material, not in a million years. Like me, though, she was there to use and take advantage of men. In her case, it was to make a move into a better career on the back of the connections to be made in a place like that. No questions are asked about your fictional CV at interviews if the person recommending you for the job is the boss.

'She went into marketing and public relations, and I went into recruitment just as I'd planned. I never saw her again until I spied her on the pier with you. Even then I couldn't place where I'd seen her before. It was Delia who was so helpful in the golf club at filling certain gaps for me, without me asking her a single question. Bless her.

'My Josh did well in the witness stand this afternoon, don't you think? He sang my praises, and then when he had the jury feeling sorry for him, he wept. I have to say I'm irritated that he felt it necessary to shake your hand when he sat next to you afterwards. I'll have to consider whether I'll file that gesture under good manners in the face of adversity or betrayal. It will depend on the outcome of this trial and the next one.

'Mrs Steele thinks that even if I'm found guilty of conspiracy in this case, I'll get a not guilty verdict for Freddie's murder, based on the circumstantial nature of the forensic evidence. No witnesses, you see. He had an unlucky brush with asphyxiation and I had an alibi. Not cast iron, but good enough to place doubt in the minds of any jury.

'Anyway, shall we see what happens next? Exciting, isn't it?'

Chapter 40

Konrad couldn't take his eyes off Lorna's face as she stood pale in the witness stand. He prayed silently for her to be strong and not to cave into the bullying tactics of Mrs Steele in her aim to place Lorna in the frame for assault and attempted blackmail.

Mr Drysdale began his examination of her statement. 'Miss Yates, you say you have no memory of the evening in question from the time of entering Mr Konrad Neale's hotel room, and that you did not notice anyone following you as you approached his room. Is that correct?'

'Yes.'

'You state that you recall nothing until you awoke after five the next morning to find Mr Neale seriously injured. What was the first thing you did?'

'I made use of a towel to try to cover the wounds on his head then I called the hotel reception to ask for help and to get the emergency services.'

'The court has heard from Mr Martin Friar, the duty manager, that room 110 was in a state of disarray when he arrived and that you were trying to care for Mr Neale and clearly in a state of shock. My colleagues have tried to persuade the jury that you carried out a deliberate attack on Mr Neale in revenge for his decision to end your relationship. Is that correct?'

'No. Konrad and I had in fact made a decision to rekindle our friendship and he had already informed his wife that he was seeking a divorce. I left that evening with no plan other than to go home to bed. I wouldn't have returned to The Management Centre if I hadn't had an urgent call from reception.'

'Did you make any arrangements with Naomi Woods to drug Konrad Neale, film yourself having sex with him, and to blackmail him as an act of revenge.'

'No, I did not. I hadn't seen Naomi Woods since I worked at La Maison.'

'But you knew she was involved in some way with a documentary that Konrad was filming.'

'I knew someone by that name was involved. I didn't think for one moment that it would be the same person.'

'The CCTV at the hotel shows Naomi Woods entering the hotel through a side entrance a short distance from Mr Neale's room, and police reports suggest that she waits for you to pass by before following you into Mr Neale's room. How do you explain that?'

'I didn't hear or see her. I know that someone forced his or her foot into the doorway and then I remember Konrad shoving me out of the way. After that, nothing. I remember nothing until the morning.'

'Mr Neale says he recalls a powdery substance being blown into your faces by the intruder. Do you recall this?'

'No. I can't remember that happening. I wish I could.'

'It would have been simpler for you to lie about that, and of course it would make my job so much easier if you had, but I confirm for the court, that you have stuck consistently to the statement you first made to the police.'

'It's the truth.'

'Do you deny that you willingly or knowingly carried out an assault on Mr Konrad Neale on the night of the thirteenth of May this year?'

'Yes, because I cannot remember and I would never have hurt Konrad. I have no good reason to.'

When it was her turn to cross-examine, Mrs Steele picked up her pen and held it delicately between finger and thumb of each hand before using it as a small baton to emphasise her questions to Lorna.

'Miss Yates, can you confirm for the court that you sent several texts from your mobile phone to my client Naomi Woods on the night in question?'

*

Annette threw another log into the wood burning stove and closed the door carefully to avoid burning herself on the cast iron. Barney pulled the cork on their second bottle of red wine. 'I miss beer, mate. Can't we risk going to the pub?'

'Maybe tomorrow, when it's all over,' Konrad grumbled. 'We can drown our sorrows or celebrate with copious amounts of beer, depending on the verdict. Right now, I can't even think about it without feeling sick.' Konrad sat, elbows on the table, swilling wine rhythmically around the bowl of his glass.

'I think it'll be okay. You could see how much the jury believed Lorna when she spoke. They know she wasn't lying and her barrister played a clever hand I thought. As for that other devious cow...'

'Naomi Woods?'

'No, I was thinking of the spiky-nosed Mrs Steele. She's something else. Intelligent, but incredibly dislikeable. I think that will be Naomi's downfall because Mrs Steele is like the villain in a pantomime and Naomi is her evil twin. They told lie after lie and I wasn't fooled for one minute by the ridiculous suggestion that Lorna and Naomi were old friends and that Naomi, of all people, was persuaded to join Lorna in blackmail and revenge for money. Naomi doesn't need money. The arguments were completely flawed.'

'You say that, Netty, but when they produced Lorna's and Naomi's phone messages from that night, the texts quite clearly showed they plotted it all together.' Barney poured a couple of glugs of red wine into Annette's glass while she cut more bread to go with the slowly disappearing cheese mountain laid out on a large wooden board in the middle of the kitchen table in the cottage at Llanrug. The Brie had all but disappeared leaving Port

Salut, Wensleydale with cranberries, and some vintage cheddar to be finished off with the selection of chutneys and olives that Annette had supplied for a late evening snack.

'Any idiot could work out that Naomi had stolen the phone, sent messages back and forth then dropped the phone back through Lorna's letter box before Naomi then drove back to The Management Centre. Harry Drysdale wiped the floor with that piece of evidence. The timings of the texts fitted exactly with the two of you having dinner then the CCTV footage in the car park when you were snogging. Lorna couldn't have sent any messages. It's a long stretch of the imagination to believe that Lorna would want anything to do with that devious manipulative bitch Naomi.'

Konrad spat crumbs across the table. 'It's more unbelievable that an intelligent young man like Josh Hawley fell for her.' He had just taken a bite of crusty bread. 'Not only fell for her but is practically mesmerised by her. Just like my Freddie.'

'Oi, spit somewhere else! You put crumbs in my wine, you thoughtless twerp.' Barney pretended to be cross.

'Sorry, didn't see it.'

'Lame excuse for bad manners, Cyclops. Didn't your mother teach you not to talk with your mouth full?'

'Now, now children, stop bickering and tell me what the detective man said today,' Annette chided the pair.

Gethin Anwell had managed to snatch a couple of precious minutes with Konrad and Barney in the gents toilets at the courts, shortly after the judge adjourned the hearing for the day. He disclosed in hushed tones that there was likely to be an appeal into the conviction of Matthew Hawley based on the outcome of the case against Lorna Yates and Naomi Woods.

'Detective Chief Inspector Anwell is a bloody decent chap. His colleagues who had investigated Helena's murder have been watching the proceedings here with interest. They reckon there's a distinct possibility that Naomi used the same drug to instruct Matthew Hawley to kill his own wife. That's why he didn't remember anything. Naomi Woods had the motive and given the evidence about her contact with the underground Chinese chemist, she had the means to kill Helena and maybe Richard too.'

'No. It still doesn't make any sense that she would then risk all that wealth and stability to bring about your downfall or kill Freddie.' Annette sat back in her chair wiping butter from her chins.

'That's because you don't think like a psychopath,' Konrad said with authority. He had been wondering about exactly the same issue for the past six months and concluded that Dr Tyrell had been the closest to explaining why Naomi had followed a path that inevitably led to her own arrest.

'Containment. That was the word Sarah Tyrell used. She said people with extreme disorders of personality seek boundaries or containment. They become out of control and driven by all the negative stuff: envy, jealousy, anger, revenge and the rest of it. But whatever they do they don't seem to achieve a sense of fulfilment. So they do even worse things. Naomi experienced most satisfaction from being destructive and seeing the results. It's all been a game that's got out of control and getting locked up will contain her.'

'What a load of old psychobabble bollocks.' Barney snorted. 'She's a twisted evil bitch. That's it. Don't dress it up in poxy medical lingo. She's a bad 'un.'

'Well said.' Annette leant against Barney and pinched his cheek. 'And anyway, where is Tessa in all this?'

'Now that's a hell of a good question.'

*

'Miss Woods, you have told the court that the digital camera you were using on the night in question ran low on battery power, which is why you stopped filming. Can you explain why you left your so-called friend, Lorna Yates, in the hotel room when you departed from the hotel, drove your hire car to the station, and then caught a train to London?'

Rupert Van Dahl had already been asking questions of Naomi Woods for twenty minutes as part of his cross-examination. She was the last witness in the case of the defence and her testimony had generated far more interest in the courtroom than anyone else's, or so it seemed to those seated in the public gallery. Konrad, who had been more impressed with his barrister as each day of the hearing passed, watched closely. He could tell by the jury's faces that they approved of his barrister's approach and his character, as well as his arguments. Rupert Van Dahl had subtly introduced reasonable doubt in Lorna's favour and managed to emphasise Naomi's guilt without compromising his role in the prosecution.

'It was part of the plan.'

'This plan seemed unnecessarily complicated. Did you ever consider that faking the kidnapping of Lorna Yates could have yielded better financial rewards than blackmail?'

At last, Konrad caught a momentary flicker of irritation flash across Naomi's face.

'No. This was her idea. Not mine. She wanted to hurt him.' Naomi raised a finger toward where Konrad was sitting.

'The court will note, for the record, that Naomi Woods has identified the victim, Mr Konrad Neale.'

'You say that the idea was the work of Lorna Yates, but is it not true that you bought the camera, you accessed the drug through your contacts in the sex industry, and you misled Freddie Neale into believing you were Chloe Jordan in order to use him against his own father. Let us not forget that it was also you who carried out the application of the drug, you who filmed everything, and you who delivered a copy of the film to the newspapers. Is that correct?'

'Yes, but that was part of the set-up to avoid Lorna being identified as the culprit.'

'Miss Woods, I feel I need to remind you that Lorna Yates was filmed by you assaulting and seriously wounding my client with a large knife. She cannot fail to have been identified.'

There was a long pause during which a staring contest between Naomi Woods and Rupert Van Dahl took place. He won.

'I put it to you, Miss Woods, that Lorna Yates was an innocent victim in this case and that the reason for your convoluted story is that you made several errors in *your* plan to bring about the destruction of my client's life. You accidentally filmed yourself, you couldn't resist sending threatening texts to him, and you have lied consistently in an effort to blame Lorna Yates who you knew had spent years trying to rebuild her life from a shattered childhood.'

'Objection. My Lord, supposition.'

'The jury will disregard that last comment. Mr Van Dahl please ensure your statements are based on fact.'

'I do apologise, My Lord.' Rupert Van Dahl looked down momentarily as if considering the risk of asking his next question. 'The court has heard that you have no previous convictions and appear to have led a blameless life. What the jury hasn't heard so far is that you gave evidence in the murder trial of your former employer, Helena Chawston-Hawley, that you were the last person to see Tessa Carlton alive when you both absconded from Willow Hall as teenagers, and that you were the person who found the body of Richard, the former colleague and younger brother of Helena Chawston-Hawley. Are these facts correct?'

'Yes.'

'You seem to attract death, Miss Woods. Was it your intention to murder my client at the hands of Lorna Yates?'

'No, just to disfigure him.'

'At the hands of Lorna Yates.'

'That's not what I meant.'

'No further questions.'

*

'I thought I was going to be physically sick waiting for that bloody woman to give the verdict of the jury. Did she think she was on MasterChef giving the decision on who would make it through the competition to the next round? My heart still hasn't recovered.' Konrad held out his shaking hands as proof. 'Thanks for giving us the place to ourselves last night, by the way. Much appreciated.'

Barney raised his pint glass. 'No problem, mate. Me and Netty booked a room at the Travelodge in Bethesda on the off-chance anyway. We were so knackered, we didn't even go for a drink to celebrate. We grabbed a disgusting takeaway, ate it in bed and slept for hours.' He slurped his beer before asking, 'What did DCI Anwell want with you today? Can't he give it a rest?'

'Bloody excellent news is what he wanted to tell me, Barney old fruit. Naomi Woods, the evil bitch, is changing her plea to guilty regarding Freddie's murder, which means we probably won't have to go through all this agony again. For the icing on top of "the cake of good tidings", the investigation into Tessa Carlton's disappearance is being considered as a possible murder. No body yet.'

'Fuck me.'

'Language. The ladies will hear you.' Konrad used his drink to indicate towards a corner table where Lorna was sitting with Annette, deep in conversation, punctuated by the odd hug.

'How's Lorna?'

'Shell-shocked. A bit like myself, I suspect. We were mobbed on the way out of court by the press, as usual. Luckily Zachary had been contracted to drive me to and from the cottage yesterday, otherwise we wouldn't have made our getaway at all. What a good man he is. He'd put chocolates, flowers, and a hamper full of food in the car, as well as a whole suitcase full of Lorna's clothing... thanks to Annette for that. He even played music all the way back to the cottage, so we didn't have to try to make conversation. I couldn't believe he had taken the risk on the verdict. The only thing he said was, "never in doubt, Mr Neale".'

'Well it wasn't.'

'It was agony. Still, it's been good to know so many people had faith in our version of events. I had to turn my mobile off last night because I had so many messages plus an indecent proposal from Gorgeous George. Apparently, my scars turn him on.'

Barney grimaced as he laughed in response. 'That poor boy. Netty says you lead him on.'

'Come off it, you don't believe that for one minute. I even had a reasonably pleasant message from Delia.'

'Now that's unbelievable. How's her new life in town suiting her?'

'Dunno, you'll have to ask Eliza. Here she comes, old soppy-bollocks in tow.' Konrad forced himself to shake hands with Eliza's boyfriend, Mason. The American accent still grated, as did the general boastfulness. Most of all, he despised the fact that his daughter's chosen man had a weak handshake, like a wet fish, thus inviting Konrad to ratchet up his vice-like grip and make Mason wince. Barney did the same, much to his friend's amusement.

'Sorry we're late, Dad. Mason had an important call from the States and it took longer than we thought.'

Should have left the wanker at home then.

'Never mind, you're here now. Are you feeling okay about Lorna being with us?'

'More than okay. I'll introduce myself. You stay here and teach Mason about the delights of proper beer. He only drinks lager.'

'Our pleasure,' Barney piped up with a devilish grin spreading slowly across his face. 'Mason, walk this way, lager boy, and let me help you with your future career. We can't have you intellectual types drinking lager; no one in this country or the whole of the UK will take you seriously as a professor of anything unless you drink real ale. Lesson one: never drink halves, always pints. Now then, we'll start you off with a golden ale. Looks harmless enough, doesn't it?'

Konrad was pretending to listen to Barney's beer lesson, but his attention was captured by his daughter and Lorna meeting officially for the first time. He held his breath until interrupted.

'Kon, another pint?'

'Yes please.' Konrad smiled amiably at the landlord who was clearly trying hard not to be overwhelmed by the famous faces in his establishment, ones that had appeared on the front pages of every newspaper in the UK that morning. He rustled up enough courage to ask, 'Will you be staying in the area for a few more days?'

'Most likely, until the dust settles. It's been a long haul but I'm glad we're finally able to venture out for a drink, and you'll probably see us again tomorrow unless the press get wind of where we are.'

'Don't worry, I've put a news embargo on the staff and the regulars. Any trouble from press intrusion and we'll throw the bastards out.'

Chapter 41

The BBC reporter pushed a microphone into Konrad's face, catching him off guard as he descended the steps of the High Court in bright summer sunshine.

'Mr Neale, how does it feel knowing your efforts have finally been rewarded?'

Konrad was able to switch easily into his professional presenter persona. His expression remained serious.

'I'm relieved of course, but mostly delighted that after four years Matthew Hawley has finally got the justice he deserves.' He thanked the reporter, put on his sunglasses, and moved off into the crowded street, determined not to be collared for any further impromptu interviews. His diary was already full of scheduled attendances for chat shows, current affairs programmes and ironically for two real crime documentaries. One investigating the murder of Tessa Carlton, whose body was still missing, and the other investigating cases of crimes committed during states of automatism.

That day in the High Court, it had been sobering listening to Naomi Woods again. Konrad had stared intently at her when she took the witness stand like a pro. This was the third time in the dock in eighteen months and Konrad wondered if the notoriety of her crimes was feeding repetitively into her psychopathy. She seemed to revel in the notoriety and play to the crowd.

As predicted, she had pleaded not guilty to the murder of Helena Chawston-Hawley even though the re-examination of the evidence had resulted in the successful appeal by Matthew Hawley and in Naomi's arrest for conspiracy to murder. She was found guilty.

Allowing the courtroom to empty, he sat alone for a while in the gallery, not praying, but in quiet contemplation, savouring the end of the most dreadful chapter in his entire life. His thoughts were of Freddie and his tears were for himself.

As he was crossing the lobby, heading for the High Court's main exit, he was approached by Mrs Steele, barrister for Naomi Woods. 'Mr Neale, could I have a word in private?'

In a smart wood panelled room, the officious Mrs Steele handed over a package. 'My client instructed me to give this to you in the event that she was found guilty today. There's a short letter giving you permission to act as you see fit regarding the contents.'

*

'That's what old Iron Breeches said?' Annette queried as she loaded the first of the DVDs into the player. She and Konrad sat in semi-darkness in the editing suite. 'Just like old times this, isn't it? Now the legal nightmares are done with, maybe we can actually finish the bloody documentary. The bosses are champing at the bit for us to be the first on air. Right, let's see what the bitch has sent.'

Annette reached for a large packet of peanuts and shook some out into her hand. She sat back to watch the monitor with interest as she popped a few nuts into her mouth.

'I thought you were on a diet.'

'I am. Hang on. Wait a minute. Before we do this, what if the DVD is an unabridged version of the night you and Lorna were attacked? You could have one of those mind melt-down moments and be lost for days again.'

'Good point. You sit with your finger on the stop button and I'll look away if it is.'

They didn't speak until the film started.

'Where the hell is this? And who's that?' Annette asked, trying to make sense of the naked limbs on the screen.

Konrad cocked his head to one side to compensate for the angle of the action in the film. 'That looks very much like

Helena being given a lesson by Naomi in the fine art of the blow job, using a strap-on dick.' Konrad was mesmerised by the scene playing out in front of him during which Naomi could be heard making encouraging comments about Helena's technique and then offering a suggestion about subtle improvements that she could make. 'This means that Naomi knew exactly what Helena was doing. She taught her. Mistress and apprentice. Naomi helped her to catch and keep Matthew. I think I know where this is going.'

'Do you? I'm too shocked to think anything,' Annette said rolling out of her chair and heading towards the door. She checked the corridor outside and then returned to her desk. 'Play the next one, but keep the volume down.'

'Oh shit. That's Josh with Helena riding him like a thing possessed. Listen. Naomi's laughing while she's filming it.

'How sick is that."

'Turn it up a bit. A little louder so we can hear.'

Konrad and Annette huddled together as they watched the scene change in front of them. They heard Naomi giving instructions. 'Well done, both of you. Very enjoyable to watch, but Helena, you're still rushing things. Take your time, swivel round and face the other way, enjoy the experience. Josh won't remember a thing, but you'll have the orgasm of your life. Then you can have another go on Daddy over there and we'll see who's the best in your opinion.' The camera panned across the bedroom to where Matthew Hawley was sitting in a chair watching his son have sex with his wife under the instruction of Naomi Woods.

'How long have I got?' Helena asked, panting slightly as she looked towards the camera. Naomi continued to film her as she rocked back, and flicked her long hair out of her face. Helena wore a beaming smile. 'I'm loving this.'

Annette put one hand up to her mouth in shock. Konrad looked at her before pressing the stop button.

'Tell me you're thinking what I'm thinking.'

'I can if you're thinking that Helena and Naomi were abusing the father and the son for their own sexual pleasure, and it very much looks as if they drugged them.'

'That would explain why Naomi became so angry when Helena made a real play for Josh. They wanted the same man. Mystery solved.'

'I find it weird that when you watch Josh, he seems to be enjoying himself, but he's drugged and won't remember any of it.'

'Let me assure you. It is weird.'

'Whoever said "the camera never lies" was wrong.'

The two friends sat in silence thinking about the implications of what they had in their possession.

'What the hell are we going to do with these discs?' Konrad asked. 'We can't show them as part of the documentary because neither of those poor men know they've been raped.'

'You're so right. It's rape. Kon, this is so bad.'

'I know. What are we going to do? If we give it to the police, Naomi Woods bags herself another trip to court and more fame for her evil deeds. But if we do nothing we're complicit in not reporting a serious crime.'

Kon and Annette pivoted their chairs to face each other.

'What a deplorable, black-hearted bitch. She knew this was the last turn of the screw, and do we believe what she says in that bloody letter about these being the only copies? She, or someone acting on her behalf, must have downloaded them from a computer somewhere.'

'Apart from the one of Lorna and me, the police have never produced another of her films as evidence. Not even a laptop, and nothing on any phone. So, I don't know is the answer to your question.'

Annette removed the DVD from the machine in front of her, and wagged it in Konrad's face. 'Let's see what's on the other disc.'

He recognised his car. The white Range Rover registration KON 1 was shown parked between trees and bushes, only yards away from a dirt track. The person holding the camera walked towards the car where Freddie sat in the passenger seat smiling and waving, fingers spread wide.

'Want to say a little something to your dad about your new job, Freddie?' Naomi's distinctive sotto voice could barely be heard over the sound of the wind blowing the leaves in the trees.

'Yes, I do.' The car window lowered, allowing Freddie to rest his elbow on the opening as he looked directly into camera. 'Hello, Dad, I'm not sorry you refused to help find me some work at Channel 7. Fuck you. I've passed my interview and I'm joining Chloe in her new business as her sales and marketing assistant. We've found some offices for the West Country branch and I'll be staying here. You can keep your money. I'm not going back to uni after the summer; I'll be too rich to care. Now if you don't mind, I'm about to get on with the rest of my life and Chloe is going to show me something new.' Freddie made a 'V' sign at the camera as he laughed excitedly. 'Come on, get in girl, put your lips around this.' There was a break in the filming before it recommenced showing Freddie's immobilised torso, tied by his neck, with a blissful look on his face.

In silence, Annette held Konrad's right hand as he wiped away the tears streaming down his left cheek.

'Bye–bye Freddie.'

Naomi's words ended the film.

Finally, after several pain-laden minutes, Konrad gained control of himself enough to speak. He had made a decision.

'We destroy the DVDs and we say nothing to a single living soul. Matthew Hawley has paid enough of a price; let him keep his son, and his dignity. Naomi doesn't have to win them all.'

THE END

Acknowledgements

A special thank you:

To Lucy, for allowing her real-life drama to turn into an inspiring idea for this book.

To Alexina, Sharon, Nicky, and Andy for their valuable time, honest opinion, and encouragement.

To Morgen Bailey for her editing wisdom.

To the amazing team at Bloodhound Books, for their faith and hard work.

To my long-suffering friends, family and neighbours for their support.

To Terry Thomas at Whistlestop on the pier, and to Liz and Dean of the Tap and Spile, Bangor, for their indulgence.

And finally, to Sadie Waggytail, for her company while I wrote, reviewed, edited and swore. She's a rubbish guard dog but makes up for it in so many other ways. X

Lightning Source UK Ltd.
Milton Keynes UK
UKHW012231050119
334976UK00001B/62/P

9 781912 175949